W9-BCG-550

FamilyVision's
New Classics For The Twenty-First Century™

Book One

Dorothy Return to Oz

By Thomas L. Tedrow

FamilyVision Press, Inc.

New York

FamilyVision Press™
An Imprint of Multi Media Communicators, Inc.
575 Madison Avenue, Suite 1006
New York, NY 10022

Managing Editor, Maggie Holmes
Cover art, Michael A. Hernandez, Jr.
Typesetter, Samuel Chapin

Library of Congress Catalog Card Number: 93-071553

ISBN 1-56969-000-6

10 9 8 7 6 5 4 3 2 1
First Edition

Printed in the United States of America

Also by Thomas L. Tedrow

FICTION

Heartbreak Trail
Broken Vows

The Legend of Grizzly Adams and Kodiak Jack
The Days of Laura Ingalls Wilder
Missouri Homestead
Children of Promise
Good Neighbors
Home to the Prairie
The World's Fair
Mountain Miracle
The Great Debate
Land of Promise

The Life and Times of the Younguns
The Younguns of Mansfield, Missouri
Frankie and the Secret
Escape From Barron Stoker
Orphan of the Ozarks

NONFICTION

Death at Chappaquiddick

SERIES CREATED

Shivers
The Satan Hunter
The Troll Family Adventures
Petz
DinoMites
The Patti Pinkerton Mystery Stories
The Step Mystery Series
The Adventures of Shelly Holmes

Dedicated to

Steven Spielberg

The greatest family filmmaker in the world.

And to

Ron Friedman

Who knows the true meaning of partnership and gave me wings.
Your marketing genius made all this happen.

God Bless My Family

To my pretty wife Carla: Good things do last forever.
You made this all possible.

To my children C.T., Tyler, Tara and Travis:
From you came the inspiration for the
New Classics for the Twenty-First Century.

To my mother, Gertrude Tedrow:
You taught me faith, courage, kindness, love, and understanding.

To my late father, Richard Tedrow:
You told me I could be anything I wanted.
I miss you every day.

Thanks to My Partners

Jack Bennett, Doug Holladay, Jarrell McCracken,
Dick Ohman, Dean Overman,
and Ron Friedman.
You have the vision to publish books for
families that read together.

Special Thanks

To Laura Carr for all your help.

And to All My Readers

Oz is where the sandman takes you.
The magic of childhood can stay with you forever.
All you have to do is believe.

CONTENTS

FOREWORD

Since my father read me every one of L. Frank Baum's wonderful Oz books during our summers at Scientist Cliffs, Maryland, on the Chesapeake Bay, I've always wanted to go over the rainbow myself. To go back to Oz and find out how that magical place had changed.

The memories of those warm, wonderful frog-croaking evenings, with the moths circling around the porch lights outside the screen door, have never left me. I can still feel the arms of my mother picking me up to take me to bed and hear my pleading for just another chapter from the Oz books.

"We'll go back to Oz tomorrow night," my father would say.

Then, after I said my prayers with Mom, I closed my eyes, hoping to feel the sleepy dust before I drifted off.

I can still remember the words of my father, as he and Mom stood at the foot of my bed, thinking I was asleep. "T can be anything he wants. I just hope he never loses the magic of being a child."

I can remember thinking, *I won't, Pop...I won't.*

Then I was off to Oz in my sleep. Flying on a magic carpet, running with the Munchkins and all the characters I'd come to know and love as friends.

I'd dance with the Scarecrow, laugh with the Cowardly Lion, and marvel at the Tin Man and all the other characters that came and went as my imagination dictated.

Who cared about the problems of the world when you were over the rainbow in Oz? I swore I would never lose the magic of being a child.

But like all of us, I did. Call it growing up, getting married, and paying a mortgage. It just seems to be a fact of life that growing up means that we get the magic washed out of our souls so we can act like adults are supposed to act.

But my promise to my father came back years later as I was reading the Oz books to my own children. It was as if my father were standing next to me, nodding approval that I was reading to my own children instead of leaving them in front of a TV.

Don't let them lose the magic of being a child, he seemed to be telling me. *And remember T, you don't have to grow old in your mind.*

I won't, Pop...I won't.

And in my mind that night, after the kids were asleep, I went hand in hand with the sandman back to Oz. I crossed over the rainbow and went back to that magical place where everything is as it ought to be.

I wasn't an adult who had to think "old" any longer, I was an adult who hadn't forgotten the magic of childhood. And when I awakened, I began the story of Dorothy's return to Oz.

I wrote it for my own children and for all the children of the world. I give this gift of eternal childhood to each of you and ask only one thing in return: that you pass it on to your own children and grandchildren. Give it to the children of relatives and neighbors.

Read to them. Take them by the hand and let them step over the rainbow. Give their minds wings so they can soar and become what they want to be.

Life is hard enough without losing the gift of imagination. All you have to do is believe.

T. L. Tedrow

FROM ORLANDO

TO KANSAS

CHAPTER 1

ORLANDO

The summer of Dorothy Gale's twelfth birthday had only just begun, and already it was the most difficult of her life. Her father was still out of work, they had the house up for sale, and her parents had begun arguing over money problems.

Since the Orlando, Florida, defense plant where her father had worked for twenty years, closed down, the only job offer he had was in Detroit, Michigan. Dorothy was heartsick at the thought of moving away from her school and friends.

Though her parents had struggled to hold on until her father could find another job in the Orlando area, nothing had come up. The income that her mother brought in was not enough to pay all their bills, so Dorothy knew that moving away was all but inevitable.

It was the first day of summer vacation, when all her friends were leaving for the beach, but Dorothy sat in her room staring at the wall. Her mother, Linda Gale, had just dropped a bombshell on her.

They wanted her to go spend the summer with her elderly grandmother in Kansas. They wanted her to leave the next morning.

"But I don't want to go to Kansas! I want to go to the beach!" Dorothy exclaimed.

Her mother wasn't going to be swayed. Their financial problems were mounting and had brought their marriage to the breaking point. So they had decided that a summer away for Dorothy would be the best thing for all.

"You're going. Your grandmother's already bought the ticket."

"Why can't I go to the beach and stay with Rita's parents?" Dorothy asked, her eyes welling up. "They'll let me stay with them."

"Because we can't afford it and I won't have you imposing on the Thomas' for the summer."

Dorothy crossed her arms and frowned as hard as a twelve-year-old girl could. "But we went last year and..."

"And last year your father was working. You know what our finances are like."

Dorothy knew but didn't want to accept the fact. She also didn't want to go spend the summer with her grandmother.

"But all the other kids are going to the beach and you want me to go to...to Kansas?" Dorothy said, as if Kansas were somewhere between Pluto and Uranus.

"That's where I met your father. It's a wonderful state," her mother said, moving about Dorothy's room, straightening up and putting things away.

Linda Gale looked at her daughter from the corner of her eye. She didn't want to frighten Dorothy, but they were nearly out of money and would have to be moving into an apartment soon.

For months, she and her husband Ed had tried to put on a strong front for Dorothy's sake, but all had crumbled when they had been forced by their bills to put the house up for sale. It was either that or file for bankruptcy.

Dorothy was pouting, so her mother said, "There's nothing wrong with Kansas. That's where your roots are."

"There's *everything* wrong with Kansas," Dorothy complained, pushing her shoulder-length brunette hair away from her face.

"You're just being silly."

"No I'm not," Dorothy said. "I remember when I was there the last time. It's hot, flat, and boring."

"You were only two years old when you were there," Linda Gale laughed.

"I bet it's still the same!" Dorothy said, so upset that she didn't catch her mother's sarcasm.

"Quit acting like a baby. Your father and I think it will be good for you." Her expression became serious. "This may be the last time you'll ever see your grandmother. She's seventy-two, you know."

"Seventy-two? You want me to spend the summer with a seventy-two-year-old woman?"

"She still gets around pretty well."

In her mind, Dorothy saw herself pushing a wheelchair along the front porch of a rest home. "Can she still walk?"

Linda Gale chuckled. "I think your grandmother will surprise you. She always does me."

"Why doesn't Dad go too? It's *his* mother."

Dorothy's mother shook her head. "Your father and I have some important decisions to make."

"Did he get the Orlando job he's been hoping for?" Dorothy asked.

Her mother shook her head and looked away. "No, it hasn't come through yet."

She blinked back what Dorothy thought was a tear and looked out the window. "But we're both keeping our fingers crossed," she said quietly, unconsciously crossing her right index and middle fingers.

Dorothy crossed hers also. "I've been saying my prayers for him," she said. Her mother nodded, still looking towards the FOR SALE sign in the yard.

Dorothy loved her father more than life itself and worried that unless he got a job soon, something bad was going to happen to the family. It was a fear that grew worse each night as she listened to her parents' arguments drift down the hallway to her bedroom.

"I wish we didn't have to sell the house, Mom."

"I know, dear," her mother said. She looked at Dorothy for a long moment, then turned abruptly towards the door. "But that's life," she said, trying to change the mood.

"I still don't want to go," Dorothy said, believing that her last chance to change her mother's mind was slipping away.

"A summer in the country will do you good," Linda Gale said, resting her hand on the doorknob.

"Then why don't *you* go?" Dorothy asked, feeling like her opinion wasn't counting for anything.

Her mother answered as she walked down the hall towards the stairs. "Because I grew up there."

"And that's why you moved away," Dorothy said under her breath.

"I heard that," Linda Gale called back, her footsteps down the stairs echoing through the house.

Dorothy heard a car door slam out front. "Hey, Dorothy," she heard her friend, Rita Thomas, call out.

Dorothy went to the window and opened it. "Hi, Rita. Hi, Mr. T," she said, using her nickname for Rita's father.

"I thought someone had bought your house?" Rita asked, standing next to the FOR SALE sign that had been in front of their house for the past month.

"The contract fell through," Dorothy said, not unhappy that the house hadn't sold. She had been hoping against hope that her father would land a good job in Orlando so they wouldn't have to move away.

"Are you going to rent the same place at Cocoa Beach this summer? My parents are taking me down today and I want to know how to contact you."

"There's been a change of plans," Dorothy said flatly, looking away for a brief moment to collect her thoughts.

"Are you going earlier then?" Rita asked.

"No," Dorothy said, feeling her eyes well up, "I'm not going at all." She locked eyes with her friend. "I'm going to *Kansas*," she said, drawing out the word like it was synonymous with going to prison.

"Kansas!" Rita exclaimed. "Who lives there?"

"My grandmother."

Rita couldn't hold back her smile. "I can't wait to hear you tell the class what you did on *your* summer vacation." Then she looked perplexed. "What do they do in the country? Play Yahtzee and go clogging?"

"How the heck should I know," Dorothy said. "The only country I know is the country music my dad listens to."

"Good luck with the cows and chickens," Rita laughed.

"Thanks a lot."

Rita left happily and Dorothy was left feeling sorry for herself. She didn't like the thought of being packed up and shipped away.

This would be her first summer away from home and she might return and find that the only home she'd ever known had been sold and her possessions were on their way to Detroit.

Then she heard her parents arguing again downstairs. *I wish they'd make u*p, Dorothy thought. *I wish they wouldn't keep arguing about money.*

"We've got to move," Dorothy heard her mother say from the kitchen.

"But I don't want to take Dorothy from her friends and school. We can make it in an apartment and..."

"Ed, you've got to face the facts."

"Facts? I can find another job. We can make it here in Orlando in an apartment."

Dorothy heard her mother stamp her foot. "You're dreaming. You've got to take the job in Detroit. At least we'd be able to pay our bills."

The problems between her parents had been building up for a long time. Dorothy had seen it coming. When her father lost his job at the defense plant, he'd acted like he was king of the mountain.

"I'll land another in a week!" he exclaimed, dancing Dorothy around the living room.

But Dorothy knew that her king of the mountain was putting on a brave front. *He didn't want to make me worry,* she sighed. *He'd do anything not to hurt me.*

It wasn't that her father hadn't tried to find work, but all the best leads were out of town. He didn't want to move from Orlando and neither did Dorothy.

But as their money dwindled away and the bills mounted up, Dorothy knew what the FOR SALE sign meant. She knew that unless he landed a job soon, that the house would be sold and she'd be living in another city and going to another school by September.

Probably in Detroit, she sighed. *Where they make cars, it snows, and they probably don't like girls from Florida.*

On her dresser was a picture of a small girl being held up in the air by her father, a handsome man in a T-shirt. The girl was Dorothy when she was five years old.

Dad loved to play the golden ruler game, she smiled. *I haven't thought about that for a long time.*

She looked at the crudely written words under the picture that she'd crayoned in when she was six years old:

GoLdEn RulER
TrEat Others right

Feeling sorry for herself, Dorothy stretched out on her bed. She laid her head back on the pillow and drifted off to sleep, to a happier time and place when the picture was taken.

In her mind she was back there again. Before the arguments. Before her father had lost his job.

CHAPTER 2

GOLDEN RULER

In her dream it was just Dorothy and her dad. She was six years old and he looked a lifetime younger, free from worries.

They were laughing in the backyard, hugging like there was no tomorrow. In her mind she was a million smiles away from the problems confronting her.

No thoughts of Kansas. No thoughts of selling the house. Just a girl and her dad, happy to be together.

"See the rainbow up there?" her father said, pointing towards the sky. Little Dorothy looked up eagerly, following his finger line to the clouds.

"Pretty colors," she said, marveling at the arc of red and yellow that hung in the distance.

"Rainbows are *pretty* special." Ed Gale smiled, admiring the wonder of nature. It was the same conversation his mother had once had with him.

"Where's the pot of gold? Over the rainbow?" Dorothy squealed.

"Maybe a pot of fool's gold," he sighed. *That's what mother said to me. I can remember the moment,* he thought.

"But if we found the gold, we'd have all the money in the world," Dorothy laughed, skipping around her father's legs.

"If you go looking for a free pot of gold, all you'll find is a pot full of disappointment." He looked at his daughter. "Life is what you make of it...how you treat others is worth more than all the gold in the world."

Dorothy was confused. "Then what's over the rainbow?"

Ed Gale brightened. "Over the rainbow is a place where everyone abides by the Golden Rule." He started to tell Dorothy what his mother had told him about Oz, but stopped. *Now's not the time.*

"The what?" Dorothy asked.

"The Golden Rule."

Dorothy scrunched her nose. "Golden ruler?"

"Golden ruler," he nodded, thinking about the term. "That's close enough. Matter of fact, that's what they should call it," he said. *That's what Mother called it...Why would Dorothy pick that name?* he wondered.

"What's the golden ruler?" Dorothy asked, grabbing his hand.

"It's the measure of how you should treat people."

"Treat the rainbow people over there?" she asked, pointing to the colorful band across the sky.

"All people. Here, there, and everywhere."

He looked at his daughter, giving her the serious look he reserved for special thoughts he wanted her to remember. "The golden ruler is simple. Do unto others as you would have them do unto you."

Dorothy closed her eyes, thinking about what he'd said. "What's *unto* mean?" she asked, opening one eye.

"Unto, ah..." her father stammered, then stopped. "Maybe I'll just make it simpler. Just remember to treat others like you want to be treated."

She repeated his words. "You mean, if you want someone to be nice, you be nice to them?"

"Exactly! Now, repeat the golden ruler," he said, making her say it until she had it right.

When he was satisfied, he smiled. "And that's the golden ruler. That's how I want you to treat your friends."

"Even bullies?" Dorothy asked suspiciously.

"*Even* bullies. That's what makes the golden ruler so special. You'd be surprised at what simple kindness will bring. Heck," he sighed, shaking his head, "might just change the world if we'd all just change our ways and abide by it."

"Lift me up. Please, Daddy!" Dorothy said, wanting to be swung in his arms.

Her father lifted her up above his head. "What's the golden ruler?" he shouted out as he tossed her up and down.

"Treat..."

"Others," he helped, catching her by the waist.

"As you want to be treated," she said, trying to catch her breath as she went up into the air and came back down again. He caught her perilously close to the ground.

"Say it again," he gently commanded.

"Treat others," they both began in unison, "as you want to be treated."

He held her out in front of him by her shoulders. Her feet dangled above the ground. "Now close your eyes," he smiled. She did as he asked without hesitation.

"Never forget the golden ruler. It's the measure of a good person."

"Yes, Dad," she said, kicking her feet. "Now can I open my eyes?"

"One...two...three," he said, then swung her up into the air. Dorothy gasped, but didn't cry out.

Her father caught her before she reached the ground. "I'll *always* be there if you need me," he smiled, hugging her tightly. "And don't you *ever* forget that."

"I won't, Daddy," she mumbled in her sleep, then felt the presence of someone in her room.

"You asleep, Pumpkin?" her father asked.

Dorothy blinked awake and smiled. "Are you okay, Dad?"

"Sure, Pumpkin, sure," he smiled, worried that the house being up for sale was a terrible burden for his daughter to carry.

Reaching over to the dresser, he picked up the picture she'd been dreaming about. "Those were happier times, weren't they?" he asked quietly, a look of concern on his face. Dorothy nodded.

"Mother said you don't want to go to Kansas." He frowned, getting to what he'd come up to her room to discuss.

Dorothy sat up. "I don't want to leave you and Mom."

He took her hand and sat down. "Your mom and I need some time to work a few things out."

"Like moving to Detroit?" Dorothy asked, looking intently into her father's blue eyes.

"That and other things," he nodded. "You'll have a better time away from here."

"But Grandma D is kinda strange and..."

"And she loves you," he interrupted, then thought for a moment. "You know, you were both born on the exact same day and she claims the exact same hour." He shook his head. "She always said that made you special...but you know how Grandma D is."

"But all she likes to talk about on the phone is that crazy stuff about the Land of Oz and..."

Her father nodded his head. "I know. That's all she liked to talk about when I was growin' up. About going back to Oz."

Dorothy gave her father a funny look. "Mom says she's got a barn full of crazy inventions."

He nodded. "I think that's why your Mom never wanted to go back and visit after the last time."

"What happened the last time?" Dorothy asked, her curiosity showing.

"That was a long time ago. You wouldn't understand."

"Try me."

Her father sighed. "Let's just say that your Mother and Grandma D had a disagreement about her tellin' you stories about Oz."

"Then why does she want me to go back now?"

Dorothy could see the momentary hurt in her father's eyes and could feel it in his words. "Because your Mom and I've got some big decisions to make and it's probably best that you're not here."

He looked into the eyes of his daughter. "Pumpkin, children shouldn't have to be worrying their summers away. You'll be grown before you know it. You don't need to be around any of this."

"But I'm twelve years old," Dorothy said, as if that were closer to twenty-one than thirteen.

"And that's why I want you to have a fun summer. Soon you'll be an obnoxious old teenager who'll give me a hard time and..."

"Oh, Dad, not that teenager stuff again."

He took another look at the picture on the dresser and grinned. "You'll be surprised what your grandmother is capable of."

"But Grandma's old and I'm too old for fairy tales and..."

"And this might be the last time you'll ever see her alive." He took Dorothy's hand. "I can't tell you how much the visit will mean to her."

Dorothy looked at her father in frustration. She was caught between respecting the wishes of her parents and her own desires.

"I don't want to go!" she finally said, firmly locking her jaw. "And I don't want to hear about Oz. I'm not a kid anymore you know."

Ed Gale crossed his arms and put on a pretend frown. "You're always saying that I act like a big kid."

Dorothy wasn't going to fall for one of his tricks. "You're different."

"There's nothing wrong with your grandmother's dreams. I grew up hearing all about Oz." Then he shrugged. "Maybe that's why I'm such a big kid, huh?" he asked, raising his eyebrows and cocking his head to the side.

"But it's not true. There's no place like Oz."

"Who says?"

"*Mom*," Dorothy said, like her mother was the final authority on everything.

"Mothers can be very wise in practical things," her father said, picking his words carefully. "But sometimes they forget about the magic of childhood."

Dorothy gave him a perplexed look. Her father shrugged. "I guess the magic kind of gets washed out of them like dirt in the laundry. It just slips away and before you know it they just sort of act...act..."

He struggled for a nice word, but Dorothy blurted out, "Old?"

Her father smiled. "I guess that's a blunt way to describe it."

"Do you believe in magic, Dad?"

"I believe in the magic of childhood." Dorothy waited for him to say something else, but in his usual way, he left it to her imagination to figure out what he meant.

Dorothy thought about what her father had said, then frowned, perplexed. "But Grandma D is *your* mother."

"So?"

"So she hasn't forgotten about magic and *she's* a mother."

Ed Gale laughed. "You got me there," he said, hugging her. He thought about all his mother's stories about the land of Oz, the Emerald City, the Tin Woodman and the Scarecrow.

No one else believed her...not even Dad. He just humored her because he loved her so much. But I believed her.

"I guess your mom is special then," Dorothy said quietly.

Ed Gale blinked, licking his lips as he collected his thoughts. "All Moms are special. It's just that my mom...well...let's just say that maybe my mom just never grew up."

"Sort of like you then?" Dorothy said, with a mischievous smile.

"Sort of," he smiled. "This visit will mean everything in the world to your grandmother."

"But I don't want to go," she said, hugging him as hard as she could, knowing that the decision had been made for her.

"I know, I know, Pumpkin, but things aren't always as we want them to be."

"I wish they were," she stammered, the first tears beginning to fall.

"I wish they were too," he said. "I wish we lived in a land of things as they ought to be. Wouldn't that be neat?"

Dorothy nodded. "Like over the rainbow?"

"Like over the rainbow. Where everyone believes in the golden ruler," her father said, hugging her like she was still just his little girl.

Dorothy nestled in his arms, melting into the love and good memories of a lifetime. She didn't want to think about leaving for Kansas in the morning. She didn't want to think about the house being sold and moving away.

She just wanted to think about a place where things were as they ought to be. Where people followed the golden ruler. Like in Oz, she sighed, wishing this feeling of warmth and security in her father's arms would last forever.

CHAPTER 3

CLICK-CLICK-CLICK

The next morning, in an attic in the small town of Osawatomie, Kansas, an old woman sat mulling over her life. The open, musty trunk in front of her contained all her secrets of the world, but her mind was drifting.

Hearing the creak of the rafters and the groan of the walls against the stiff prairie wind that blew across the farm, she cleared her throat, looking around. *This old house is like me: old, broken down, and ready to go.*

Though the house needed painting and buckled boards needed replacing, it was the only house she'd ever lived in, not counting the orphanage she'd been raised in. But that was long ago and though she'd never learned who her parents were, the old woman truly considered Auntie Em and Uncle Henry to be them.

Auntie Em and Uncle Henry. Those were the names they liked to be called. They raised me. Left me their farm.

Dorothy Gale, who now liked to be called Grandma D, thought about how much the house had changed since she first arrived with her cloth suitcase in hand.

It used to be just a one room shack. Four walls, a floor and a roof. Weren't no trees on the flat prairie back then so every board was precious. Had to take the wagon miles just to find new fence posts.

Though they were probably poor by most standards, Grandma D remembered how rich her life had been in that one room they all lived in. Though they'd expanded the house over the years, the memories of that little room they started out in remained a bright memory.

We had just a rusty cook stove, some cracked dishes, a mended table, and three chairs. They slept behind a sheet in a bed in the corner and Uncle Henry had made me a small bed in the other corner.

I'll never forget looking out the window at the prairie that stretched forever to the edge of the sky, thinking I'd never want to live anywhere else. God had put me in this time and place for a reason, so I swore I'd never move away. That was a promise I made and a secret I never told anyone.

But there were other secrets that she'd kept hidden in the attic. Grandma D looked into the trunk again.

She'd never shown anyone the secrets she'd hidden in the trunk. Never in sixty years, since she'd been taken to Oz by the tornado and brought back to Kansas by clicking the ruby shoes.

Though she wanted to share her secrets, she had never shown them to her family or friends. Not to Auntie Em or Uncle Henry, who'd willed her the same house that she'd gone to Oz in. Not to her friends or even to her late husband, Roy.

The secrets in the trunk would have proved to everyone that Oz was real. But Grandma D felt that showing what she had would destroy the magic.

Most everyone in the county thought she was just an eccentric, old woman, a crackpot who tinkered with strange inventions and painted strange pictures of fairytale creatures.

Though no one had believed her about the tornado taking her to Oz, Grandma D knew where she had been. If she hadn't seen the Emerald City with her own eyes, she wouldn't have believed it existed either.

But she'd been there, so Grandma D didn't care what people thought: Oz existed. It was in a far away, magical place just over the rainbow...and she'd been there.

But getting back there was something she'd never been able to figure out how to do in sixty years. Her only link to Oz and the proof of her visit, which she'd never shown to anyone, was in the trunk.

In front of Grandma D were the once-ruby shoes, a newspaper and a small child's snow-shaker crystal ball—the kind you shake to make the snow fly around inside.

The shoes were the same ones she'd taken from the Wicked Witch who had died when the house had crushed her. Grandma D could still remember the Good Witch Glenda's words as she sat on her ruby throne:

> *"The ruby shoes have magical powers. And one of the most wonderful things about them is that they will carry you to any place in the world in three steps. Just three steps in the wink of an eye. Just click them together three times and command the shoes to carry you wherever you wish to go."*

Then she kissed me and the shoes took me home. Grandma D looked at the shoes. *Why won't they work now? Why won't they carry me back to Oz?*

She remembered how she'd clicked together the heels of those same shoes sixty years ago, saying, "Take me home to Auntie Em." *In an instant I was whirling through the air. Couldn't see anything but the wind until I found myself sitting in the middle of the Kansas prairie.*

Grandma D sighed. *Auntie Em found me running toward the house in my stocking feet. The ruby shoes must have fallen off as I tumbled head over heels.*

"Where on Earth did you come from?" Auntie Em called out, taking me into her arms.

"From the Land of Oz," I told her.

Though I tried to convince her that everything I said was true, she and Uncle Henry just told me I'd been dreaming. I thought it was a dream too. That Oz didn't exist. But then I found them.

Grandma D nodded, then shook her head. *Never told anyone what I found in the tornado's wreckage. Found the shoes and then I found the newspaper and the snow-shaker crystal ball.*

Grandma D picked up the snow-shaker ball. To anyone else, it looked like a child's toy from Kmart, with just a small green castle inside. But Grandma D knew that when you shook it, it became the Emerald City, glistening with all the beauty that she remembered.

She shook the snow in the ball, watching the flakes dance around until they settled. Then the ball began to glow and she could see the Emerald City.

It's been sixty years since I was there, Grandma D thought. *I want to go back just once more before I die.*

She sat there looking at the crystal ball, wondering how many thousands of times she had sat there, shaking the ball and peering through the snow at the sparkling city.

"Guess I might be a bit crazy," she mumbled to herself. "Believing in a place which I saw just once and never saw again."

If it hadn't been for the copy of *The Emerald City Times* that she'd found in the tornado's wreckage, Grandma D might have doubted her own sanity. But the newspaper was the *real* proof of Oz.

The Emerald City Times was magical, because the headlines and the articles changed each day, which was how she kept up with the events in Oz over the years.

Grandma D looked at the headline:

WHEN WILL DOROTHY RETURN?

"When?" she whispered. "That's what I've been asking all my life."

The headline changed again:

DOROTHY, PLEASE COME BACK!

"How?" she said, holding the newspaper up. "Tell me how?"

The headlines had been changing like this for the past week. Grandma D knew that something was happening in Oz and they needed her back.

But neither the headlines nor the stories told her what was wrong so she was left to guess. *I wonder what they need me for? What could it be?*

She looked at the shoes she'd taken from the Wicked Witch. The once ruby shoes were still red, but they didn't have any rubies.

She slipped the old shoes on her feet and clicked them together. "Take me back to Oz."

The click-click-click of the shoes made a lonely sound, answered only by the dust swirls and the creak of the floorboards.

"Why won't they work?" she asked herself in frustration. "I've got to get back to Oz."

She picked up the bag of rubies and pondered the mystery that had bothered her for sixty years. *Why did the rubies fall off my shoes when I came back? Why won't they stay on when I glue them back onto the shoes?*

No matter what kind of glue she used—Super Glue, Elmer's Glue, wood glue—the results were always the same. The rubies would just drop off. And without the rubies, they weren't ruby shoes, which made all the difference in the world.

With a deep sigh, Grandma D looked again at the newspaper and snow-shaker. Sometimes she still wondered why she hadn't shared the contents of the trunk when the kids at school had mocked her on the playground, all those years ago. But even then, Grandma D felt that to show anyone what she'd brought back would destroy her only link to Oz.

No one knew that in the trunk was the proof that the Land of Oz existed. That the Scarecrow, Tin Man and Cowardly Lion had all been real, not figments of a young girl's imagination. That the pictures of the Wizard and all her Oz friends that she'd painted over the years as a hobby were not made up dreams.

But over time, Grandma D had given up trying to convince people about the land over the rainbow. She was content to live peacefully on the farm she called Ozcot, keeping Oz alive in her heart and mind, following the headlines on *The Emerald City Times*.

In her own crazy way, Grandma D had spent her life trying to return to Oz. The barn was full of inventions and contraptions she'd put together in hopes of finding a way back.

They were wind machines of all shapes and sizes. Inventions that came from dreams. Contraptions that came from books.

Crazy machines that could feed off electricity, thunder, and lightning, and produce winds that could make another tornado to take her back to Oz.

Though she knew it would be dangerous if she was able to create a tornado, Grandma D had long ago come to the conclusion that the only way she would get back to Oz would be to ride another sky-high tunnel of fury. That was why she had spent all her time and money on the machines she'd dreamed up.

But none of them had worked. She sat frustrated in the attic, knowing that Oz needed her but not knowing how to get there.

It's got to be something about the rubies falling off the shoes. If they'd just stay on, I know I could get back.

"Make these shoes work," she commanded, as if she had magic powers.

"Take me back to the Land of Oz." She clicked the heels again, feeling foolish, wishing that, just for once, the magic sparkle would happen again. But nothing happened.

A whoosh of wind hit the house, shaking it more than usual for a Kansas summer. Then another gust of wind shook the rafters.

Through the window Grandma D saw the makings of a dust devil in the distance. She knew that something was going to happen soon. She could feel it in her bones.

But she didn't know how, what, or when.

It was in the air, in the wind, and in the way her inventions and contraptions in the barn had begun to move around on their own. It was in the way that lightning and thunder had been crackling over the farm more and more.

Oz wanted her back. All she had to do was figure out how to make a tornado to get there.

A burst of wind shook the attic window frames, sending small pieces of rock-solid putty falling to the floor. "I hear you," she said to herself, as if the wind were sent from Oz.

Grandma D walked over and looked out the window. Though it was just early summer, the wind and dark skies reminded her of that time sixty years before when the tornado struck and lifted her to Oz.

I wonder if Alexander has gotten the new machine to work? she wondered, looking towards the barn. Alexander Bean was the boy she'd hired to help work on her inventions.

He was a local twelve-year-old, frail boy with glasses. The farm kids liked to tease him and called him *bookworm*, because he read so much. Grandma D had hired him for his book sense. Alexander thought that she was just a crazy old lady who liked to make crazy machines.

Got to see if he's found a way to make the wind work backwards and forwards at the same time. It was a theory she'd developed, after watching the dust devils created by crop-dusting planes taking off in different directions.

But without my ruby shoes, I can never get back. She clicked them again. "I want to go see the Wizard." Nothing happened at all.

Why won't the shoes work? she wondered, looking down.

Grandma D closed her eyes, gritted her teeth and clicked her heels. "I want to go back to Oz!" she said again, sounding like a magician in a low budget movie. The only thing that moved was the dust in the attic.

It was nearing the same day of the month when the tornado had struck sixty years before. And for some reason, whether it had something to do with the stars, moon, tides, or whatever, Dorothy Gale knew that Oz needed her.

The goose bumps and shivers that reading the newspaper headlines gave her convinced Grandma D that Oz was in trouble, serious trouble.

She shook the snow-shaker crystal ball again and looked at the Emerald City. "Bring me back," she pleaded in a soft whisper. "I'm ready to help. I'll do anything you need."

Though she could see the Emerald City in the crystal ball, she was no closer to getting back to Oz at that moment than she'd been in sixty years.

Peering closer at the beautiful, green castle, Grandma D saw a banner unfurl from the top of the tallest building. *HELP!* was written in big, bold letters.

Grandma D shook the crystal ball again and the banner flapped in the snow flurry. A shiver so cold that it felt like ice crept up her spine as another banner appeared: *COME NOW!*

Then, in front of her eyes, the headline of the newspaper dissolved and a new one appeared:

THE WIZARD NEEDS DOROTHY

"Oh gosh," she whispered, "I know somethin' bad's happened."

Grandma D closed her eyes and concentrated. "I'm ready!" she shouted, clicking her heels. "I want to go off to see the Wizard. He needs me." Then she looked down at the rubyless shoes.

Grabbing up the bag of rubies, she clicked her heels again. "Take me to the Emerald City."

"Nothing!" she said in frustration.

She counted to ten and clicked them again...and again and again and again. Finally, her knees and ankles aching from all the clicking, she leaned against the rocker and asked the newspaper, "How do I get there?" she whispered.

When she'd regained her strength, she straightened up and positioned the shoes exactly as she'd done in Oz. Grandma D clicked the heels of her rubyless shoes three times and spun around, commanding the shoes, but nothing happened. She clicked them again and spun around, but the only thing that happened was her joints cracked.

"I'm trying," she cried out. "I'm ready to go!" she shouted.

From the first floor, an old man called out, "Are you talkin' to yourself again?" Grandma D stopped and looked towards the stairwell.

Doc Jones, who had known Grandma D since grade school, looked up towards the attic. "Did you hear me Dorothy Gale? Where are you ready to go to? To the loony bin?"

"*Yes I heard you* and *no* I ain't goin' to the loony bin and *no* I *ain't* talkin' to myself," she shouted back, irritated for being disturbed when Oz was calling her back.

"Then who were you talkin' to?" he shouted, enjoying the thought of how irritated she probably was.

Grandma D *was* irritated. "The man in the moon. Now leave me alone."

"I can't hear you so good," Doc shouted back. "Come over to the stairs so I can hear you better." Grandma D walked over to the stairwell and looked down.

"You know, Dorothy Gale," Doc said, smiling, "if you weren't so gall-darn hard to get along with, why I might just ask you to marry me one day."

"Well, I guess I'll just stay the way I am so we can stay the way we are."

"What exactly are we?" Doc asked.

"We're two old people who're too old to be gettin' married."

"Never too old for love, Dorothy Gale. You best learn that before you die."

Grandma D saw the hurt in Doc's eyes and sighed. She knew that Doc had been crazy about her since grade school. And she also knew that if it hadn't been for the Korean War and his being drafted, they'd have gotten married.

But that was a long time ago and she'd met her husband Roy while Doc was gone and...*and the rest is history*, she thought. *Old history. Ancient history. Not worth thinking about or getting worked up over what could have been.*

Doc looked up at her. He had never loved and would never love another woman but Dorothy Gale. It was the pledge he'd made in the sixth grade when they'd shared their first kiss under the Thompsons' stairs.

He'd lost her when he'd been drafted into the Korean War, and when he came back, he knew he could never love anyone else. So he'd stayed a bachelor, content to remain friends with Dorothy and her husband Roy. But now that Roy had died, he wanted to start up where they left off before it was too late.

"You just hush and get ready to go to the airport," Grandma D said, knowing he was about to start talking about marriage again.

"But the plane hasn't even left Orlando yet."

"Don't matter. Takes you longer to get ready than there's hours in a day."

Doc Jones looked back up at her. "If you'd just consent to marry me, I wouldn't have to spend so much time comin' back and forth between your place and mine."

"Just hush and call the airline to check if it's on time."

Doc shook his head. "Don't see why you're so worried about seein' her, seein's how you..." Then he stopped and held his tongue.

"Say it."

"No," Doc said. "That wasn't right of me."

Grandma D let down her guard just a bit. "No, go on and say it. I haven't seen my own granddaughter in ten years because I've spent all my money on my inventions in the barn."

Doc tried to ease her conscience. "They could have come to see you."

"They did the last time and every time they asked me to come visit them, I always made up some excuse or some reason I couldn't go."

"Better late than never," Doc shrugged. "Say, speaking of being late, did you pay that property tax bill yet?" Doc asked, frowning. He knew she was always late paying her bills and had more than once rushed down to the power office to keep her electricity on.

"I told you, it ain't come yet. Don't you ever listen?" Grandma D said, irritated.

Doc stood his ground for her own good. "Don't know why you're the only one in the county who ain't got their tax bill yet. I still say you should call them up and ask where yours is before Ozcot ends up on the courthouse steps."

Grandma D grunted in frustration. "If the taxman don't want to send me a bill, then that's fine with me. No tax news is good news if you ask me."

"You're playin' with fire. You ought to just go and find out what you owe and pay it."

She didn't want him to know that she'd spent the property tax money she'd been saving on her latest tornado machine. "Just go to the airport and get my granddaughter."

Doc kicked the side of the stairs harder than he intended and hurt his foot. "Will you let me pay it for you then?"

"No! Then you'll probably think you got a right to move in and marry me."

"Things could be worse, you know." Doc adjusted his belt and then looked up intently. "Don't be comin' to move in with me if you end up gettin' evicted."

"That's a promise, you old fool. I'd rather live in the barn."

Doc chuckled. "You won't even have a barn if they evict you."

Grandma D sighed. "Now get goin'. That Kansas City airport's a long way off."

Grandma D watched her old friend shake his head and walk towards the kitchen. She had no idea how worried he was about the taxes on Ozcot not being paid.

He'd seen the courthouse auctions for farmers who hadn't paid their property taxes and was worried half to death that in her stubbornness, Grandma D would suffer the same fate.

Just wish she'd get it over with and marry me, he thought, shaking his head as he looked at the stack of bills on the kitchen counter.

He picked up the power bill, marked OVERDUE, and put it in his pocket. *Guess I'll just pay this later. She'll never know.*

Grandma D had no idea that Doc had been paying most of her bills and covering her bad checks at the bank. Doc knew that she spent every dime she could find on her inventions in the barn. That was just the way that Grandma D was and one of the reasons he loved her so much.

Ozzie, Grandma D's dachshund, scratched at Doc's leg. "I ain't feedin' you no more, you darn weener dog," he grumbled, nudging the dog away with his foot.

Ozzie turned in circles, then rolled over. "Oh, all right," Doc said. He always gave in when Ozzie did a trick.

Opening the refrigerator door, Doc looked at the food he'd brought over for Grandma D that morning. That was another thing she never seemed to notice.

"Let's see. You like prunes?" he laughed. Ozzie lay down and put his paws over his eyes.

"No, I guess you don't."

Doc reached back into the refrigerator, moving aside the milk and orange juice cartons. "Ah-ha," he smiled. "Try eatin' your cousin," he said, opening a pack of hot dogs. Ozzie sniffed the meat and sat up.

"Here's a weener for a weener dog," he laughed, tossing it to the small dog. Ozzie grabbed the hot dog, which was half as long as he was, and scampered under the kitchen table.

Up in the attic, Grandma D trudged back over to the trunk and picked up the Oz paper again. "I'm ready to come back. I want to come back. But the rubies won't stay on the shoes."

Putting the paper down, she held up the bag of deep-red stones to the bulb hanging from the ceiling. The stones glistened, reflecting light spots onto the nail-filled ceiling boards.

She click-clicked the shoes one more time for good measure before putting them back into the trunk. It had been a daily, secret routine she'd done since she was twelve years old.

The wizard needs me for somethin', she worried, looking at the headline.

The newspaper headline was the only way she'd kept up with what had happened in the Land of Oz over the years. She stood in the dusty attic, thinking about those changes.

The Wizard's son is still running things. Ura Wizard's got to be about my age now. I wonder what he's like?

Then she chuckled and thought of her old traveling companions, the Scarecrow, Tin Woodman and the Cowardly Lion. *They were such wonderful friends.*

She was sad when they'd died of old age, almost within months of each other, and remembered how she'd wept when she read the headlines on *The Emerald City Times*.

Grandma D closed her eyes, trying to push thoughts of her old friends away, and then the nightmare came back to her. It had been occurring and reoccurring for days.

It was a nightmare of a woman dressed in black. With dark, blazing eyes and lips the color of blood. The daughter of the Wicked Witch had come to haunt her.

CHAPTER 4

WICKED WITCH

Grandma D had been having disturbing visions of Ima, the Wicked Witch of the North, daughter of her old enemy, the Wicked Witch of the West.

She knew what Ima looked like from the pictures she'd seen in *The Emerald City Times*, and had read the stories about how her beautiful face was just a mask for her true ways.

The nightmares came almost daily now. Grandma D gritted her teeth, pinched her arm and tried to wake herself up, but nothing worked. She was under the witch's power again.

Standing in front of her was the Wicked Witch's daughter, Ima Witch, dressed in black and pointing her long, blood-red fingernail. Though she didn't wear a witch's hat, her hair was done up in a swirling style that ended in a point.

Around her neck was a dark green necklace. At the end, glowing green in the darkness of the attic with venomous, ruby-red eyes, hung an evil-looking dragon.

"Hello, orphan girl," Ima taunted. "Dorothy, you look about one step removed from the grave."

If Grandma D had noticed, she would have seen that the shadow of the witch's face looked different than her appearance; that there was even a hat on her head, but Grandma D was too frightened.

"Leave me alone. You're just a nightmare," Grandma D said, blinking. She thought she saw the tongue of the dragon slither out from the necklace, as it stretched its wings.

Ima nodded. "I'm your worst nightmare, yes, I am," Ima whispered, moving around the attic. She stopped and petted the dragon necklace. "Do you like my little...dragonfly?" she smiled, leaning down and kissing the dragon's cheek.

Grandma D covered her face. "Go away."

"You want to pet Itsa?" Ima asked, holding out the glowing green pendant. "Itsa Dragon...get it? *It's a* dragon." Ima chuckled at her own joke. "I like that name. Don't you?"

The eyes of the dragon came alive as it turned its head and hissed, then slowly flew off.

Grandma D watched the dragon fly towards her, then clicked her heels. "Leave me alone," she pleaded, as the dragon flew slowly around her head then returned to Ima's necklace.

"You'll never return!" Ima shouted. "Oz will soon be mine!"

"No," Grandma D whispered, covering her heart with her hand.

"Yes!" screamed the witch, throwing her head back in wicked laughter. "You're too late to help the Wizard!"

"I won't listen to you!" Grandma D said, covering her ears and closing her eyes.

"Then listen to this," Ima said, lowering her voice. "I'll tell you who your parents were."

Grandma D's eyes opened slowly. She looked at the witch. "Do you know? Do you know who my parents were?"

"Of course," Ima grinned. "And I'll even write their names down for you." A pencil and paper appeared in front of the witch.

"Oh, please," Grandma D whispered, watching Ima write out two names.

"Yes, old Dorothy, these are the names of your parents," she teased, waving the slip of paper around.

"Please give it to me."

"All right, but you might need some light to read what I've written." Ima snapped her fingers and a flame appeared on the tip of her right index finger.

"Here," Ima cackled, "is this better?" she asked, putting her flaming finger to the page.

"Oh, no, please don't!" Grandma D said, but the paper burned to a crisp in an instant.

Then in a poof, Ima was gone. Grandma D looked around.

"It was just a dream. Just a dream," she whispered, closing her eyes to collect her thoughts.

Was I dreaming? What if she did know who my parents were? I'd give anything to know.

Unable to hold back her tears, Grandma D sobbed, remembering how some of the children at the one-room school had taunted her about being an abandoned baby. "Nobody wanted Dorothy, nobody wanted Dorothy," they'd sing during jump rope.

Taking a deep breath, she composed herself. "That was just a bad dream," she announced to herself, rubbing the tears from her eyes.

If she had just turned, Grandma D would have seen the proof that her nightmares were real. For inside the snow-shaker crystal ball, a cackling witch was flying around the Emerald City on a broom. It was Ima, the wickedest witch in the history of Oz!

Behind her came a flying troop of little witches who had someone tied up like a deer, hanging from below their brooms. It was the Wizard of Oz whom they'd tricked into leaving the magical Emerald City. Once outside the walls of the city, he lost his powers.

The newspaper headline erased and a startling new one appeared:

WIZNAPPED!

But Grandma D didn't see it. She stood with her eyes closed, trying to come to grips with what she thought she'd just imagined.

Grandma D felt a strange tingle and blinked open her eyes. "That's strange," she shivered, looking around.

Inside the snow shaker, Ima Witch did loop-de-loops on her broom, pointing to the Emerald City and then pointing back to herself screaming, "Oz is mine. Oz is mine." But Grandma D didn't hear her because the witch's voice was muffled by the glass.

"Guess I just got chilled," Grandma D mumbled, adjusting her collar button and pulling her sweater together. The newspaper headline erased before she saw it.

The wind hit the house again. Grandma D looked at the date on the newspaper. *It's the right date and the weather's almost the same. Maybe the nightmares mean something.*

She looked down. *Everything's the same except me. I've gotten older. I'm not the young Dorothy that Oz is expecting.*

Then she shook her head in frustration. *My granddaughter couldn't be comin' at a worse time*, she thought, worried about the weather and the upcoming sixtieth anniversary of her trip to Oz. *What if a tornado hits and she gets hurt?*

But she knew her son was having financial and marital problems. He'd never been able to keep a secret and when he asked Grandma D to take care of Dorothy for the summer, she couldn't refuse.

But if Oz brings me back, I can't say no. Whether she's here or not, I'll have to go back. The wizard needs me.

For a moment she saw it all happening again. The sky turning black. Animals shrieking in fear. Dust and branches flying through the air, knocking out the windows.

The memory was so real, so visual, that she grasped the rocker to steady herself. In her mind, the house was being picked up and spun around and around and around.

She heard a witch laughing, but was frozen with fear. From inside the crystal ball, Ima Witch had appeared again, but Grandma D didn't see her or the tied-up Wizard she'd suspended over a dark pool of water.

In Grandma D's mind, she was tumbling head over heels in the tornado in a house that was being taken from Kansas to the Land of Oz. The same house she was standing in.

Then as if the whole world came to a halt, the house crashed and she was in Oz. For a magical moment, Grandma D was twelve-year-old Dorothy Gale again.

"I'm back," she whispered, not knowing that she was dreaming in the attic.

Inside the crystal ball, Ima Witch was bent over with silent laughter, twirling her hands, leading Grandma D through the fake dream.

Ima shook her head, trying to hold back a laugh. "She thinks she's back in Oz! That old fool doesn't know she's dreaming!" she said to the dragon.

Ima's cackle shook the walls as she danced around and sang. "Here's Dorothy's favorite song—with a few words of my own," she laughed, and parodied the words to the melody:

"Somewhere...over the graveyard..."

Ura Wizard, the kindly old man, struggled at the bonds that held him. "Leave Dorothy alone!" he commanded.

"Mr. Wizard himself speaks," Ima laughed, spinning around.

"That wasn't nice."

"You make me cry crocodile tears," she mocked, fluttering her eyes. Small green teardrops appeared on her cheeks, then disappeared.

"Hmmmmm," she said, scratching her chin, "maybe old Dorothy will like *this* song:

"Oh what a terrible morning, oh what a horrible day..."

"You're rotten to the core!" Ura Wizard shouted, straining at his bonds.

"I know it," Ima winked.

"There're no words to describe you," Ura sputtered.

"Sure there are," Ima smirked. "Here's my favorite baby witch rhyme:

"Witches are made of
Evil and spells and all things verboten
To be a good witch,
You've got to be rotten."

Her laughter bounced off the walls. She looked again at the image of Grandma D that was floating in front of her.

"Let's see how she likes the Munchkins," Ima snickered.

A horde of little flying witches surrounded Grandma D's image. In her eyes they were the Munchkins. She didn't know the witch had cast a spell on them.

"Oh, my little friends," Grandma D whispered. "I'm so glad to see you again."

One of the little witches bent down and picked up a bug. She bit it in half and offered the other half to Grandma D, who thought it was a candy treat.

"Oh, thank you," Grandma D grinned, taking the bug in her hand. The troop of little witches snickered.

"You won't get away with it," Ura Wizard said. "You'll never control Oz."

Ima looked at him and smiled. Her red lips seemed to have a life of their own. "I've already gotten away with it," she whispered, "and soon Oz will be mine."

"Never!" Ura shouted. "I'm the Wizard of Oz!"

"You're the wizard of nothing. Here's some wind for a windbag," she said, drawing in a deep breath. Then she blew it toward the dangling wizard and he rocked back and forth.

Below him sea monsters with shark fins broke the surface, snapping at him. "They'll banish you from Oz when they take you to court," Ura said, eyeing the creatures below him.

"Court is in session!" she shouted, raising her arms and parting the water of the big tank. The finned monsters jumped from the water, snapping at the dangling Wizard. "Do you like my pool of lawyers?" she cackled.

"I command you to stop," Ura shouted.

"Shut up!" Ima sneered, "or I'll let the ropes bite you."

The Wizard looked at the snakes that had wrapped themselves like knots around his wrists and ankles. The snakes opened their jaws. Below him the hungry, evil creatures were waiting to eat him.

Grandma D was oblivious to it all, happy in her mind to be back in Oz. "That's right, Dorothy old girl," Ima cackled. "Just one step at a time," she commanded.

Each time that Ima moved her hands and fingers in the air, a part of Grandma D moved. First a leg, then a hand, then another leg.

Grandma D looked around the attic, thinking she was in Oz. She didn't know that it was all an evil tease.

"I'm in Oz," she whispered, taking a tentative step forward in her rubyless shoes.

Ima moved her hands like a puppeteer, aiming Grandma D's awkward steps, one at a time, towards the open stairwell.

"Just one more step," Ima giggled, seeing that Grandma D was poised to tumble down the steep stairs.

"Wake up, Dorothy, wake up!" Ura Wizard shouted.

"She can't hear you," Ima cackled. "She thinks she's back in Oz."

Ura closed his eyes. Grandma D was teetering back and forth near the fifteen foot drop.

The witch moved her right hand, trying to get Grandma D to step down to her death, but her leg wouldn't move. "What's wrong with her," Ima mumbled. With a snap of her left fingers, Toto appeared, barking for Grandma D to come forward.

"Toto, oh my sweet Toto, you're still alive!"

Grandma D stood with one foot poised over the top step. In her mind she was back in Oz.

The Tin Woodman waved her forward. "Come on, Dorothy, we're waiting for you." In the distance were the Scarecrow and the Cowardly Lion.

Ima whispered, "Welcome to Oz, Dorothy," watching Grandma D begin to lean forward. "Thanks for dropping in."

Grandma D smiled but didn't put her foot down. Ima snapped her fingers and the Scarecrow and Cowardly Lion appeared in front of Grandma D, waving her forward.

"Welcome back!" they shouted. "The witch is dead!"

"I'm so glad to be back," Grandma D muttered, "Here I come."

Grandma D smiled. I'm back. I'm going to stay in Oz forever, she thought, looking around as she stepped forward. Then the house was shaken by such a violent burst of wind that it knocked her backwards, away from the stairwell.

Blinking her eyes, she looked around. Oz was gone. She was back in her attic. *It was all a dream,* she thought, wanting to cry.

The windows and rafters shook with the wind outside. "What's happening?" she said loudly, getting up and walking to the window.

Small dust devils bounced across the barnyard followed by leaves pulled loose from their branches. *Something's goin' to happen soon. Something's goin' to happen,* Grandma D thought, feeling chilled again.

Behind her, the face of Ima Witch filled the crystal ball with a leering, frightening scowl, whispering, "You'll never return to Oz. Oz is mine. Oz is mine." The dragon on her necklace opened its mouth and hissed. A sheer curtain rippled behind her in the breeze.

Grandma D looked around. "Must have been the wind. Just the wind whispering," she said quietly, trying to convince herself.

"Soon you'll be gone with the wind," Ima whispered with a hiss. The silken curtain behind the witch flapped forward, settling around Ima's head.

The outline of the curtain formed a long, pointed witch's hat on Ima's head. She lifted the curtain up and pushed it away, then leaned down and kissed the dragon.

With a long, venomous cackle, she dissolved. All that was left in the ball was a flurry of snow flakes and a dragon's tongue which licked the inside of the glass sphere.

CHAPTER 5

GOOD-BYE

"Do you have everything?" Ed Gale asked his daughter for the fifth time. He was oblivious to the crowd around them at the Orlando International Airport.

"Yes, Dad," Dorothy sighed. "You've got to calm down." She adjusted her backpack.

"It's just that we've never sent you away alone like this and..."

"And I'll be all right," she smiled, kissing his cheek.

He looked down at the flashy red sneakers he'd given to her as a present. "They really do look kind of wild."

Dorothy moved her feet. She loved the shoes but felt uncomfortable receiving such a gift when they were so short of money.

"They're...they're really neat, Dad. You shouldn't have."

Her father shrugged. "I got a good deal on them and, heck, you only live once," he grinned.

The ticket agent picked up his microphone. "We will begin boarding Flight 412 to Kansas City momentarily."

Dorothy looked at her father. Crazy thoughts raced through her mind. *What if I never see him again? What if he and Mom are divorced by the time I return?*

Her father recognized the scared look in her eyes. "Everything will be all right, Pumpkin. I promise you. When you get back I'll have a job and we'll burn the FOR SALE sign together."

"Oh, Daddy..." she hugged him. "I hope we'll like Detroit."

"Detroit? We're going to stay in Orlando. You got to believe, kid. Something good's goin' to happen."

Dorothy knew he was trying to make her feel better, but she had resigned herself to moving. There was something about being sent away for the first time by herself that had forced her to confront reality.

"Just as long as we all stay together," Dorothy whispered.

Her father looked into her eyes. "There's nothing going to happen like you're hinting at. Your mother and I have had some arguments, but it's nothing we can't work out."

"I wish Mother could have come," Dorothy said, looking at the people who were boarding the airplane.

"She wanted to but..." Ed Gale looked away, letting his words trail off.

Dorothy knew that her mother couldn't get off work and would have come if she could have. But they needed the money and her mother couldn't risk losing her job.

"Last call for boarding for Flight 412 to Kansas City," the ticket agent blared out.

"Here," her father said, stuffing a small rubber band-held roll of bills into her jeans pocket.

"No, Dad," she protested. "I've got the money I saved baby-sitting."

He shook his head. "I sold some of my tools in the basement. It's not much. But fifty dollars will help, I hope."

"Sold your tools!" she exclaimed. "But those were Grandpa's and..."

"And he'd have wanted me to do what I did. That's the way Dad was."

"Miss?" the flight attendant at the gate called out. "Are you going to board?"

"Yes, she is," Ed Gale answered. He looked at Dorothy. "Remember, though Grandma D may seem eccentric, she's just a child at heart."

"I know. That's all you've been telling me since we left the house."

"Just be kind to her and humor her stories about Oz. They're kinda fun to listen to."

"Mom says Grandma D really believes that she went to Oz and..." Dorothy hesitated.

"And what?" her father asked.

"Nothing," Dorothy said, not wanting to hurt her father's feelings or cause any more problems between her parents.

Ed Gale picked up Dorothy's carry-on bag. "Grandma D's not crazy. She may tell tales, but she's *not* crazy." He took her by the arm and marched her to the gate.

"I'll see you in four weeks, okay?" he smiled.

"I'll miss you," Dorothy said, unable to hold back her tears.

"And I'll miss you, Pumpkin. Now get on that plane. Knowing your grandmother, she's probably already waiting at the gate for you."

Dorothy kissed his cheek then turned to go. At the entrance to the ramp, she stopped. "I'll understand if you have to sell the house and move us to Detroit."

"Orange juice costs too much in Detroit," her father laughed. "Now fly to Kansas and remember the golden ruler."

"I will. I love you, Daddy," Dorothy said, blowing him a kiss.

Ed Gale blew a kiss back and watched her until she went around the corner. *I hope Dorothy can handle my mother.*

Once Dorothy was inside the plane, there was no turning back. The doors were closed and locked behind her and the last, heavyset man who stumbled aboard.

I guess I'm really going to Kansas, Dorothy thought, making her way down the aisle. The man huffed and puffed behind her, sweating profusely.

Putting her bag and backpack under the seat in front of her, Dorothy squeezed into the window seat and looked out. *I'll miss you, Orlando.*

The sunlight through the window reflected off her new red sneakers. She blinked back a tear, knowing that her father had probably given up eating lunch for two weeks to afford them.

She saw that the big man was standing in the aisle, looking around. *I hope he doesn't sit by me.*

There were plenty of empty seats on the plane, and Dorothy crossed her fingers. But then he started slowly towards where she was sitting.

Guess I'm really having a run of bad luck, she thought, as the man wedged himself into the seat beside her. She smiled at the man, then turned her face towards the window. *I hope he's not a talker,* she thought. *I just want to suffer in silence.*

"Never seen sneakers like that," the man said, trying to be friendly.

"My dad got 'em for me."

"Your dad must be pretty neat," he said, looking at the bright, shiny sneakers, shaking his head. "Can't imagine my father buying me shoes like that when I was your age."

Dorothy looked at the red sneakers and nodded. "My dad *is* pretty neat."

In what seemed just a few minutes, the plane was off the ground. *I'll miss you Walt Disney World. I'll miss you Universal Studios,* Dorothy sighed, looking down at the theme parks below.

There on the horizon was what appeared to be a rainbow. *That's a good sign*, Dorothy smiled, thinking about her father and the place where things were as they ought to be.

As the plane settled into its route, Dorothy opened up the airline magazine in the seat pocket and found the map. Locating Kansas, she tried to find the small town where her grandmother lived.

"Where's Ozawatomie?" she mumbled to herself, running her finger over the map of the prairie state.

"Oatomie?" said the man next to her, putting down his book.

Dorothy looked up and smiled. "I mean, *Osa*watomie," Dorothy said, not wanting to explain the Oz nickname her grandmother had given to the town.

"It's right there," the man said, pointing the tip of his finger to an invisible spot on the map. "It's just south of Kansas City, north of Fort Scott, east of Emporia and west of..."

Dorothy mumbled, "Nowhere."

The man looked up and smiled. "Not nowhere," he said, sensing that she was going someplace she didn't want to go. "But it is a pretty small town."

"Ever been there?" Dorothy asked.

"Once. But that was a long time ago."

"Same for me," Dorothy nodded. She looked back at the map. "And not a beach in sight."

The man laughed. "Young lady, finding a beach, lake, or even a pond in Osawatomie is probably harder than finding a pot of gold at the end of that rainbow out there."

Dorothy looked through the window. "There's *not* a pot of gold at the end of the rainbow you know."

The man was clearly embarrassed. "I know, it's just an old myth and..."

Dorothy interrupted, shaking her head. "What's over the rainbow is a golden ruler."

"A what?" asked the man, half wishing he hadn't started the conversation with the girl if she was going to turn out to be strange.

"A golden ruler. That's what my dad says anyway."

The man shrugged. "Whatever you say," he said, settling back into his seat to continue reading his book.

Ozawatomie, Dorothy thought, closing her eyes, trying to remember what her father had told her about the farm she could not remember visiting ten years before.

And Grandma's farm is called Ozcot. And she's got pictures she's painted of the Tin Woodman, the Scarecrow and the Lion all over her walls.

Dorothy giggled, not caring what the man next to her might be thinking. *She used to have a dog named Toto and now she's got a dog named Ozzie.*

Dorothy felt like laughing. *Everything's Oz to Grandma D. Oz...Ozcot...Ozzie...Ozawatomie...Ozmania.* She giggled to herself again.

*And she likes to wear red shoes and...*Dorothy looked down at her red sneakers and smiled. *Grandma D will like these I bet.*

Dorothy tried to think about the flight but her thoughts drifted back to the Oz tales that her father had told her. He knew by heart the stories that his own mother had told him.

Grandma says she ran down a yellow brick road and danced with little people. That there's a bad witch who flies on a broom and the Wizard is really a nice man and Grandma's been waiting for a tornado to hit Ozawatomie again to take her back to Oz and...

She opened her eyes with a start. *Tornado!*

She tapped the man on his arm. "Say, mister. Do they get tornadoes around Osawatomie?"

The man thought for a moment. "Hasn't been one round that part of Kansas in close to sixty years."

"That's good," Dorothy smiled.

The man thought for a moment. "'Course they do get some freak windstorms down those parts, but I guess that's just part of livin' in Kansas."

"But no tornadoes, huh?" Dorothy asked.

"None during my lifetime, anyway."

Dorothy let out her breath with relief. "That's good, because I wouldn't know what to do if I saw one."

"If you see one," the man said, shaking his head, "you better say your prayers. No telling where you'll land if one of those things picks you up."

"You can say that again," Dorothy smiled, closing her eyes. "Just ask my Grandma D."

The man looked at her like she was crazy. "Kids," he mumbled, turning back to his book.

But Dorothy didn't hear him. She had slipped off to sleep, dreaming about she and her father burning the FOR SALE sign on their house together when she returned. Just as he had promised.

If only dreams were true, she thought, knowing she was dreaming.

I want my life to be back like it was. Like it ought to be. Like things are over the rainbow.

Suddenly the plane shook and Dorothy opened her eyes, catching her breath. The man next to her dropped his book as the plane rocked back and forth.

The captain's voice came over the intercom. "Folks, that was just a strong wind we weren't expecting. Bit unusual this high up, but this is the storm season in the Midwest so you never know. I've put the FASTEN SEATBELT light on and would appreciate your keeping them fastened for the rest of the trip."

Dorothy felt a little better, though she made sure her seatbelt was tight. Then she heard it.

Dorothy looked around and heard it again. *Laughter. I hear a woman's taunting laughter.*

Dorothy looked around but none of the people on the plane were laughing. Everyone was either looking out the window, reading or sleeping.

She thought about asking the man next to her if he had heard it, but decided against it. *Might think I'm just a silly kid.*

Moving around until she got comfortable, Dorothy was just about to settle in for a nap when she heard it again.

"Go home, silly kid, go home," said an evil-sounding voice that seemed to be right inside her ear.

Dorothy looked around. "Did you hear that?" she asked the man, feeling a river of goose bumps run up her arm and down her spine.

"Hear what?" the man asked, putting his book down and looking at her.

"The laughter."

The man cocked his head, but heard nothing. "Young lady, is this some kind of joke?"

Dorothy shook her head. "Guess it was the wind," she mumbled, feeling embarrassed.

She turned back to look out the window and cried out in fright, putting her hands over her eyes. A dark-haired, laughing woman, all dressed in black, was pointing at her!

"Oh my goodness!" Dorothy whispered.

"Stay away from Kansas!" Ima hissed, circling her finger in the air at Dorothy. "Go home, before it's too late!"

From the glowing necklace around her neck, the dragon's tongue crept out and slithered up along Ima's arm until it circled around her finger.

Dorothy pushed back from the window, bumping the man.

"What's wrong?" the man asked, now thinking about moving to another seat.

Dorothy dropped her hands and slowly opened her eyes. She looked out the window and saw only the clouds rushing by.

"Nothing," she whispered, "nothing at all."

The man turned back to his book, but Dorothy couldn't shake the feeling of dread that came over her. It was like a shiver had been injected into her soul.

That looked like a witch, she thought. *And what was that thing with the tongue around her neck?*

Then she shook her head. *There's no such thing. Witches aren't real,* she thought, closing her eyes.

Leaning her head against the window, Dorothy rested. On the other side of the glass, the slithering tongue of the dragon crept along the outside, inches from her face, then disappeared.

The crackle of an announcement came over the intercom. "Folks, we just crossed the Mississippi River. We expect to be landing in Kansas City in forty-five minutes," the captain of the plane said over the intercom.

CHAPTER 6

OZCOT

"Doc, you're gonna be late to pick her up," Grandma D said, pushing Doc Jones out the front door of Ozcot.

"Hold on, woman," the seventy-two-year-old man said, adjusting his coat.

"Come on, you old fuddy-duddy," she smiled. "You're pickin' up my twelve-year-old granddaughter, not going out on a date."

He looked in the mirror and adjusted his bow tie.

"Will you quit fiddlin' with your hair, what's left of it," she said, poking him in the side.

"Some women say I'm rather handsome for my age," he said, defensively.

"And those women are probably blind. Now you go on and get to the airport," she said, handing him his hat.

Doc Jones stopped at the door. "Will you just think about marryin' me?"

"Well, I told you, Doc, I just want to keep things the way they are."

"I'll ask you again, what exactly are we?" he said with more emotion in his voice than he intended.

Grandma D quickly composed herself. She put the thoughts of what had happened out of her mind and recognized the hurt in Doc's voice. *I better stop this before it gets out of hand.*

Grandma D cleared her throat. "We're *exactly* a couple of old coots who've been friends for longer than most people live, and what could have been won't ever be so it's best to stay the way we are."

Doc blinked, trying to figure out if she'd answered his question or not. "And what are we?" he persisted.

"We're good, *good* friends and it's best we stay that way," she smiled, squeezing his hand.

"But we could be more than that," he said taking her hand in both of his.

"And we could get to drivin' each other crazy if you're thinkin' what I think you're thinkin' again."

"Better late than never," he winked. "And I've been waitin' a long, long time to marry you."

"And my granddaughter's probably been waitin' a long time for the old coot who's supposed to be pickin' her up. Now go on and pick up Dorothy. It's been a decade since I last seen her and I can't wait to see how she's grown."

"And tell her your stories," Doc mumbled, adjusting the brim of his hat.

"What did you say?" Grandma D asked, thinking about the vision of Oz she'd had in the attic.

"Just don't go fillin' her head with all them Oz stories," he complained. He swung his hand forward like he was giving a grand tour.

"It's bad enough you got pictures you painted of scarecrows and dumb-lookin' tinmen everywhere without you goin' and gettin' this girl to think you're crazy." He looked at the picture on the wall of what she'd told him was the Emerald City of Oz.

Doc heard Grandma D's dog bark outside and shook his head in disgust. "And you even named your weener dog Ozzie."

"Quit callin' Ozzie a weener dog." She hated the slang name for the breed.

"Okay, he's a hot dog."

"He's not a hot dog."

"A sausage dog?" he grinned, hunching up his shoulders, making an expression like the old comedian, Stan Laurel.

"Ozzie's not a sausage dog either. He's a dachshund."

"And you named him after that crazy Wizard of Oz you're always talkin' about."

"I did not!" Grandma D said, stamping her feet in frustration. "I named him after Ozzie on *The Ozzie and Harriet Show*. Named the cat Harriet. You know that."

"And you named your farm Ozcot. And you're always wearin' red shoes, clickin' 'em together when you think I'm not listenin'."

"Because I was given the ruby shoes in Oz."

"And I was given my false teeth by the king of Siam." Doc saw that he had gotten her goat and was relishing the devilishness.

"And where are those rubies that you've never shown me?"

Grandma D set her jaw. She didn't want to talk about Oz now. Not until she figured out what was happening.

"Doc Jones, you know I can't tell you that." She took a deep breath. "I never should have told you anything about them."

Doc shook his head in disgust. "That's what you always say. I ain't never seen one of 'em."

"Because the rubies are a secret." *And won't stay on the shoes.*

Doc looked her in the eye. "I still say you sold the rubies and bought all the paint that you used to paint all these dumb pictures."

"I did not!"

"If you got any rubies left, you ought to sell them to get some money to fix up this place." Doc shook his head. "House and barn need a new coat of paint."

Grandma D shook her head. "Can't sell the rubies."

"Tell that to the taxman when he comes 'round to take your farm."

She looked aside, deep in thought for a moment. "The rubies fell off when I came back from Oz. Strangest thing you ever saw."

"So you paint all your shoes ruby red and go around like you're at a Halloween dance all year long," he said, looking down at the red shoes on her feet.

Grandma D moved her feet, uncomfortable with his stare. Harriet the cat dashed between Doc's legs and headed towards the barn.

"And you've got a barn filled with crazy machines," he said, reaching down to pick the cat hair off his pants.

"They're not crazy," she said, folding her arms. "They come from my imagination."

"Dreams from an asylum if you ask me. You go into town and start tellin' people that you've been workin' on a tornado-makin' machine. Just see the looks they'll give you."

"It's my secret. I should *never* have told you."

"Who else would have helped you put all them contraptions together and not cart you off to the loony bin?"

"Since you've gotten so old and crotchety, I've had to hire me that young neighbor, Alexander Bean, to help put my ideas together."

"Alexander the bookworm," he said derisively in a mocking tone.

"Nothin' wrong with reading," she said, defending the frail twelve-year-old boy who helped around Ozcot.

"He reads so much that he's goin' to get his nose chopped off by a book one day."

"Oh you're just actin' ignorant," she said.

Doc shook his head. "That boy spends all his time readin' books, chargin' you by the hour for things I got to do and undo later for free."

"You know I appreciate what you've done," she said, feeling awkward at the reminder of how helpful Doc had been over the years since her husband Roy died.

"'Course now, if you'd just marry me, I could be here twenty-four hours a day to help out and..."

"There you go again," Grandma D said, walking over towards the fireplace.

Doc took another look at the picture above the mantel behind her. "Oz...phooey," he said.

"It's real and I was there," she said defensively, looking up at the picture of the stout and stately, Wizard of Oz. *And they're calling me back,* she wanted to add.

"You just got dropped on your head during that tornado and you ain't been the same since." He regretted the words the moment he'd said them.

Grandma D's eyes flared. "You didn't have to say that!"

"I'm sorry," Doc said, fidgeting around. "But you talk about that Oz place every second like you were gettin' ready to go back any moment."

"You never know," she sighed, calming herself down. She walked back over and stood at the open door, thinking about the vision of Oz again.

Jessie Lee, the handsome African-American paperboy, rode up the dusty driveway and tossed the afternoon paper onto the porch. "Hey Oz lady, how you doin' today?" he called out.

"I'm doin' fine, thank you, Jessie," Grandma D laughed.

"Seen any witches 'round here today?" Jessie shouted out, raising his eyebrows like he was part of a conspiracy. He circled his bike in her driveway.

"Not today, maybe tomorrow," she said, shaking her head, not wanting to think about the nightmare of Ima the Witch.

"Well, let me know if you see that bully bear hidin' 'round here again," he said, referring to John Bear, the community bully who'd picked a fight with Jessie the week before in the middle of the road in front of Ozcot.

"I'll keep an eye out," Grandma D volunteered.

She watched the young grade school child ride off like there was no tomorrow. "I wish I were that age again," she said, more to herself than to Doc.

Doc shook his head. "You know he's cheatin' you on the change he gives you when you pay your bill."

"I know," Grandma D said. "I just keep hopin' that he'll stop on his own without me tellin' on him."

She looked back to watch Jessie turn the corner on the driveway. "It's just a few quarters. Probably don't make much difference with all the big crooks we've got runnin' around."

Doc set his lips tight in frustration. "I keep tellin' you. It's from little crooks that big crooks grow. Teach 'em right while they're young and they'll be good citizens later."

"But he's gettin' better. Jessie shorted me only a quarter this week," Grandma D said, as if that was just a cat's hair from being honest.

"You didn't teach your son that cheatin' was all right, did you?"

"I guess you're right," Grandma D sighed.

Doc looked again at all the pictures that Grandma D had painted over the years. He turned back to the woman he found so exasperating. "I don't see how Roy put up with you all those years."

"He loved me," she said flatly.

"But did he love all this Oz stuff?" Doc asked, looking at the picture titled *The Wizard Of Oz* that hung over her mantel. He'd always hated the mixture of greens and yellows that seemed to glow in the dark.

"Roy was a good man. He understood me. Yes, he did," Grandma D said, looking down at the small, framed picture of her handsome husband taken twenty years before he died.

Doc watched her eyes and knew he'd lost out to Roy again. "I best be goin'," Doc said, pushing through the screen door.

He clumped slowly down the porch stairs and walked past the Ozcot sign and the wooden statues of the Tin Man, Scarecrow, and Lion that Roy Gale had chopped from trees with his ax and mounted next to the mailbox.

Ozzie barked at him from the barn. Harriet stretched on the roof, too tired to care whether Doc was coming or going.

"Ozzie the dog and Harriet the cat. *Ozzie and Harriet*. I always hated that show," he grumbled to himself.

Dorothy watched him walk towards the old Dodge he'd parked next to the barn. *God just planned our lives different than we imagined, Doc. What we talked about as little kids, kissin' behind the schoolhouse, just wasn't meant to be.*

Then she looked at the picture of Roy again. For a moment she was lost in thought, thinking about the man who'd captured her heart. The man she'd had her only child with.

And you even changed your last name to Gale so that I'd still be Dorothy Gale when the tornado came again to take me to Oz. You were a good man, Roy Gale. A good, good man.

Doc Jones tooted his horn as he drove past the front of Ozcot. Grandma D waved back. Alexander Bean, whom Doc called the bookworm, looked out from the barn to watch the car drive away.

Doc mused, *That old woman's been waitin' for a tornado to come since we were in grade school. Everyone thought she'd had her brains knocked loose by that old storm, the way she talked.*

Before he was past her property line, he heard the loud roar of a souped-up engine behind him. "Go on by, Hot Rod," he said, waving his arm for the woman in the car behind him to pass.

Willa Watkins, the prettiest, richest, and meanest woman in Osawatomie raced by in her black sports car, leaving him in a cloud of dust.

"Woman's got more money than brains," he grumbled, tooting his horn back at her.

He watched the raven-haired beauty speed off down the road. He'd disliked Willa's mother, who had been the tattler of his grade school and disliked her daughter even more.

Grandma D had refused to sell Ozcot to Willa's mother and now Willa herself had made her intentions known of wanting to own Ozcot no matter what the cost.

"Can't understand why that Willa can't build her subdivision without Grandma D's land," he sighed, shaking his head.

The wind picked up the dust in front of his car. The branches of the scattered trees bent towards the road. He was saddened by the number of farms that were for sale or had been abandoned over tax liens.

"Hope that old woman pays her taxes 'fore she's evicted and sent packin' to Oz."

A large tumbleweed, followed by brush and small branches of all shapes and sizes, bounced across the road. Then a cloud of dust momentarily blocked his view but was gone before he could bring the car to a stop.

Ima watched him from her castle. "The old fool's a meddler, is he," she nodded.

Closing her eyes, she concentrated, sending her vision off over the rainbow. The mirror in Doc's car appeared fogged. He rubbed at it but it didn't do any good.

Doc adjusted the outside mirror and looked at the dark horizon. He didn't notice Ima's eyes staring at him from his rearview mirror.

Doc clicked the radio on. "And reports of dust devils have come in from Emporia and a small twister reportedly touched down on the outskirts of Topeka."

Doc looked out over the prairie land. *This is tornado weather if I've ever seen it,* he thought, rolling up the window. Ima's eyes faded from the rearview mirror as a cloud of dust enveloped the car.

CHAPTER 7

CONTRAPTIONS

Grandma D made her way to the barn, holding her skirt down against the unusually strong gusts of wind. "Alexander. Alexander Bean. Are you in there?" she called out.

Getting no answer, she continued towards the old barn that was older than she was. Then the boy stuck his head out. "You callin' me?" he asked, pushing up his thick glasses.

"That's your name, isn't it?" Grandma D nodded, entering the barn.

The wind pulled the door shut with a bang behind her. She gave a quick glance at all her inventions that were stored in the barn.

The barn was filled with contraptions of all shapes and sizes. Wheels, levers, knobs, engines, and pulleys, were hooked together with everything from bailing wire to shoestrings.

"You been tinkerin' or readin'?" she asked, giving the boy a stern look.

The thin, pale boy shook his head. "No, Ma'am, I've been workin' like you asked me to."

His glasses slipped down the end of his nose so he pushed them back up, then took them off. Using his T-shirt on which was written, READ YOUR WAY OUT, he cleaned off his glasses and stuck them back on.

Grandma D looked at the pile of books on the workbench behind him. "Workin' huh?" she smiled, pinching his nose. "You got to quit fibbin' before your nose grows like Pinocchio's."

"I just read during my break times," he said. His cheeks blushed at being caught in the fib.

"Nothin' wrong with readin'," Grandma D said. "Just like your shirt says."

Alexander self-consciously hunched his shoulders to cover over the saying on his shirt. Grandma D picked up a book on physics. "Kids your age read this stuff?"

"Most kids I know don't like to read," Alexander said, matter-of-factly. "Or write much either."

"How do they get by in school?"

"You get by just by showin' up." Alexander shook his head. "Kids call me a bookworm. But I like to read."

"Better than those music videos I see on TV," Grandma D said, making a face. Grandma D felt a wave of sympathy for the boy. "Reading takes you to faraway places in your mind, doesn't it?" Alexander nodded.

Grandma D picked up another book, *Wind, Magnets and Perpetual Motion Theories.*

"What are you readin' this for?" she asked, not noticing that the blade on the big machine in the center of the room turned halfway around, then stopped.

"To figure out why your invention is actin' so strange," Alexander said, watching the machine from the corner of his eye to see if it moved by itself again.

"Strange?" she asked. But before the boy could answer, the machine answered for him.

The newest and biggest contraption, the one that had come to Grandma D in a recent dream, stood in the center of the barn. It was moving around like it was supposed to but had never done before.

"Did you change something on it?" Grandma D asked, watching the machine creak back and forth on its base.

A tingle of excitement crept over her. *Is this a sign? Is this going to get me back to Oz?*

The machine was awesome, standing thirty feet high and wider than the silo which stood at the back of the barn. It had an old windmill blade in the center and a crop-duster propeller hooked behind it. The blade and propeller were supposed to make the wind move backwards and forwards at the same time.

Hooked to the blade and propeller shafts was a rusted, old oil derrick, to increase the wind speed. The derrick was connected to a Rambler station wagon's engine to add power to the wind, which was mounted in the food trough of the pig that had died in the snowstorm of '66. The food trough was for balance.

Alexander had attached a rabbit's foot, a bag of four leaf clovers, his good-luck penny-on-a-string and a strange assortment of odds and ends he felt the machine needed since, as he put it, they were operating on little more than a wing and a prayer.

"The propellers have been movin' by themselves all morning," Alexander said, giving the contraption an odd, fearful look.

His eyes seemed magnified behind the thick glasses. They followed the huge windmill blade as it spun slowly around, shaking the rabbit's foot. The crop-duster propeller moved halfway, then stopped, making Alexander's lucky penny-on-a-string jump.

Grandma D walked over to it. The machine's switch was on *off* but the blade was moving.

She looked back up at the blade. "Must be the wind," she grumbled.

"I don't think so," Alexander said. "It was movin' by itself when it was quiet outside. The crop-duster prop moved too." He looked perplexed.

"Just the wind," Grandma D said. "Or maybe you need new glasses."

Just the wind, Alexander mimicked in his mind, standing there in a dead calm. Then the rabbit's foot seemed to jump around on its own.

"Must be some static electricity in the air," Grandma D said, looking at the foot dance.

She turned to face the boy she'd hired to help her build her tornado machines, but behind her the engine of the Rambler sprang to life with a loud, sputtering roar.

Grandma D jumped back. "Turn it off!" she said, covering her face at the smoke that belched out.

"It's not on," Alexander said, pointing to the on-off switch.

"Must be a short in it somewhere," Grandma D said, moving the switch back and forth, trying to shut the machine off.

But that didn't work and the engine roared louder and the windmill blade spun faster and faster. Then the crop-duster propeller seemed to come to life and the barn turned into a wind tunnel.

"Move back!" Grandma D shouted, pulling Alexander by the arm.

The blade spun round and round, pulling at the old Ford pickup truck axle that held it. Behind it, the propeller was spinning so fast it was a blur.

The arm of the oil derrick was going up and down so fast that it seemed to be trying to dig a hole to China. The lucky charms were spinning in opposite directions. The whole contraption looked like it was going to kick loose from its frame and fly into space.

The winds outside shook the barn as if calling to the blade and the propeller to join them. Grandma D's dress lifted up and the pages of Alexander's books flapped like cards being shuffled. Lightning cracked and thunder pounded overhead.

"Hold on!" Grandma D shouted over the noise.

The winds and crosswinds whipped through the barn. The other machines teeter-tottered on their bases like dominoes.

The dust was so thick that it took a moment for Grandma D to recognize the hay from the loft that was flying around like a snowstorm. Alexander's glasses were covered with a film of dust.

The barn seemed to almost shake loose as the winds outside battered to join the winds they'd created inside.

"It's a tornado," Alexander screamed, grabbing up the pile of books he'd brought to read while he was supposed to be working.

Tornado! Grandma D thought with hope. *I've got to get my ruby shoes on.*

"I've got to go!" she screamed, racing for the barn door.

"Where you going?" Alexander called out.

"To Oz, back to Oz!"

But as quickly as it started, the machine and the wind outside came to a dead stop. Grandma D looked around in the eerie calm. A sense of defeat and depression came over her.

A flutter of hay from the loft lifted up in the stillness and fluttered down around them. "That's strange," Grandma D said, looking at Alexander.

He shook the straw from his hair. "Real strange," he said, looking at the machine like it was an alien creature. He pushed his glasses up to the bridge of his nose to get a better look, but they slipped back down.

Then the roof seemed to lift up on its own and settle back down. "Meant to ask you about that too," Alexander said, "how you hinged the roof to move like that."

Grandma D felt another eerie chill come over her. *I haven't felt this way since I was in the witch's castle.*

Up in the attic the trunk shook back and forth. No one heard Ima's muted laughter that came from inside the crystal ball.

Nor was anyone there to see the top of the trunk pushed up by her cone-shaped hair. The Wicked Witch was watching.

CHAPTER 8

Doc Jones

Dorothy got off the plane looking around for her grandmother. She heard the chorus of the song, *Kansas City*, playing through the loudspeakers of the airport.

I guess I'm in Kansas, she thought.

Dorothy turned slowly, trying to see if she recognized any of the older ladies waiting around the gate. *Where's Grandma D?* she wondered.

"You must be Dorothy," said a spry, elderly man behind her.

"I am," Dorothy said, turning with a questioning look in her eyes. "And who are you?"

"Excuse me," he said, taking off his hat. "I'm Doc Jones. A good friend of your grandma's. She couldn't come get you and asked me to bring you back to Oz."

"To where?" Dorothy said, with a slight, involuntary laugh.

"I mean, to Ozcot," Doc said, scratching behind his ear. "That old woman calls everything Oz," he grumbled, taking Dorothy's carry-on bag from her hands.

"You mean like Ozcot?"

"Like Ozcot," Doc sighed. "Come on," he said, walking off. "Hope you like this song, 'cause they're always playin' the dang thing every time I come here."

Dorothy caught the line from the song, "they got some crazy little women here....".

Whoever wrote that was probably talking about my grandma. Then she frowned. *That wasn't nice.*

"Are you coming?" Doc called back.

Dorothy hesitated a moment, then tagged along behind him. "She didn't tell my dad that you'd be coming."

Doc said over his shoulder, "She didn't tell me I'd be coming either until this morning. But you know how your grandmother is."

"Not really," Dorothy said, looking around at the airport crowd.

Doc slowed down until she caught up with him. "That's right. You ain't been out here for 'bout..." he paused, trying to remember.

"Ten years," she volunteered.

"That's 'bout right," he smiled. "Last time you were here you were still in diapers and cryin' up a storm."

Dorothy blushed. "I wasn't *still* in diapers."

"No, I guess you weren't," he smiled. "But you've sure grown up since then, haven't you?"

Dorothy shrugged. "I'm twelve years old you know."

"Thought you might be 'bout eighteen," Doc smiled. Dorothy didn't know that he was teasing her and straightened her shoulders, suddenly feeling very mature for her age.

"I can't tell you how excited your grandma is 'bout you comin'. Guess you're pretty excited 'bout comin' back here, huh?"

Dorothy shrugged, not answering.

Doc saw the unhappy look that was gone in a flash. "Rather be with your friends in Florida?"

Dorothy nodded. "I've never been away from home before by myself."

Doc smiled. "You're not by yourself. You're gonna be with your Grandma D."

"How many animals does she have?" Dorothy asked, figuring that all farms had animals.

"None left in the barn, 'cept for the mice. Harriet the cat hangs out there."

Dorothy remembered that her father said Grandma D liked dogs. "Does she still have a dog?"

"Got Ozzie, if you can call him a dog. He's a worthless mutt if I ever saw one."

"What kind of dog is he?" Dorothy asked.

Doc made a face and shook his head. "He's just a weener dog."

"A what?" Dorothy laughed.

"A weener dog. You know, one of them long, yappy dachshund weener dogs that ain't much bigger than a Polish sausage and probably tastes worse."

Dorothy thought for a dozen steps, then said, "Why'd she name him Ozzie? Ozzie sounds like something you'd name a collie."

"Named him after her favorite TV show, *Ozzie and Harriet*. But I think she named him after some rare fungus."

Dorothy looked perplexed. "*Ozzie and Harriet*? Is that a new show?"

Doc just shook his head and kept walking. Dorothy took a double step to catch up. "Does Grandma D still talk about Oz all the time?"

Doc took her hand and laughed. "Why, you're gonna be hearin' so much 'bout Oz and wizards and all that kind of half-baked stuff, that by the end of the summer you won't know whether you're comin' or goin'."

That's what I'm afraid of, Dorothy thought as they headed down the escalator.

They went to the baggage claim area and pulled her bags from the conveyor belt. Doc talked up a storm about everything, anything, and nothing in particular.

On the way to the car, Dorothy asked, "How long have you known my grandmother?"

Doc chuckled. "I'm older than dirt and I've known her 'bout that long." He saw that Dorothy didn't understand. "I've known your Grandma since we were five years old, and since we're both seventy-two, why that's about sixty-seven years."

"Sixty-seven years," Dorothy whispered, whistling in surprise.

"Long time," Doc said, a serious look on his face. "Known that woman a long time."

Though she was only twelve, Dorothy caught something in Doc's voice that made her think he was more than just a friend to her grandmother. But since she was only twelve years old, she didn't know how to ask him. So she decided to wait until a better opportunity came up.

After putting her bags into the trunk of his dusty Dodge, Dorothy asked, "Which direction is Osawatomie?"

"You mean, *Oz*awatomie?" Doc smiled, starting up the engine. Dorothy nodded. "Well," Doc said, closing one eye, pretending to be serious. "It's just south of Kansas City, north of Fort Scott, east of Emporia and west of..."

Dorothy stopped him. "I've heard that before."

Doc chuckled. "Lot of things get told over and over in Kansas. Guess it goes with our prairie roots."

He guided the car through the airport gates and headed south. "Laura Ingalls Wilder lived all around this state and the cowboys came up the Wichita Trail," he said, trying to make polite conversation.

Doc took Interstate 35, then caught Route 169 and made a beeline south towards Osawatomie. Dorothy half-listened to Doc as she watched the flat Kansas countryside pass by.

"And you'll like Osawatomie. It's the birthplace of the Kansas Jayhawk, and old John Brown fought one of the first battles of the Civil War there and..."

Dorothy felt tired and grumpy, not wanting to think about *The Little House on the Prairie* or the Civil War. She wanted to think about the beach.

"'Course, some folks might say we got our skeletons. The Republican Party of Kansas was begun by Horace Greeley in our little town and...say, are you listenin' or are you sleepin' with your eyes open?" Doc asked.

Dorothy blushed. "Sorry."

"Now listen up and I'll tell you some history 'bout Kansas they should have taught you in school."

Dorothy tried to listen but she wasn't in the mood for a history lesson. There was sun to the west but darkness to the south and east, which was the direction they were heading.

"Storm coming up?" Dorothy asked, interrupting him.

Doc looked out the window and coughed. "Weather's been actin' weird lately."

Dorothy raised an eyebrow at the teenage word he used, but let it pass. "You mean storms?"

"Lots of dust devils and things."

"Dust devils?"

Doc smiled. "Forgot you're from Florida. Dust devils are kinda like mini-tornadoes, 'cept they don't do no damage. But they're weird. Really weird."

Dorothy turned her head, having never heard a person over thirty use the word *weird.*

Doc caught her glance. "I kinda like that word. Weird. Sort of describes your grandmother, you might say," he chuckled to himself. He turned to Dorothy. "Picked it up from some of the young boys who come 'round the farm."

"Boys?" Dorothy said.

"Finally said something that caught your attention, didn't I?" he chuckled.

"I thought Grandma lived alone."

"She does," Doc said, "but there's Jessie Lee, the paperboy, and John Bear, the bully from the next farm over, and Alexander the bookworm and..."

Dorothy looked at him like he was crazy. "Sounds like a fraternity. Who's the bully?"

"You mean John Bear?" Dorothy nodded. "He's just a big, misunderstood kid. His folks are gettin' a divorce and I guess he just doesn't know how to handle it."

That made Dorothy think about the arguments her own parents were having, so she went silent. Doc saw her sullen look and tried to cheer her up. "If you like to read, you'll like the bookworm."

Dorothy looked over. "Does he like that nickname?"

"I just sort of named him that. I'm always catchin' him readin' on the job in your grandma's barn and..."

That caught Dorothy's attention. "Job? I thought she didn't have any barn animals left."

"She don't. But he sort of helps her with her inventions when I'm not around and..." Doc looked away, hoping to change the subject.

"What kind of inventions?" Dorothy asked, now convinced that she was going to the wrong place at the wrong time in her life.

She felt like she was riding with a strange Mr. Rogers, on her way to visit a woman who believed in witches and...Doc interrupted her thoughts.

"Your grandma, she's one smart cookie, you know."

"If you say so." Dorothy pouted, feeling sorry for herself again.

"You'll be surprised at what she's put together." He realized he had opened up the can of worms again and looked ahead towards the road.

Dorothy waited for him to tell her more, but he didn't volunteer any more information. "What kind of inventions?"

Doc sighed. "I think I've said too much already. I'll let your grandma explain the things she invents." He nodded and mumbled to himself. "Like to see her explain them things myself."

Dorothy closed her eyes, thinking about the fifty dollars in her pocket. *How much does it cost to take a bus to Orlando?* she wondered.

They rode in silence until they passed the city limits sign for Osawatomie. Doc exited the highway at Main Street and headed away from town.

Dorothy looked at the farms and what appeared to be mostly older people doing the things that older people do.

I'm going to be spending my summer in a Kansas rest home. This must be a nightmare, Dorothy decided, pinching herself to wake up. But nothing changed.

She watched the flat countryside pass by. "How come there're so many farms for sale?" she asked, looking at all the signs and thinking about the sign in front of her own house back in Orlando.

"Times are tough out here in the farm belt. Only thing doin' well is the government and that's 'cause it just raises taxes to spend what it don't have."

Dorothy cocked her head, trying to follow his conversation. Doc sighed. "You're too young to understand 'bout money things."

No, I'm not, she thought, knowing that it was the lack of a job that had brought on her father's money problems which had resulted in their house being up for sale.

She looked at the FOR SALE signs on the farms along the road ahead, feeling a new sense of understanding for the problems of others that she'd never had before in her life.

Then she heard the roar of an engine and a sleek, black sports car went zooming past. "Who's that?" Dorothy asked, curious as to who the dark-haired woman could be in a car that probably cost more than any of the houses in town.

"That's Willa Watkins. Sort of the town witch if you ask me."

"Witch?" Dorothy said, startled, thinking about the horror books she'd read.

"I shouldn't have said that," Doc said. "But she's a mean one, she is. Got all highfalutin' when she lived in Detroit with her husband."

"Detroit?" Dorothy said, thinking about her father's job offer.

"Dee-troit," Doc said. "Can't imagine livin' in that awful place."

"Have you ever been there?" Dorothy asked.

Doc shook his head. "Nope, and I never will. Kansas City, St. Louis, heck any city you name and I wouldn't want to live there."

"Why's she living back here then?" Dorothy asked.

"Willa's husband had a heart attack." Doc honked at a farmer and waved. "If you ask me, her husband probably died of a nightmare, wakin' up one evenin' and seein' the witch he'd married."

"She can't be *that* bad," Dorothy said.

"No, you're right," Doc nodded to himself. "She's not that bad. She's *worse*." He glanced over at Dorothy with a serious look. "She probably sweeps her house clean on the same broom she flies around on." He held his straight face as long as he could, then finally broke out into a big grin.

"Maybe she's hard to get to know," Dorothy said, trying to act her age around a man who was definitely not acting his.

"I know her mother and they're both alike. Only thing that Willa Watkins cares 'bout is herself and that there subdivision she's tryin' to build near your grandma's farm."

"What's grandma think about it?"

"Not much," Doc said. "But Willa's a persistent one and will haunt your grandma till her dyin' day unless she sells Ozcot to her."

Dorothy turned with a concerned look on her face. "Grandma D's not going to sell the farm, is she?"

"Not in this lifetime," Doc said flatly. A dust devil passed in front of them.

"What was that?" Dorothy asked.

"Just a dust devil," Doc said. "Sort of a mini-tornado."

"You ever seen a tornado?" she asked.

Doc nodded. "Kids 'round here used to practice tornado drills each spring in school." He pointed to a closed down elementary school on the right. "We used to kneel in the hall with an open book over our head and say a prayer."

Dorothy thought about it, then asked, "Do kids in Kansas still do tornado drills?"

"Naw."

"Why not?" she asked.

" 'Cause you can't pray in school no more. If a tornado's comin' at you, the only thing that can save you is a prayer. So what's the use of practicin' a tornado drill if you can't pray?"

Dorothy tried to understand what Doc was saying, but needed to think about it.

Doc nodded to himself. "That school's where I first met your grandma," Doc said.

"You *really* knew her in grade school?"

Doc nodded. "We held hands in second grade. I carried her books until the fifth, and we kissed under the Thompsons' stairs in the summer of sixth grade when we couldn't find a bottle to spin."

"What'd you need a bottle for?"

Doc looked at her like she'd just dropped in from another planet. "Don't you kids still play spin the bottle?" Dorothy shook her head. "How 'bout post office?" Dorothy shrugged.

Doc sighed deeply, biting his bottom lip. "Well, your grandma and I sure did."

Dorothy saw the far-off look in his eyes, which confirmed her earlier suspicions that Doc was more than just a friend to her grandmother.

"You like my grandmother, don't you?"

Doc was momentarily taken aback, but then in his normal blunt style, hit the question head-on. "I've liked her all my life. Ain't no secret 'round these parts. Even her husband Roy knew it."

Dorothy was silent, thinking about what he had said. Doc didn't want to upset her, so he said, "Weren't nothin' wrong with lovin' someone from a distance. I was respectful and all."

"Have you and Grandma...ah...talked about how you feel?"

Doc shrugged. "'Till I'm blue in the face. Thought when Roy died she'd want to start up where we left off. But..." he let his voice trail off.

"But what?" Dorothy asked.

"Nothing. Your grandma was an orphan. Now she wants to find out where she came from 'fore she puts any more names on her tree."

"Names on her tree?"

"Family tree. Just my luck to be stuck in love with the same woman all my life and not have her want me 'cause she don't know who her parents were."

They rode in awkward silence, then Doc said. "One day you'll find that you might have common sense up here," he said, tapping his head, "but your heart just don't seem to get the message."

"I...I think I understand," Dorothy stammered.

Doc shook his head. “I doubt it.”

He turned the car into a rural driveway. “Well, here it is,” Doc smiled.

Up ahead was Ozcot, her grandmother’s farm that was stuck out in the middle of nowhere. Dorothy looked at the aging house and barn that needed paint. She wanted to ask Doc more about his relationship with her grandmother, but decided to wait.

Dorothy looked around. *And not a beach in sight, not even a lake or a pond*, she thought, wondering what Rita was doing at that moment. *She’s probably trying to flirt with the lifeguard,* she thought with disdain, as if a twelve-year-old girl could compete on the beach with the high school girls.

Doc parked the car in front of the wooden statues of the Scarecrow, Tin Woodman and Cowardly Lion. He caught Dorothy’s raised eyebrows as she looked at the wooden characters looking out over the Kansas prairie like they were trying to find their way home.

“Welcome to Oz,” he said sarcastically, making a sweeping gesture with his arm as he stood outside her car door.

Ozzie the dog came yipping up. “Don’t let that weener dog scare you,” Doc said.

“I like dogs,” Dorothy smiled, leaning over and scratching the dog’s head.

Doc heard noises from inside the closed barn. “Your grandmother’s probably in the barn. Let’s put your things inside and I’ll tell her that you’re here.”

Dorothy straightened up. The flat, Kansas prairie land seemed to stretch endlessly in all directions.

All she could think of was *The Little House on the Prairie* TV show that she’d watched years ago. She turned in a half circle.

“Come on, Dorothy,” Doc called back, trudging up the stairs with her bags in hand.

Dorothy put her backpack over one shoulder and looked down at her red sneakers. *Can’t imagine a pioneer crossing the prairie with red sneakers on,* she thought, smiling to herself.

As she approached the house, she looked for a rainbow, but there was none in sight. The only thing on the horizon was what looked like a dark, building storm.

Hope that's just a dust devil. She shivered, trying not to think about tornadoes. She didn't notice the roof of the barn shaking.

CHAPTER 9

Reunion

Inside the barn, Grandma D grabbed Alexander's hand away from the switch. The boy had turned the big machine back on for an instant, but she'd managed to turn it off before it had a chance to sputter and spin.

"Don't go foolin' with that," Grandma D said looking up at the roof. "We got to figure out what happened before we turn it on again."

Then she heard Doc calling out her name. "My granddaughter's here!"

"How old is she?" Alexander asked, pushing back his glasses and straightening his T-shirt.

Grandma D winked. "She's twelve years old and might just like a boy who can read those books and figure out what in the heck made this machine do what it did."

Alexander blushed. "Don't tell her the kids call me Bookworm." Then he looked down. "No girl would like a kid called Bookworm."

Grandma D ruffled his hair. "One day you'll find that all that readin' did you a lot more good than those kids who do nothin' but hang out down at the quick shop in town."

"Just don't tell her, okay?"

"I won't," she said. "Now you get to work. I'm payin' you by the hour and want my money's worth."

Grandma D opened the barn door, but saw only Doc's car. "Guess she's already inside," she said, stepping over a mud patch, wondering what she would have told her granddaughter if she'd been in the barn when the machines went crazy.

Dorothy put her backpack down on the sofa in the living room. Doc saw the expression on her face.

"Every picture in the whole place is about Oz," he said, looking around.

Dorothy walked over to the picture of the Wizard of Oz above the mantel, then turned and gazed at a large oil painting of a younger Dorothy with the Tin Woodman.

Doc looked at the painting and then at Dorothy. "You favor your Grandma. Anyone ever told you that?"

Dorothy shrugged. "I think my dad did, but I'm not sure."

"Yup," Doc continued, "you got the same hair and eyes." He looked at the picture again and then closely at Dorothy's face. "And you got the same nose and chin."

Grandma D came through the front door. "Doc Jones, are you fillin' my granddaughter's head with gunk?" she asked, but she was immediately taken aback by the resemblence.

"I was just remarkin' at how much you two looked alike."

Grandma D looked at Dorothy. "Come here and give your grandmother a hug."

Dorothy stood, frozen to the throw rug. "Grandma D...I...I..."

"Well, if you won't come hug me, I'll come hug you," she said, stepping forward and wrapping her arms around the girl.

Grandma D looked at the picture of herself when she was the same age as Dorothy. *She does look like me. Change her hair and you'd think she was me going to Oz sixty years ago.*

It didn't take them long to get comfortable with each other and Doc excused himself to go into town to run a few errands. He didn't want to tell Grandma D that he was going to stop by the tax office to see why they hadn't sent a property tax bill for Ozcot.

In the kitchen, Grandma D poured Dorothy a cold glass of milk and set out some fresh chocolate chip cookies she'd baked. "You're not too old for milk and cookies, are you?" she laughed.

"I don't think so," Dorothy said, hungrily eyeing the cookies.

After a few minutes of family catching up, Dorothy said, "Doc told me that he's known you since grade school."

Grandma D shook her head. "Known him a long time, sometimes I think maybe too long...." Her voice drifted off. Oz was all she wanted to think about.

Dorothy wasn't quite sure what her grandmother meant and said, "I think Doc really likes you. I can't understand why he hasn't asked you to get married."

Grandma D coughed, not used to children and their new awareness of such things. "He probably asks me every day."

"Asks you every day to marry him?"

The old woman nodded. "Drives me crazy too."

Dorothy thought for a moment. "Why don't you marry him?"

"I'm not ready yet, Miss Mind-Your-Beeswax," Grandma D said, already regretting the words.

"I...I'm sorry," Dorothy said.

"No, I'm sorry. Shouldn't have said that."

Dorothy took a sip of milk, then asked, "Don't old people get married?"

"Sure they do, but not this old girl." Grandma D stood up. "Now, that's enough of this talk. Let's show you around."

"I can't wait to see your inventions in the barn," Dorothy said, wiping the milk from her lips with the napkin.

Grandma D dropped her smile. "What did that old man tell you?" She didn't want anyone or anything standing in the way of her getting back to Oz.

Dorothy gulped, not sure what to say. "Nothing. He just said that you were an inventor and had some things you'd made in the barn. That's all."

Grandma D kept her eyes glued to Dorothy's, then changed her expression back. "I just tinker now and then. Kind of a hobby I do by myself. Best you be stayin' out of there. Don't want you to get hurt."

Dorothy stood up. "I can't wait to meet Bookworm."

Grandma D suspected that Doc had told the girl more than she let on, but didn't want to pursue it at that moment. "Don't call him that when you meet him. He doesn't like the nickname. Come on, I'll show you your room."

Dorothy stopped at the doorway to the second floor bedroom. It was like she'd stepped into a time warp. Everything in the room seemed from a museum.

Grandma D smiled. "This was your father's room. He just sort of kept things the way he liked them as a kid."

Dorothy looked around. Old metal warplanes hung from the ceiling. Baseball cards were arranged like a playing field diamond on the wall, still held in place by yellowing Scotch tape.

The bed was a small single, the size a grade school child would use. The dresser was half the size of Dorothy's back home. On top of it were lead toy soldiers, an autographed baseball and a silver-framed picture of her mother, when she was a younger, high school girl.

Grandma D walked over to the dresser. "Your father was in love with your mother from the moment he saw her. Said he saw her at a dance and knew then and there that he was going to marry her."

"Dad said that?" Dorothy asked, thinking about how her parents argued now, not imagining them together as young sweethearts.

"He sure did," Grandma D nodded. "Said that dark-haired girl with the flashy eyes and hot temper was just the thing he needed to help him grow up."

Dorothy pursed her lips and looked around the room which was a child's delight. "But his room is so...so..."

"It was just the way he wanted it. Didn't seem no harm to me. I told him that everyone should grow up on their own schedule but that you don't have to grow old. You know what I mean?"

Ozzie ran into the room, pulling at Grandma D's dress. "What's wrong, Ozzie?" The dog yipped and ran to the doorway where he did turns and circles.

"He wants you to do something," Dorothy said.

Grandma D heard Alexander shout her name from the barn outside. She went to the window and saw the boy waving his arms from the barn.

Throwing open the window, she shouted, "What in tarnation are you making all that racket about?" Dorothy looked out over her grandmother's shoulder.

"It's happenin' again!" Alexander screamed, pointing towards the barn. The barn door slammed open and a blizzard of hay came flying out as the roof lifted up a good foot off the walls.

"What's in there?" Dorothy whispered, having never seen anything like that.

"Nothing," Grandma D said, closing the window. "Just farm stuff."

"Farm stuff?" Dorothy asked, looking at the barn.

Grandma D nodded. "Nothin' you need to worry about."

The whole trip had been pretty strange so far, so Dorothy wasn't quite sure what to make of this latest development. "Just as long as we don't have any tornadoes, I'll be fine."

Grandma D turned her face and fidgeted with her dress. "You unpack. I'll be back in a few minutes."

Dorothy looked out at the boy in the yard. They locked eyes for a moment.

"Come on, Alex," Grandma D said from the yard.

Alexander followed behind Grandma D and struggled to pull the door closed against the wind.

"Just farm stuff, huh?" Dorothy mumbled, shaking her head. "Kansas is really...really weird," she sighed, using Doc's word.

Upstairs in the attic, Ima Witch watched Dorothy from the crystal ball. The top of the trunk lifted up in the shape of a witch's hat.

"Welcome to Kansas, deary," Ima whispered. "I've got a *weird* surprise waiting for you in the attic."

CHAPTER 10

RATS

Dorothy started unpacking but couldn't keep her curiosity down. *What are they doing in the barn?* she wondered. *I swear I saw the roof lift up and down.*

She looked around the room for a moment, then walked back to the window. *If they're doing something crazy, I'm going to hitchhike home,* she decided, feeling strange as she looked around the room at her father's boyhood toys.

As she picked up the trophies and whatnots of her father's life, she thought about returning to school. *"What did you do this summer?" they're going to ask me and I'll say that I went to visit my sixty-two-year-old grandmother who thinks she went to a place called Oz and builds strange things in her barn and...*

She heard something rattling and thumping in the attic. Like something was trying to get out. Upstairs the trunk moved back and forth. Then it stopped.

"Hope there aren't any rats in the house," she mumbled, opening up her suitcase. She'd always been deathly afraid of rats and had been that way ever since she was a little girl.

The thumping began again and it sounded right over her bed. "I'll never get any sleep if this continues," Dorothy said, walking out to the hall.

She saw the open attic stairs and could hear the thumping even louder. "Maybe it's the dog," Dorothy said, never having heard a rat or mouse make a noise that loud.

Wonder if Kansas rats are big rats? she thought, stopping at the bottom of the attic stairs. Her worst fear was coming back.

Dorothy heard the noise again and gulped. *I hope it's not a rat. I'm scared to death of rats.*

Ima read her thoughts. “Soooooooooo you don’t like rats? Well, say cheese,” she cackled, turning in a circle and snapping her fingers. The shadow behind looked far different than her face.

Ima did a little jig. “Come out, come out, wherever you are.” She moved the crystal ball around and saw a little mouse in the corner of the attic.

Ima moved her hands and the mouse stopped moving. The witch smiled, nodded, then rhymed:

> “Hickery dockery dick,
> The rat appeared real quick.
> So go to the stairs and bite on her hair,
> Hickery dockery dick.”

The little mouse in the corner of the attic suddenly turned into a rat—a rat the size of a German shepherd.

“Go kiss Dorothy,” Ima whispered, moving the rat forward with her hands, using her invisible powers. The big rat moved towards the stairs, twitching its nose and baring sharp teeth.

Dorothy heard the rat’s steps. “Doc?” she called out. “Is that you, Doc?” she barely whispered, knowing he’d already left but not knowing anything else to say. The only answer was a louder thump.

Then Ima imitated Doc’s voice. “Yes, it’s me, Dorothy. Come on up here, I want to show you something.”

Ima snapped her fingers and cast Dorothy into a trance. “I’m coming right up, Doc,” Dorothy called back.

Ima silently laughed in the snow-shaker crystal ball, watching Dorothy’s every move. The witch moved her hands around, making Dorothy step forward, trying to bring her up the attic stairs.

Ima grinned and whispered inside the trunk, “Just one step at a time, my sweet. Come to Ima. Come on.” The rat’s tail moved back and forth, like a thick pink cable.

Ura Wizard grunted and groaned behind the witch. A thick snake had wrapped itself around his head and was sitting with its head resting on the bridge of the Wizard’s nose.

The rat moved his head around, sniffing the air. "Think of Dorothy as a big piece of cheese," Ima commanded. The rat moved its jaws up and down in hunger.

Dorothy went up the first step and Ima smiled. "Come to dinner," Ima whispered, her head turning a complete circle on her shoulders. Dorothy was now fully under her spell.

Dorothy looked up the stairwell, oblivious to the rat that was staring hungrily down at her. "Hi, Doc," she smiled, thinking the rat was Doc Jones.

The rat looked over the edge but Dorothy was caught in the witch's trance. "Step up, deary. One small step for mankind and one large step for ratkind," the witch cackled.

The thick, baseball bat-sized tail of the rat drooped over the stairwell, hanging in front of Dorothy's face. But Dorothy was under the witch's control and didn't see it.

Ima smiled and commanded the rat with a rhyme. "Open your mouth and close your eyes, think of Dorothy as a cheese surprise."

The rat opened his mouth, ready to bite as Dorothy edged up another step.

Ima cackled. "Maybe we should invite some more friends to dinner," she smiled, seeing three mice cowering in the corner at the sight of the big rat.

Ima did a jig as she spun in a witch's circle. As she rhymed, the three mice changed and followed her directions:

> "Three fat rats,
> As hungry as can be.
> They all went over to take a bite,
> To chew on the girl who'll taste so right,
> Oh have you ever seen such a wonderful sight,
> As three fat rats."

As she spun out of her jig, Ima snapped her fingers and now there were four rats looking over the edge, waiting to bite Dorothy.

"Come on, Dorothy," Ima called out, imitating Doc.

"I'll be right up," Dorothy said, stepping up the next step.

Then the house was hit by a strong gust of wind. Windows rattled and the front door burst open.

The noise made Dorothy blink and she grabbed onto the stair rail. The wind came up the stairs, blowing into the attic in a strange way.

"*Curses!*" shouted the witch, seeing that her spell had been broken. She shook the trunk back and forth in anger.

The front door banged against the wall. The rats changed back into mice and scampered into the corner.

The door banged again. Dorothy shook her head, trying to clear it, then ran down the stairs to close the door and looked out.

The barn's roof was shaking! Dorothy dashed out, forgetting all about the thumping in the attic.

Inside the barn, havoc and confusion had taken over. "Shut it off!" Grandma D shouted.

"It's not on," Alexander shouted back, pointing to the *off* switch. The rabbit's foot flew off into the air.

The windmill and propeller blades were spinning blurs. Pointed in different directions, they were creating crosscurrents of wind which pushed at the sides of the barn.

The blades were spinning wildly. The oil derrick was pumping up and down. Everything seemed to be working except for one thing. The engine wasn't turned on.

Dorothy stood at the entrance, awestruck by the strange array of odd-shaped machines in the big, musty barn. *What in the world?* she questioned. A flying object came towards her and she reached out and caught it.

She looked in her hand and saw a rabbit's foot. *This is too much!* she thought, her eyes wide.

Then the Rambler station wagon engine roared to life and Alexander tripped over Grandma D's leg as he moved backwards. The wooden portals and back door of the barn burst open.

Grandma D spun around and saw Dorothy standing there. Alexander was too caught up in trying to shut off the machine to notice the pretty girl.

Grandma D started forward, but Dorothy didn't move. The old woman looked at her granddaughter, then leaned over and shouted towards her ear. "Give us a minute to shut the machine off."

Dorothy shouted back. "What are these inventions supposed to do?"

Grandma D searched for words. "They're...they're...to make..."

Suddenly the engine shut off and the blade and propeller came to a halt. Alexander shouted out, "Tornado! I think the machine's ready to make that tornado you've been wanting, Mrs. Gale."

Alexander turned to see Grandma D's expression and the look on Dorothy's face.

Dorothy whispered, "Tornado?"

"Let's go back into the kitchen," Grandma D said, taking Dorothy's hand.

Alexander saw the rabbit's foot in her other hand. "I was afraid I'd lost that for good," he smiled, taking it.

"It just flew at me and..." Dorothy stopped.

"Guess you got all the luck," he smiled.

"I don't think so," Dorothy said, looking back one more time as her grandmother led her out the door.

"It's a long story," Grandma D began, as they walked towards the old, clapboard farmhouse.

But all Dorothy could think was that it was a long way back to Orlando from her father's boyhood room on the second floor and her tornado-making grandmother.

Grandma D began with how she'd come as an orphan to live with Auntie Em, how the tornado had taken her to Oz, and everything that had happened in that far away land.

By the time her grandmother finished, they were sitting in the living room, under the watchful eye of the Wizard of Oz, who stood above the mantel in the big, green oil painting.

"And that's the story of Oz and my tornado machines," Grandma D said, feeling foolish. "You don't know how wonderful it was to be home again."

"That's quite a story," Dorothy said, not knowing what to think. "But why do you want to go back?"

"It's just something I have to do. I can't explain it."

"Well," Dorothy smiled, "I'm glad you told me. It answers a lot of things I didn't understand that my dad told me."

Grandma D felt a wave of relief. She felt better having told Dorothy everything, even about the secrets in the trunk. *Guess I needed to talk about it,* Grandma D thought.

"I'd only heard bits and pieces of the story from Dad and you over the years."

"I didn't want to have to tell you everything at once, but I guess it's better this way," Grandma D sighed. "Kind of felt good to tell someone everything."

"But you said that everything's changed. Why do you want to go back?" Dorothy asked.

"I just do. It's something I want to do before I die. I just feel like I belong back there," she sighed, not wanting to tell Dorothy how hard it had been for her, growing up as an orphan.

"Oz sounds mighty strange, really weird," Dorothy shrugged.

Grandma D looked at the girl. "Oz is a special place. It's not like some Shirley Temple or Judy Garland movie. Oz is up here," she said, tapping her temple, "and in here," she nodded, covering her heart, "and over there," she said, pointing off towards the horizon.

"But if it's there, why do you need to go back then?"

"Because I do," Grandma D said flatly.

"And you really think that your machines can make a tornado to take you back to Oz?" Dorothy asked, hardly believing that she was really having this conversation.

Grandma D nodded. "I know they're wantin' me back."

"Can I see the newspaper in the trunk in the attic?"

"Not now. But soon," Grandma D said. For the first time in sixty years she was actually considering showing someone her secrets.

Dorothy made a pouting face. Grandma D smiled. "I'll show them to you tonight."

"Promise?" Dorothy said.

"I promise," Grandma D said. "But you got to promise to keep it a secret." Dorothy nodded.

They both heard the thump from the attic and looked up. "I think you've got mice," Dorothy said.

"*All* attics in Kansas got mice," Grandma D smiled. "Now let's go out and get you introduced to Alexander properly."

Ima watched them go from inside the ball. "Go home," she whispered. Her words sent flurries of snow around her image. "Go back to Orlando, young Dorothy, before it's too late."

But her words were muffled by the snow-shaker glass and the lid on the trunk. Ima licked her index finger, then spun around with her finger in the air, chanting her witch's incantation:

"Blood is red,
Witches dress in black.
Dorothy Gale,
You'll never come back."

On her way to the barn, Grandma D grabbed her heart. "What's wrong?" Dorothy asked.

"I just felt a sudden chill," the old woman said, feeling like something she couldn't put her finger on had just passed from her life.

For the first time in her life she felt like she would never get back to Oz. The feeling cut through her like a hot, sharp knife.

Ima cackled and pointed her finger at the image of young Dorothy, which floated in front of her in the crystal ball.

Dorothy stopped next to her grandmother. "I feel a chill too."

Ima laughed and wet her other index finger. She spun in the opposite direction, finger in the air, the shadow behind her outlined the invisible hat on her head.

The snow flurries reversed direction as she chanted:

"Your parents will divorce
Your house will be sold,
You'll move to Detroit
Where you'll always be cold."

A feeling she couldn't explain, suddenly came over Dorothy and she started crying in front of the barn door.

"What's wrong, child?" Grandma D asked.

Dorothy sobbed so hard she couldn't speak. It was as if all the tears she'd been holding back in Orlando came flooding out of her.

"I...I...I'm worried that Mom and...and Dad are divorcing...and.... and...they're selling the house and..."

Grandma D hugged her like a mother. "I think you need to talk some things out with your old grandma. Why don't we take a walk through the fields and see what's botherin' you."

She looked at the girl and remembered how she'd felt when Auntie Em and Uncle Henry had taken her in as an orphan. Never having known her parents, Grandma D had always wondered what it would be like to worry about them, but then she put it out of her mind.

Got to stop hurtin' myself. I'll never know who my mother was...or who my father was. I don't think Doc will ever understand. I'm just an orphan who knows how much love little girls need.

As they walked through the fields, Dorothy told her grandmother about the arguments of her parents. About the house being sold and their moving to Detroit.

Dorothy poured her heart out to Grandma D, and in turn, Grandma D apologized over and over for not having seen her in ten years.

They looked at each other in a new light and both felt at peace, little knowing of the troubles soon to come.

CHAPTER 11

THE WIZARD

Inside the crystal ball in the attic trunk, Ima threw back her head in laughter. The dragon on her necklace hissed with glee.

Ura Wizard glanced around the room. He was helpless to protect Dorothy and unable to escape from the monsters that swam hungrily below him.

The shelves were lined with candles, skulls, and jars of snakes, rats, toads, and spiders, and old, musty books.

There was no way out. The door to the hall was locked and the drop outside the window was a thousand feet or more. There were three doors in the room.

On one was written PETTING ZOO, on another was a sign marked HEAD ROOM, and on the third was labeled BROOM CLOSET. He looked at the door. *What's the petting zoo? What's the head room?*

Ura felt a bead of sweat trickle down his nose. Another crept along his spine. *I'm trapped*, Ura said, his hopes sinking.

Without Dorothy, Oz will be lost, Ura worried. *Ima will take control and turn all that is good about Oz into evil.*

Come back. Please, Dorothy. Come back, he said, concentrating all his thoughts and energies into that message he sent over the rainbow. But he knew that the moment he had stepped out from the protection of the Emerald City, that his powers were all but gone.

Ima popped her arm into the air like she was catching a ball. "Did you lose something, Wizzie?" she laughed. Without waiting for an answer, she tossed his thoughts back to him.

The Wizard listened to his thoughts whisper back at him as they bounced off the walls of the witch's castle, hitting his head as they passed by with a jarring jolt.

"You're no longer the Great Wizard," she sneered, pointing her finger.

"And you'll never rule Oz," he said, with more bluster than belief.

Ima cackled. "Oz will soon be mine," she smiled, dancing around the room.

"Leave Oz alone," he demanded.

She shook her head. "I've got big plans for Oz and the Emerald City."

"Plans? What plans?" Ura asked, worried now that the land over the rainbow was going to be destroyed.

Ima grinned. "I just want to redo my castle." She looked around the room, pretending to concentrate on the flooring. "How do you think these floors would look in yellow?"

"Yellow?" Ura said.

Ima nodded. "Yellow. Like in yellow bricks. Seems there was a give-away sale after you left the Emerald City and..."

"What did you to do our beautiful yellow brick road?"

Ima giggled. "I just had my little witches pull up the bricks and put them in the basement. They'll be safe with me until the rebuilding begins."

Then she frowned. "But first I need to put up a little bridge."

"What kind of bridge?" Ura asked suspiciously.

Ima winked and blew him a kiss. He felt the smack of her lips like a slap on the face. "I think I'll just put a teeny-tiny four lane highway over the rainbow."

"You can't!" Ura said loudly. "You can't open Oz up. Too many people will want to come."

"That's just the point," Ima smiled. "I think that Oz will make a wonderful theme park."

"A theme park?"

"Yes," Ima sighed, spinning around. "Maybe I'll call it Oz Land, or Ima's Studios." Then she giggled. "How about Six Witches Over Oz, or maybe Witch Berry Farms, or WitchWorld?"

With a demonic laugh that chilled the room, Ima pointed her finger at the Wizard. "Yes indeed, I'll turn your little paradise into a pot of gold. I'll charge fifty dollars a day to get into my family-value experience. I'll sell Oz franchises all over the world. That's what's really supposed to be over the rainbow, isn't it? Just one big golden parachute of greed, eh, tizzie-whizzie?"

"But you'll ruin Oz!"

"Look what's happened to Christmas," Ima chuckled. "I bet you don't even know whose birthday it is." She spun around, cackling. "And what's Easter become? Nothing more than some silly rabbit's do-drop-in to spend money. Greed—I love it!" she shouted, shooting lightning bolts from her fingers.

Then Ima closed her eyes, rocking back and forth. "Yes, Mr. Wizard, greed rules a world filled with porkers fighting at the trough. When the world's lost its way, it's up to the witches to show them what they really want—isn't that right?" she cooed dangerously, flashing her dazzling eyes.

"The people won't stand for it!" Ura shouted. "Oz is the last refuge for hope, the last place safe for imagination. Without Oz you can't preserve the magic of childhood."

"Who cares?" Ima chuckled. "Do you really think that people who don't even know their own history will care about the future when they don't even understand how they got to the present?"

Ima gazed through an image of a television set up on the wall. "Look at that," she nodded. "That's all the people care about over the rainbow. They're preoccupied with the present. They care only about now without regard to later."

Ura watched the images in horror.

Ima shook her head. "No, Wizbag, it'd be too easy to blame all the misery on me. They did it to themselves and made it easy for evil to rule."

Ima flicked the channels until it became a blur. "Control of the airwaves is control of the conscience of the world. And I'll fit right into the world of television, don't you think?" She batted her eyes, pretending to flirt.

"That will never happen to Oz," Ura snorted.

"Oh, but it will," Ima said gleefully. "Television is the world's electronic baby-sitter that blurs the difference between truth and fiction. Once I'm in control, I'll put up an electronic curtain around the world and feed them their own desires, call them my ideas, and make a fortune."

"No one will believe you."

"Sure they will, and when I get finished, fiction will be truth and truth will be lies. History will be curbside trash, just yesterday's mail. Who needs books when you have TV?"

"But the people of Oz elected me!" the Wizard screamed. "Well, you're not in Oz."

"I'll never go along with your plans for Oz," Ura said defiantly, "and I'm the Wizard of Oz!"

"Oh, you'll go along with it," she laughed. "I'll make you the doorman, maybe even let you sell tickets if you're lucky."

"I won't do it," Ura said, eyes glaring at her.

"You will or I'll turn you into a duck—a dead duck," she laughed.

"You wouldn't dare."

"Don't tempt me, you old windbag. Wizard? Hah! You're just a fizzie-wizzie. Nothing but a humbug like your father who thought he was some kind of P.T. Barnum with all his smoke and mirrors." She looked at him and snickered. "The Great Wizard of Oz. He was pathetic."

"That wasn't the way he was! Father Wizard got off course but I've straightened out Oz and..."

Ima silenced him with a snap of her fingers. "Your father was nothing but a politician and you're nothing but a snake-wrapped sushi lunch for my...goldfish!" she screamed, pointing to the monsters swimming below.

For a moment they all turned to gold and jumped up at him. Then she shrieked with laughter and disappeared in a flash. The door marked PETTING ZOO slammed shut by itself.

Ura closed his eyes as the witch's laughter echoed off the walls. The Wizard did his best to ignore it and concentrated as hard as he could. *She wants the golden ruler. That's what she needs to control Oz.*

With Oz unprotected and Ima having the ruler, nothing will stop her...nothing.

He closed his eyes and willed with all his might. *I've got to save the gold. I've got to keep her from getting it.*

He heard strange sounds come from behind the PETTING ZOO door. Then he heard her singing:

> "Old McWitchy had a petting zoo,
> Of things you'd hate to keep.
> That like to bite on children's toes
> When they are asleep."

Ura wished he could cover his ears to her singing. *Why did I let her trick me? Why?*

Beyond the walls of the Emerald City, the Wizards of Oz, Ura and all those who had reigned before him, had virtually no powers at all. They ruled Oz from within the Emerald City where their powers were supreme in the Land of Oz.

But once outside, they became weak. It was the secret of the Wizards that no one was to ever know. But somehow Ima had figured it out. She'd enticed him to come out with images of his late father.

Why did I fall for that? Ura berated himself. He'd heard of what she'd done to the Munchkins and knew she was making threats against the Emerald City.

Father Wizard said the witch might try it. He said, "Watch out for witches bearing gifts." Why didn't I close my eyes...why?

But he hadn't. Ura Wizard had seen the images of his father, calling him to come out from the protection of the Emerald City. To come out and play as father and son once more.

Once outside the gates, the Wicked Witch blocked his path back into the Emerald City. With his powers weak and growing weaker, he tried to go around her, but it was no use.

A hundred little witches dropped down and tied him up. Now he was a prisoner in her castle, locked far away from his beautiful Emerald City.

He felt the golden ruler pushing against his back, as one of the snake bands moved. *Give me strength,* he wished, drawing from all the powers of the Wizards over the ages. *Give me the strength to protect the golden ruler.*

The yellow brick road was gone so he had to act fast. *The golden ruler will save Oz if I can get it into Dorothy's hands. Oz needs all the friends it can get. We need Dorothy back.*

Closing his eyes and whispering the secret magic chant, passed down from Wizard to Wizard, Ura willed with all his might that the simple, foot-long stick of gold should float from his pocket.

Slowly, slowly the stick of gold came out from the hidden pocket inside his jacket and floated up above the tank. Ura felt his powers weakening. He wasn't sure if the gold stick would make it out of the castle.

Finally, after using virtually all of his energy, he willed the golden stick to the ledge of the immense stone windowsill. It wavered in the air, unsure of whether it should leave its master's hands.

Ura nodded to the golden stick and whispered:

> "Fly with the wind,
> Brave heat and cold.
> Hide in the rainbow
> Where values are gold."

"Get to the rainbow," he whispered. "Go as fast as you can."

With his last ounce of energy, Ura sent the golden stick flying through the air. "Godspeed," he whispered. "The golden ruler belongs in the Emerald City. But the rainbow will keep you safe until Dorothy gets here."

Then in a blinding flash, Ima reappeared. She closed her eyes and moved to the edge of the tank. "We checked your cape, but it wasn't there."

"What?" Ura asked, knowing what she was looking for.

"Don't play games with me, whizzie. Where's the gold?

"Gold? What gold?" he asked, playing for time. "You mean the goldfish?"

"I have no time for your games. Where's the golden ruler?" she screamed, her words oozing with hatred.

"It's gone," he smiled.

"Where?" she asked, circling around the water tank in panic.

"It's gone back to Oz. By now it's safely away from your evil hands and..."

Ima screamed the scream of centuries of evil, locked up in her blood. With a terrible fury to witness, she spun in circles like a whirling dervish.

A mirror appeared in the air and she came to a halt, though her hair kept blowing in the breeze she left behind. Ima preened herself, running her ruby-red, long fingernails through her raven black, shoulder-length hair.

"Pretty as a picture," she whispered, blowing herself a kiss. The imprint of her lips appeared on the mirror.

She looked over at Ura. "Make it easy on yourself and tell me where it is." Ura shook his head. "Okay then," she said coldly, blowing a chilling breath over towards the Wizard. In a second he was frozen solid.

Ima grinned and held up the mirror in front of her.

> "Mirror, mirror, Ura's in the freezer,
> Is the gold hidden on that old geezer?"

The mirror moved back and forth. "It isn't, huh," Ima said.

She looked at the Wizard. "Then where is it?"

"I don't remember where I left it," he said, through chattering teeth.

She sighed deeply, then gripped the mirror tightly and whispered darkly:

"Mirror, mirror that I hold,
Show me where I can find the gold."

Ima did a double take. The mirror showed nothing but clouds.

Gritting her teeth in rage, she shook the mirror, and left it hanging in the air in front of her. Leaning forward, her lips nearly touching the glass, she whispered coldly:

"Mirror, mirror in the air,
Is my gold in the clouds out there?"

The mirror nodded. The clouds in the reflection parted and Ima could clearly see the golden ruler speeding through the air towards the rainbow that separated Oz from the world.

"You did this!" she screamed, spinning around and pointing at Ura. "You sent my gold to the rainbow."

The green dragon on the necklace came alive and crawled out and up onto her shoulder. The dragon stretched its wings and hissed.

"Back Itsa," she snapped, and the dragon went back into the necklace, leaving his tongue to flicker in and out.

Ima looked at Ura. "You've upset Itsa Dragon. He doesn't like anyone to displease me." The dragon darted out across the room and lashed the Wizard's face with its tongue.

Ima was in a rage. "You should have given it to me," she said sinisterly.

"Then your plans are ruined," Ura laughed. "By now the golden ruler is probably in the rainbow."

Ima waved her hands in a circle over her head and the image of the flying golden ruler appeared just as it was entering the rainbow. The witch covered her face as if she was being hit by scalding water.

"That's enough!" she shrieked, and the image dissolved. She looked at Ura. "No one will stop me from taking the magic of Oz and turning it into my golden goose. But I need to think."

She waved her hands in the air and a dozen little witches flew in. They sat on the ceiling, waiting for Ima's orders, eating bugs.

"Let the music begin," Ima nodded.

The little witches swallowed their bugs and began playing strange-looking instruments that appeared in their hands. Ima bowed to the air.

What's she doing? Ura wondered.

Ima turned as if she heard his thoughts. "Dancing gives me time to think," she said, moving in circles in a strange dance step.

Ura looked at the wall and saw the shadow outline of a terrible monster in her arms, but saw nothing or no one dancing with her.

Then he looked at her shadow outline and back at Ima. He blinked his eyes. *She's not wearing a witch's hat!* he thought, but her shadow figure was clearly wearing an tall, pointed hat.

Then he looked closely at the outline of the face in the shadow. Ima was considered a dark, raving beauty. But the face in the shadow had a long, pointy nose, a crooked chin, and the biggest, ugliest wart that he'd ever seen with hairs that seemed to be alive. Obviously, the shadow showed the witch as she truly was, without a magic spell cast over her appearance.

She looks just like her mother, Ura gulped. *No, she's the* ugliest *thing I've ever seen.*

Then he looked at the door marked HEAD ROOM and shivered. *I wonder what's in there?*

When the song was over, the little witches flew away. Ima held out her hand. Ura heard what sounded like a grunting kiss.

"Come back later, darling," Ima whispered to the invisible figure.

But the kiss led to a bite on her hand. The Wizard watched the back of her hand open up in a jagged bite mark. But no blood came out.

He knew that it was rumored that witches didn't bleed because their blood had dried up from being so wicked, but he had never seen the proof.

"Oh, you naughty boy," Ima said, taking her hand away.

Then she turned to the Wizard and unfroze him. "I just love to dance," she sighed, spinning in a circle. "I was the belle of the witches ball last year."

Ura tried to trick her. "Why don't you take off your hat?"

Ima started to reach above her head, then stopped. "Don't play games with me, fizzie-whizzie. You might not like what you see."

"I already don't," he said.

"Who cares?" she smiled. "Are you ready?" she asked, raising her eyebrows.

"Now what are you going to do?" Ura asked.

"You'll see," she cackled.

With the tip of her broom, she stirred up the water in the tank below the Wizard. Fins and sharp jaws emerged.

"Guess who's dying to meet you," she laughed, twirling in a circle and disappearing in a puff of smoke, leaving the Wizard to twist in the wind.

The door marked BROOM CLOSET slammed shut by itself. Inside the secret room, Ima looked over her collection of prized flying brooms.

"Let's see," she said quietly, picking up a short, stubby broom. "No, this won't do. That's for cave flying."

Ima walked down the racks of brooms, picking up and examining some long, sleek brooms with tight wrapped straw ends.

"Aha!" she smiled, "this will do."

Taking it out, she went to the window and floated up to the ledge. "Come on, Itsa," she said. "Time to go bye-bye."

The dragon slid off from the necklace and slithered up to her shoulders, wrapping its tail around her neck. Wetting her finger, Ima held it up to test the wind.

"Perfect," she nodded, "perfectly rotten weather. The best to fly in," she said, jumping off the ledge into the clouds.

Ima flew off on her broom, determined to see if she could get the golden ruler back from the rainbow. She wanted to make the Wizard sweat, knowing that she had to keep him alive until the golden ruler was back in her hands.

"But after that," she whispered to herself as she flew through the air, "if he doesn't go along, I'll have him stuffed."

CHAPTER 12

JESSIE

Dorothy felt so much better after her walk through the fields with her grandmother, that she went straight to the phone to call home. A stranger picked it up on the first ring.

"Century Twenty-One open house," said the voice.

Dorothy froze. *Open house?*

"Hello?" said the voice on the line.

"Ah, this is Dorothy Gale. Is my mother there?" Dorothy could hear strange voices in the background.

"I'm sorry, dear, but we're having an open house. Your parents will be back after five. Do you want me to leave a message?"

Dorothy didn't know what to say. "Ah, no, that's okay."

They're holding an open house. I bet the house will be sold and they'll move to Detroit while I'm up here in Kansas. I won't even get a chance to say good-bye to my friends.

"Did you speak to your mother?" Grandma D asked from the kitchen.

"They weren't home," Dorothy said. "Think I'll go out for a walk."

"Keep your eye out for storms. They come quick during summer."

"I will," Dorothy said, opening the front door and heading out.

She walked down the drive and was up near the next property line before she realized there was a commotion up ahead.

"Give me a paper," a big, heavy-set boy said rudely.

It was John Bear, the neighborhood bully. He grabbed the paper out of Jessie Lee's hands, but only knocked it to the ground.

Jessie stood his ground. "You can't have one for free. They're for my customers."

John Bear grabbed Jessie by the shirt collar and cocked back his arm. “You better give me one,” he said, lowering his tone, “or I’ll knock your block off.”

Jessie Lee shook his head. “Why don’t you pick on somebody your own size?”

“’Cause I like pickin’ on you,” Bear said.

Dorothy stepped forward. “Let him go!”

Her voice was so loud and unexpected that Bear let go of Jessie’s shirt. Dorothy stepped between them.

“Only bullies pick on people smaller than them.”

“I just wanted a paper, that’s all,” Bear said sheepishly.

“For free,” Jessie added. “Wouldn’t pay for it.”

“He was tryin’ to charge me thirty-five cents for a twenty-five-cent paper.”

Jessie looked slighted. “I have to add a carryin’ charge.”

Dorothy looked at Jessie. “Why don’t you just sell it for what they cost? You’ll still make your commission.”

Jessie shook his head. “You mind your business and I’ll manage mine. Okay?” he said, picking the paper up off the ground and putting it back into his sack.

Dorothy looked between them. “You two make quite a pair,” she said, shaking her head. “One’s a bully and one’s a shark.”

Jessie Lee got back on his bike. “Where you from anyway?”

Dorothy smiled. “I’m from Orlando and I’m...”

John Bear interrupted. “She’s spending the summer visiting with her grandmother.”

“How’d you know?” Dorothy asked.

Bear shrugged. “A town this small you know everything.”

“You’re the Oz lady’s granddaughter?” Jessie asked, astonished that such a young, pretty and city-looking girl was visiting Osawatomie.

“That’s my grandma,” she nodded.

Jessie pushed off on his bike. “She told you ’bout Oz yet?”

Dorothy’s expression changed as she wondered how to react. “Maybe.”

"Well, maybe you're kind of crazy like she is," Jessie laughed. "See you 'round like a donut," he shouted, riding off down the road.

"See ya," Dorothy smiled.

"And I like your red sneakers," he called back. "They make a real fashion statement."

"Thanks," Dorothy said quietly, feeling awkward.

John Bear spat out a cuss word, talking to himself.

"Don't say that," Dorothy warned. "I don't like cussing."

"I'll cuss if I want to," Bear said, eyes glaring.

"Then you won't cuss around me," she said, walking off.

Bear watched her head back up the small rise towards the fenced fields. He thought the cussing would impress her, but he was very, very wrong.

With a heavy heart and not a friend in the world, Bear trudged back to his home. *Guess she thinks I'm no good too,* he thought. *Just like my dad said,* he choked, his eyes welling up.

Dorothy wished she were home, but knew she wouldn't get far on the fifty dollars in her pocket. A funny feeling came over her, like someone was following.

She looked around and shrugged it off, but it kept coming back. Finally, she spun around.

"Who's there?" she called out.

But there was nothing but the wide Kansas prairie. "I swear, I felt someone near me."

Above her, a dark cloud stood up from the white, billowy blanket of clouds that covered the sky. It was shaped like a witch with a pointed hat, riding a broom.

CHAPTER 13

Ima Says

Doc drove slowly towards Osawatomie, mulling over his feelings for Grandma D. The storms in the distance seemed to be getting closer, but Doc didn't seem to notice as he headed towards the bridge over the Pottawatomie Creek.

Maybe I've been wastin' my time waitin' for her, he sighed. *Never had more than a few friends I could really count on,* Doc decided. *Could count 'em on one hand with about three fingers left over. Just Roy and Dorothy. Husband and wife. Husband of the woman I've wanted to marry darn near all my life. Now he's dead and there's only Dorothy left. My best friend and the woman I guess I've always been in love with.*

He thought of the other girls that had eyed him in high school, but dismissed the thoughts. *Guess I'll never know what could have been with any of 'em. Heck, guess I'll never know what could have been between me and Dorothy if I hadn't been drafted in the Korean War.*

He passed by a farm truck and waved out the window. *Guess Uncle Sam will never know how much I gave up for my country when I went off to war. Went off to war and lost my girl—lost my heart—lost my heart and soul.*

Suddenly, a chilling breeze blew inside the car. Doc shivered and rolled up the window. "Feels like winter out there."

The wind that preceeded Ima back to the castle leaked over the rainbow. Ima was in a bad mood. A very bad mood.

She hadn't been able to pull the golden ruler from the rainbow and now she didn't know what she was going to do. All she knew was that she couldn't let Dorothy Gale come back to Oz.

Ima said a witch's chant and clapped twice, opening up her window to the world over the rainbow. She was focused directly on Doc.

"So you're an old fool who loves old Dorothy." Ima put her ear to the glass. "Tell me where you're going," she whispered.

Doc looked around as if he'd heard someone. "I'm goin' to town to pay Dorothy's property tax. Don't want her to lose her farm."

Doc then blinked. "Why did I just say that? I must be gettin' old."

Ima snapped back. "So she might lose that pile of dirt, will she?" Ima cackled.

She snapped her fingers and saw that there was a property auction on the courthouse steps. In the sheriff's hands were the deeds that were being sold.

Ima put her eyes to the glass and pulled the image closer. Among the papers was the deed to Dorothy Gale's farm. Ozcot was going to be sold for unpaid taxes!

Ima danced a jig of delight, then remembered that Doc was going to try to save her farm. Snapping her fingers, she saw Doc driving towards town.

With a sinister whisper, Ima put her lips to the glass and said, "Do you remember Simon Says?"

Doc looked into the rearview mirror. "Of course I remember Simon Says." He saw a pair of eyes—Ima's eyes—looking at him.

He started to blink, but her eyeballs started moving back and forth, hypnotizing him. "Well, old man," she whispered through the rearview mirror. "If you know Simon Says, you'll love Ima Says."

Doc was looking into the mirror, not at the road. Ima smiled. "Just do as I say and you'll have a smashing time."

"I'm ready to play," Doc said in a monotone voice.

"Okay," Ima said, turning the mirror around so she could see the road ahead. There was a truck approaching in the other lane. "Ima says to veer to your left." Doc eased the car over into the on-coming lane and headed straight towards the truck.

"Good," Ima whispered. She turned the mirror back. "Ima says to push the gas pedal down."

Doc nodded and pushed the gas pedal to the floor. The car lurched forward. He didn't hear the truck's horn as the car raced straight ahead on a collision course.

"Ima says to smile." Doc smiled. "Ima says to smile wider...'cause you're on Ima's funniest home video."

As the car sped forward, Ima giggled to herself. "I'll love watching replays of this later."

On the steps of the courthouse, Ozcot came up for sale. The sheriff took a deep breath and sighed. *Can't understand why that old woman didn't answer my letters.*

In the audience, Willa Watkins raised her hand. "I'm just telling everybody here that I'll pay more than the place is worth."

The sheriff cleared his throat. "The taxes owed on this property are twelve hundred dollars. That's the minimum bid."

"I bid ten thousand dollars!" Willa shouted, standing up. She knew that no one would even bid against her if she came out strong on the first bid.

Just a mile away, Doc Jones' Dodge sped forward. The truck driver had thought Doc was just some kid playing chicken and humored him. But as the car got closer, the big eighteen wheeler was going too fast to brake quickly.

The trucker looked for a place to pull over, but there were kids on both sides of the road. Bracing for the impact, the trucker tried one last blast of his horn.

Ima spun around shrieking, "Ima says *die!*"

She looked at the image of certain disaster and cried out, "Ima says, right on, Doc, right on!"

Doc, thinking that he was commanded to veer right, jerked the wheel. With barely twenty yards between Doc and the truck, he edged the car back into his lane as if he had all the time in the world.

Ima's jaw dropped. "Curses!" she screamed.

Doc hit a large pothole and bumped his head against the roof. The impact jolted him out of the trance.

He blinked. "Musta been daydreaming," he said, trying to clear his mind. "Better go get a checkup," he mumbled, turning towards the tax office which was in the old city hall building.

He saw the sheriff conducting what he knew was another property auction for unpaid taxes, and shook his head as he got out of his car. More poor souls losing their farms.

"And if no one else wants to bid, Willa Watkins has bought the deed to the Gale farm."

Doc stopped in his tracks. "Did you say the Gale farm, Sheriff?"

"I'm sorry Doc, but you're too late."

Willa stepped up and snatched the deed. "Now I can build my subdivision. Nothing can stop me now."

"There must have been a mistake," Doc stammered, walking towards the steps.

"We sent her at least four notices," the sheriff said.

"But she said she didn't get a single one," Doc pleaded.

"They all say that," Willa snapped, shaking her head. "All the tax cheats and dead beats blame it on the U.S. Mail."

She looked at Doc. "I'll be by to tell that crazy old lady to get ready to move." Willa turned to the sheriff. "And if she don't get out, I'll be coming to you to evict her."

Willa walked off laughing and got into her sleek, black sports car and sped off in a blaze of burning rubber. Doc turned to the sheriff and said, "But Dorothy's always paid her taxes late. You know that."

"Not this late."

"But you know how Dorothy is and..."

The sheriff held up his hands. "I'm sorry, Doc. I like Dorothy, but my hands are tied. The law's the law and the law says that unless property taxes are paid, you lose your land."

"But she didn't get any tax notices."

"I put one in the mail myself." He looked at Doc. "I'm sorry. I really am. But there's nothing I can do about it."

* * *

Ima was watching it all from the crystal ball. She moved her hands and the image changed to Willa Watkins speeding down the country road towards Ozcot.

"There's a woman after my own heart," she nodded. "Kind of even looks like me," Ima said.

Willa picked up the deed to Ozcot on the seat beside her and kissed it. Ima chuckled.

"She's doing all my dirty work for me," Ima smiled. "Soon Dorothy Gale will be evicted from her farm and all those tornado machines will be taken apart."

Then she closed her eyes and scratched her chin. "But why didn't old Dorothy Gale get those tax notices?"

With a spin to the left and a spin to the right, Ima pointed her index fingers together, then rolled them in the same direction, circling like a wheel. The image in the crystal ball started going in reverse as the days in Willa's recent past were shown to her.

"What were you up to?" Ima whispered, looking at the images of Willa moving backwards as she moved the clock back.

Ima was looking for something. "Aha," she cackled, "there it is." She stopped the image, then rolled her fingers in the opposite direction until she had it right.

Ima watched Willa Watkins steal the tax notices from the Ozcot mailbox. "I thought so!" Ima laughed. "You are a witch after my own heart," she laughed.

With a blink of her eyes, Ima rolled her fingers in the opposite direction and sent the days spinning foward until the image was back to the present. Willa Watkins was speeding towards Ozcot to give Dorothy Gale the bad news.

"Let's see how old Dorothy Gale enjoys this how-do-you-do," Ima cackled. "Call it a welcome wagon...witch's style."

CHAPTER 14

City Girl

Jessie Lee delivered the rest of his papers, then doubled back around to see if he could spot the city girl again. He saw young Dorothy in the distance, walking along the top of the fence of John Bear's property.

Hope that old bull's in his pen, he worried. That bull was the meanest animal he'd ever seen.

Dorothy was walking along like there was no danger in the world. *Dumb city girl. Guess I better go check.* He doubled back, happy that he had another excuse to see Dorothy again.

Standing on the fence, Dorothy laughed to herself, happy to be a little girl for a little while. Walking step by step, she carefully walked along the top boards, keeping her feet sideways for balance.

A dark, witch-shaped cloud hovered above her. Inside the crystal ball, Ima nodded. "Be careful, dearie," the witch whispered. "And that's no bull."

Ima moved her hands and changed the picture. The big bull was snorting inside his pen, pawing the ground. He'd seen Dorothy.

"But that one is bull—all bull!" Ima shouted, howling with laughter.

Dorothy couldn't see the big bull standing behind the scrub in his pen. She hummed a tune as she walked along the fence top, then remembered a childhood verse.

"Humpty Dumpty sat on a wall," she said, moving forward carefully. "And Humpty Dumpty had a great fall."

Dorothy stopped on one of the posts and rested. "All the king's horses and all the king's men," she said, stepping onto the next board.

Ima put her hand to her mouth and giggled, finishing the verse for herself. "Couldn't save Dorothy from the bull in the pen."

With a snap of her fingers, the bull pushed against the door of his pen and raced out.

As Jessie got closer, he could see that the bull was coming down the hill towards Dorothy. *I know he's spotted her red sneakers. I know it.*

In fact, the bull had seen Dorothy and movement had transformed his trot into a thundering dash. Dorothy heard his clumping hooves and began losing her balance.

"Oh, no," she cried out, not feeling the breeze from the shadow of the witch's broom that was pushing her forward.

Dorothy fell into the bull's pasture. "Help!" she shouted, struggling to get to her feet.

The dark cloud overhead was moving in circles. Back inside the crystal ball, Ima was dancing with glee. "Help yourself!" she laughed.

Oh, gosh! Jessie thought. *That bull's gonna kill her.*

Jessie dropped his bike and ran towards the fence. "I'm comin'!" He vaulted over the fence without thinking of the consequences.

"Get back!" he shouted, waving his arms at the bull.

Ima stopped her dance and pushed her face against the image. "Leave her alone. She doesn't want help!"

"What'd you say?" Jessie asked, turning his head towards Dorothy.

"I said help," she whispered, eyeing the bull.

"Thought I heard somethin' else," Jessie said.

The animal stopped and snorted. Jessie said to Dorothy quietly, "Just get up easy like and climb back over the fence."

Ima shrieked in anger. "Curses. This girl leads a charmed life!"

"Get back Mr. Bull. This is Jessie Lee talkin'."

Dorothy did as Jessie instructed. "But what about you?" she whispered back as she topped the fence.

"That's a good question," Jessie said.

"And here's the answer," Ima whispered from inside the crystal ball. She poked the image of the bull with her broom. "Move it, you slab of beef."

The bull jumped forward.

"Back now, Mr. Bull," Jessie said, moving his hands slowly up and down to calm the animal down.

Ima poked the image again and the bull took another step. "Let's see how fast that paperboy can run," she cackled, poking the bull's image with all her might.

The bull bellowed and charged forward. "Run, Jessie!" Dorothy screamed.

Jessie jumped to the left, rolled down a small incline, then sprinted for the fence, and vaulted back over. The bull was only a split second behind.

"That was a close call," Dorothy said, helping Jessie up.

"You're just askin' for trouble, walkin' on a bull's fence with silly lookin' red sneakers on," he said, dusting off his pants.

Dorothy looked down at her shoes and gasped. "Red. Is it the color or the movement bulls hate?"

Jessie interrupted. "That was pretty dumb."

Dorothy glared. "How was I to know there was a bull over there?"

"That's 'cause you're just a weird city girl." Jessie tried to frown but broke into a smirk.

"That's Doc's word," she grinned. Her anger vanished with his smiled.

"No," Jessie said. "Doc got the word from me."

They both heard a car come speeding down the lane. Over the rise in front of them, Willa Watkins flew towards them in her car.

Jessie's bike was still in the road. "Oh no," he mumbled.

Willa saw the bike in the road at the last minute and ground her brakes to a skidding halt. "Whose bike is that?" she shouted out, her face red with anger.

"It's mine, Miss Watkins," Jessie said.

"Well, move it!" Willa shouted. "I haven't got all day."

Dorothy was shocked by her rudeness. "You shouldn't shout at him. He didn't mean to leave it there."

"Oh yeah," Willa sneered, "then why did he leave it there? For his health?"

Dorothy shook her head. "And you don't have to be rude about it."

"And who are you?" Willa asked. "You're obviously not from around here."

Dorothy didn't like the woman and wanted to end the conversation. "I'm from Orlando and I'm staying with my grandmother and..."

Willa broke up laughing. "So you're the granddaughter. Hope you enjoyed the short visit."

"I just got here," Dorothy said, perplexed.

"And you're just about to leave," Willa smiled.

Jessie looked between them. "What are you two talkin' about?"

"Nothing that concerns you, paperboy," Willa snapped. She turned to Dorothy. "I suggest you start packing your bags."

Dorothy had heard enough. "And I think you should go learn the Golden Rule."

"I do," Willa chuckled. "She who has the gold, rules."

"You're not very nice," Dorothy said, looking Willa straight in the eye.

Suddenly, Willa opened up her car door. Dorothy took two steps back onto her grandmother's property.

Willa marched towards her. "Stay off my grandmother's property," Dorothy warned.

"Stay off my property," Willa said.

"What are you talking about?" Dorothy asked.

Jessie shook his head. "Yeah, what are you both talkin' about?"

Willa unfolded the deed from her pocket. "I just bought your grandmother's farm, so why don't you go pack your bags and head back to Florida?"

"Because I'm here for the summer, that's why," Dorothy said defiantly.

"Consider this the shortest summer on record," Willa chuckled.

Dorothy stood speechless as Willa drove away in a cloud of dust. Her laughter seemed to echo long after she was out of sight.

Jessie Lee shook his head. "Guess the only thing I can say to you is, hello and good-bye."

"Hello and good-bye?"

"Yeah," Jessie shrugged. Hello, I just met you and good-bye, you're leavin'."

"She can't own Ozcot," Dorothy said, ignoring his words. "It belongs to my grandmother. It's her link to Oz."

"Missing link," Jessie mumbled.

"What?" Dorothy asked, not having heard him.

"If Willa Watkins got the deed, then your grandma's goose is cooked. I'd go home and start packin' my bags if I was you."

Dorothy cleared her throat. "But you're not me," she said, running up the hill to warn her grandmother.

Jessie watched a strange shadow follow behind her. The sun was partially blocked by a cloud shaped like a witch on a broom. It cast an evil darkness over Dorothy and over Ozcot, which made Jessie shiver.

"Glad I'm not you, girl," he said, getting on his bike and riding away.

The witch's shadow with the pointed hat followed Dorothy as she headed back to her grandmother's house.

CHAPTER 15

EVICTION

Willa Watkins raced up the driveway to Ozcot and skidded to a halt. She looked at the carved statues of the Oz characters and made a face.

"After I tear this old house down I'll burn you for firewood," she said, looking at the Tin Woodman, the Scarecrow and the Cowardly Lion.

Ozzie jumped down the porch stairs and ran barking towards her. "Get back, dog!" Willa shouted.

Grandma D opened the front door and watched. "He won't hurt you."

"If he bites, I'll sue," Willa said, kicking at the dog.

"Come on back, Ozzie," Grandma D called out.

Willa watched the dog run off. "I came to tell you that by law you have ten days to move out."

"What on earth are you talking about?" Grandma D asked, stepping out onto the porch.

"I just bought this dump at the tax auction. You got ten days to vacate or I'll have the sheriff evict you."

Grandma D felt faint. "I never received any tax notices. They can't..."

Willa shook her head. "They can and they did. You didn't pay your taxes and I bought the farm. It's as simple as that."

"But I didn't get a tax bill," Grandma D said, feeling dizzy.

"They sent you at least three. That's the law. You tax cheats are all alike," Willa said, looking around. She started towards the barn.

"You can't go in there!"

"I just want to see what I bought," Willa said.

Grandma D stepped quickly down the stairs and caught up with the younger woman. "This is my property. I want you to get off."

"Not for long," Willa said, eyeing the barn. Then she shrugged. "Doesn't really matter about that barn. I'll just have to tear it down along with your old clapboard shack."

Grandma D struggled to hold her tongue. Willa grinned. "You should have sold this place to my mother years ago. You could have made yourself a nice, tidy little profit and been living in a retirement home in Florida by now."

Willa gave Grandma D a wink. "Now, you've got less. You don't have the money, you don't have the land and...you're home-less," she laughed. "Get it?"

"I got it," Grandma D said, feeling herself build to a slow fury. "Now get out!"

Willa laughed all the way to her black sports car. When she opened the door, Ozzie ran up and nipped at her leg.

Willa kicked him away and turned to Grandma D. "If that dog comes with the property, I'm gonna take him to the pound and have him gassed." She sped away in a cloud of dust.

Dorothy came running up, out of breath. "Grandma D! That woman told me that..."

Grandma D nodded. "Willa Watkins said she owns Ozcot."

"She doesn't, does she?" Dorothy whispered.

"Where's Doc when I need him?" Grandma D sighed. Coming over the rise she saw his car. "Never been happier in my life than now to see that old man."

Doc had come to tell Grandma D the bad news but when he saw Willa Watkins driving away from Ozcot, he knew she'd beaten him to it.

Grandma D and Dorothy told him what Willa had said and Doc told them about the auction.

"What are we going to do, Doc?" Grandma D asked.

"We? How come it's only we when *we* is in trouble?" he smiled.

Grandma D took his hand in hers. "I need your help, Doc. I got to hold onto Ozcot. Somethin's happenin' in Oz. They need me and..."

"Oz, Oz, Oz," he said, disgustedly. He looked his old friend in the eye. "If you ever had a need for money...big money...now's the time."

"But I'm just barely gettin' by on Roy's pension and..."

Doc held his hand up for silence. "Only way you're gonna stop Willa Watkins is to go pay the taxes and raise some ruckus. Heck, you might even have to stoop and hire a lawyer."

"But where am I gonna get the money? I can't ask you to pay it," Grandma D said.

"I've got fifty bucks," Dorothy volunteered.

"That's sweet of you, dear," Grandma D smiled, "but I'm afraid we're talking about a lot more than fifty dollars."

"I'll put up the money for you," Doc said. "You know I will."

"No," Grandma D said, "I've got a few things I can sell and..." She stopped. A feeling hit her that was like a ton of bricks falling on her shoulders.

Maybe I'll never get back to Oz. Maybe I should forget the dream and...

"What are you goin' to sell?" Doc asked. "All you got are pictures you painted of Oz and them tornado contraptions that ain't never gonna work."

Grandma D took a deep breath and looked from Doc to Dorothy. "I can sell 'em."

"Sell what?" Doc asked.

"The rubies."

"No, you can't!" Dorothy said. "They're for your ruby shoes."

"You mean you really got some rubies?" Doc said, not knowing whether to believe her or not.

Grandma D nodded. "Got a bag full of them. Upstairs in the attic."

She turned and headed towards the house. Dorothy looked at Doc and then at her grandmother. She was about to find out if Oz really existed, if there were such things as ruby shoes. Young Dorothy felt very nervous.

"Come on, Doc," she said, grabbing his hand.

"I think I'll wait out here," he said.

"But Grandma's goin' to get her rubies and...and..."

Doc shook his head. "I've been kiddin' and not believin' her about Oz for close to sixty years."

"So?"

"So I don't want to know. I don't want to know what's up in that attic."

"But you've got to help. Grandma D needs you."

Doc shook her hand loose and pushed her gently forward. "I'll help her out, you don't have to worry about that."

Dorothy felt drawn to the attic and started towards the house. "Come on, Doc. Please come. Don't you want to know the truth?"

"No. The hardest thing to accept in this world is the truth. Let this old man live with what he's believed all his life. Okay?" he said, staring at her.

A gust of wind whipped dust between them. The darkening sky cast a shadow over Ozcot.

Dorothy looked into his eyes and knew that what lay in the attic would challenge his life. That what awaited her in the attic would challenge and probably change her life.

Lightning cracked in the distance and a rumble of thunder swept over the prairie like a kettledrum solo. The whole world seemed to darken without warning.

"You better get on inside," Doc said. "It's gonna storm."

"But where will you be?" Dorothy asked.

Doc nodded his head. "I'll be in the barn. I'll see what the bookworm's up to."

She watched him go, then turned towards the house. A bolt of lightning hit the rod on the peak of the house.

Up in the attic the trunk rocked back and forth, as if someone wanted to get out. In the room where Dorothy was to sleep, the toys moved by themselves.

She heard the thumping in the attic and thought it was her secrets in the trunk. But inside the trunk, across the rainbow, the wicked witch was moving her hands, drawing Grandma D towards the stairs.

"Sell the rubies...that's right...sell the rubies," she said, rubbing her hands together. Ima knew that once they were out of Dorothy Gale's hands, that she'd never be able to get back to Oz.

"And she thought the rubies had to be on her shoes," she cackled. "What a fool!"

Grandma D moved her foot as an old wind-up toy car sped across the floor. As the thumping from the attic grew louder, she watched the jack-in-the-box handle spin around. A familiar song plunked out.

Inside the trunk, Ima danced around, singing the children's song. And just as the clown popped up, Ima jumped into the air with her hands outstretched.

The mice in the corner watched the old trunk change shape. It looked like a witch was trying to break out.

Dorothy felt the rain and rushed towards the door. Behind her hail scattered across the lawn like golf balls.

She covered her ears at the sound of the thunder, which shook the walls of the house. Opening the front door, Dorothy fell against the wall as lightning cracked behind the hills.

The wind blew around the house as the threatening skies from the east moved closer. Black clouds raced overhead. Hailstones pounded against the roof. Thunder boomed in and with the lightning bolts dancing across the eaves, it sounded like the world was being turned upside down.

All heck's breakin' loose, Dorothy thought, holding onto the doorjamb. The trunk rocked back and forth across the attic floor but the thunder and hailstones muffled the sound.

"Grandma D, where are you?" she called out.

"I'm upstairs," Grandma D answered. "Come with me to the attic."

The trunk stopped moving. The outline of Ima that the trunk had made around her body settled back down. Only the point of her shadow hat was visible.

CHAPTER 16

RUBY SHOES

Grandma D took Dorothy's hand as she came to the bedroom. "Let's go," she nodded. "You need to see what I got up there."

The wind-up cars and toys in the bedroom moved around, bumping into the walls. "What's causing that?" Dorothy asked.

"Has something to do with Oz," Grandma D nodded, watching the old, red fire truck roll across the floor.

Dorothy picked up her backpack for no real reason except that it made her feel better. They took the attic stairs, one step at a time.

"I...I'm scared, Grandma," Dorothy whispered.

"Nothin' to be scared of," Grandma D said. *I hope.* She gulped.

Wind blew the front door open and it seemed to come up the stairs, grabbing at their legs. "What's happening?" Dorothy whispered, as what sounded like baseball-sized hailstones pounded the roof.

"Oz is callin' Dorothy back," Grandma D said.

"How do you know?" Dorothy asked, not knowing what to believe anymore.

"I know," the old woman said. "It's been sixty years to the day since the tornado took me over the rainbow. They need me back."

A shrieking wind blasted around Ozcot. They heard a window snap shut and break from somewhere down below.

"Then why don't you go?"

Grandma D stopped near the top of the stairs. "'Cause I don't know how to get back there." The pointed hat shape that stuck up from the trunk slipped back down until it was normal again.

Dorothy frowned. "But if Oz is calling you back, they must have a way for you to go back."

"That's what I've been thinkin'," she said, stepping up the last step to the floor of the attic. "But I've got to save Ozcot. That's the most important thing in the world to me right now."

"But...can't you let Doc pay your tax bill?" Dorothy asked, ducking her head as she stood next to her grandmother.

"I've let him do too much and..." She stopped and looked over at the trunk. "Did you see that trunk move?"

Dorothy looked over and shook her head. "Is that where you keep the rubies?"

Grandma D nodded. "And the copy of *The Emerald City Times* and the snow-shaker crystal ball I told you about."

"For real?" Dorothy asked, looking at the trunk in awe.

"For real," Grandma D smiled.

Grandma D stepped towards the trunk, but Dorothy grabbed her arm. "Wait," she said.

"Why?"

Dorothy shivered. "Doc said he didn't want to be up here when you opened it."

"Roy once told me the same thing. He never came near the attic the last ten years of his life," Grandma D said quietly.

"Maybe I ought to go back downstairs," Dorothy said, turning to go.

"You've got to stay," Grandma D said, gently taking Dorothy by the hand. "I need someone to witness the truth—to witness that Oz is real. That there's a place over the rainbow where things are as they ought to be and everybody lives by the golden ruler."

"The what?" Dorothy said, remembering her father's words: *Over the rainbow is a place where everyone abides by the golden ruler.*

Grandma D nodded. "He told you, didn't he?"

"Who?"

"Your father. He told you about Oz and the golden ruler."

Dorothy nodded.

From somewhere outside, they heard a trainlike sound. "Oh my gosh," Grandma D said. "It's a tornado." They didn't know it was Ima playing a trick, trying to get them to panic.

But then the sound died out and was muffled by the rain and hail. "What should I do?" Grandma D moaned. "Sell the rubies or listen to Oz?"

The trunk seemed to move towards them, but neither one was sure of what they saw. "I want to show you my secrets," Grandma D said, taking Dorothy's hand.

"But...but..." Dorothy protested.

"No buts about it, young lady," Grandma D smiled, then the corners of her mouth fell. "But I guess that really doesn't matter if I'm going to sell the rubies, does it?"

"You're not going to sell the rubies," Dorothy said, trying to pull away. "I'll just go tell Doc and..."

"And I want you to see what's in the trunk," Grandma D said, taking Dorothy's arm and spinning her around. "If I got to sell the rubies, I at least want someone to know that I wasn't crazy. That I really did go to Oz."

The trunk seemed to take on bigger-than-life dimensions in Dorothy's mind. Grandma D moved in the swaying light of the solitary bulb.

Ima watched them walk forward. "Just take the rubies and sell them. That's right. Pay your taxes and die a sweet old age in Kansas."

Ozzie came running up the stairs and sniffed at the trunk. Grandma D knelt down and undid the clasp.

"Are you sure it's okay that I see this stuff?" Dorothy asked, putting down her backpack.

"You're kin," Grandma D said. "I don't think it will do any harm."

Ozzie sniffed at the trunk again and ran yipping towards the stairs. "What's wrong with him?" Grandma D asked, turning away from the trunk.

"I don't know," Dorothy said. Neither one saw the point of the witch's hat push the top of the trunk up. Before they turned, the trunk went flat again.

Grandma D took a breath and slowly lifted the lid. Dorothy gasped as the ceiling light reflected off the rubies and the crystal ball.

"These are my secrets," Grandma D whispered, holding up the sparkling bag of rubies.

"They're beautiful," Dorothy gasped. "There must be a million dollars worth in there."

"Not that much," Grandma D said. She put the bag back down and lifted up the crystal ball.

"And this is how I see Oz," she smiled, holding the snow-shaker up for Dorothy to look at.

Dorothy peered at it closely. "But I don't see anything."

Ozzie pulled at Dorothy's pants leg. "What's wrong?" she asked, looking at the dog.

Grandma D shook her head. "Dog's spooked about somethin'."

Ima's leering face pushed against the inside glass of the snow-shaker, but Dorothy was looking at her grandmother.

"Just let me put the dog downstairs and I'll show you Oz," Grandma D said. Dorothy turned back to look at the crystal ball but Ima had already vanished.

"Here, let me show you," Grandma D said, taking the snow-shaker. She shook it until the snow flurried around then handed it back to Dorothy.

Dorothy looked into the glass, but all she saw was white. "I still don't see anything," she whispered.

"You will."

Then Dorothy gasped. "I can see something!" Through the falling flakes of snow, something was glowing green.

"Is that...?"

Grandma D nodded. "That's the Emerald City."

"That's awesome," Dorothy whispered.

"That's a good word to describe it," Grandma D said quietly.

"Then Oz is real? You really went there?"

"And look at this," Grandma D said, holding up the newspaper.

Dorothy blinked as the headline changed in front of her eyes:

DOROTHY MUST COME BACK TO OZ!

Grandma D shook her head. "I wish I knew what the emergency was."

"Don't you know?"

"All I know is that something's happened and..." The headline changed again.

THE WIZARD'S BEEN WIZNAPPED!
WHO WILL SAVE THE WIZARD?

"Oh, no," Grandma D said.

"Oh, yes!" Ima cackled, watching them from her castle. "Now pick up the rubies and take them to a pawnshop or something. Sell them quick so I can end this game."

The Wizard concentrated with all his might trying to send Dorothy Gale a message. *Rainbow...think of rainbows...rainbow...think of rainbows.*

Ima whipped around. "What are you thinking about?" she screamed.

She cocked her ear. "Rain...rain..." Unsatisfied, she jumped up and grabbed a thought from the air. She put it to her ear and listened.

"Rainbow!" she shrieked. "Don't tell that old crow to think of a rainbow!"

But it was too late. The pleasant thought from the Wizard was heading over the rainbow to Kansas and into Dorothy's ears. The Dorothy from Orlando.

Young Dorothy looked at the headline, then back at the Emerald City inside the crystal ball. "You've got to go back," she said to her grandmother.

"I can't," Grandma D said flatly.

The wind died down outside. There was an eerie calm. Grandma D walked over to the window and looked out. A rainbow was on the horizon.

"What am I going to do? What am I going to do?" the old woman moaned.

Dorothy saw the old ruby shoes in the trunk and picked them up. "Put these on."

"They don't work," Grandma D sighed. "I've been tryin' them on every day for sixty years."

"Put them on," Dorothy pleaded. "Maybe they'll work this time and you can go save the Wizard. He'll know how to save Ozcot."

Grandma D reluctantly tried on the shoes and clicked them together three times. "Take me to Oz." She waited a moment, then shook her head.

"Click them again," Dorothy said.

Grandma D hit the heels together three times and commanded the shoes, but nothing happened. She looked at Dorothy and frowned.

My granddaughter looks just like me when I was that age. She's twelve years old, born on the same day and it was sixty years to the day that I went over the rainbow. Maybe they're not callin' me. Maybe...

Turning to look at the rainbow one more time, Grandma D saw the dark storm building behind it. She bent down to take off the shoes.

"What are you doing?" Dorothy asked. Ozzie came back up the stairs whining about the approaching storm.

"Hurry, put these on," Grandma D said, handing the shoes to Dorothy.

"But they're yours," she said, taking the shoes. She felt a tingle.

"Put them on. You've got to hurry."

"Why?" Dorothy asked, taking off her red sneakers.

"I just have a feelin' that somethin's gonna happen."

When Dorothy had the shoes on, Grandma D opened up the bag of rubies and spread them around her feet. "But you've got to sell the rubies to save Ozcot and..."

Grandma D shook her head. "Someone's got to save the Wizard. Maybe it's you. Maybe you're the Dorothy they're calling back."

From the other side of the rainbow up in the top room of the dark, stone castle, Ima gasped and fell back.

"What am I going to do?" she screamed, running and banging her head against the wall.

"Give up." Ura Wizard smiled.

"Never!" Ima snapped. She closed her eyes and concentrated.

Mother made the rubies fall off those shoes to keep Dorothy Gale from coming back to Oz. But will the same spell keep the rubies from going back on the shoes if young Dorothy puts them on?

Ima watched, trying to come up with a plan.

Grandma D put her hand on Dorothy's shoulder. "Now click them together three times."

Ima coughed, trying to catch her breath. "No...no..." she whispered, watching Dorothy click them once.

"Look, Grandma," Dorothy gasped. The rubies seemed to move on their own.

"Now the second time," Grandma D said. "Click them again."

Dorothy did and the rubies edged closer. "It's working."

"It's you they want," Grandma D nodded. "You're the Dorothy that's going back to Oz."

"Nooooooooooooooooooooooo!" Ima screamed. The fury of her anger was frightening to behold.

The witch spun around in a circle. She pointed her fingers towards the ceiling. The air crackled with electricity as tiny lightning bolts jumped from the tips of her fingers.

"Click them again, Dorothy," Grandma D smiled, "and tell the shoes to take you to Oz."

The rubies were vibrating next to the shoes. Ima shouted as she spun in an ever faster circle:

> "Rubies this is you-know-who,
> Stay away from those old shoes!"

Dorothy clicked them the third time and whispered, "Oz...please," but nothing happened.

"Try it again," Grandma D said.

Ima spun in the other direction and shouted:

> "Toe cheese, rats and smelly shoes,
> Rubies don't go near those shoes."

Grandma D bent down, then straightened up and looked around. "Try 'em again," she said to Dorothy.

"Curses!" Ima screamed. She clapped her hands above her head and stood on one foot chanting:

> "Trick or treat,
> Smell those feet,
> Rubies, rubies,
> I repeat.
> Stay away,
> Stay away,
> Don't go near
> Those shoes today."

Though Dorothy clicked the shoes twice more, still nothing happened. The trunk lid closed behind them with a loud bang.

"I smell a witch," Grandma D whispered, looking around. "Where are the Munchkins when I need them?" she said to herself.

Dorothy gulped and couldn't speak. She tapped her grandmother's arm and pointed to the snow-shaker.

Inside the crystal ball, the face of Ima Witch appeared. "Ding dong...and you thought the witch was dead." Ima spun around, shrieking with laughter.

"Who's that?" Dorothy whispered, turning to her grandmother.

Ima cackled. "I'm a new friend of your old grandma. Just call me Ima...'cause I'm a witch." She pointed at Grandma D. "You asked about the Munchkins...let's just say they had a change of heart."

"Where are they?" Grandma D whispered.

"They're right here," Ima laughed, pointing to a troop of little witches who flew behind in a circle through the air.

"What have you done to the Wizard?" Grandma D shouted.

Ima chuckled. "I thought you'd never ask. He's right here. He's having a swinging time," she laughed. The image of the Wizard, tied up like a trophy deer and swinging over the tank of monsters, came into view.

"Let him go," Grandma D pleaded.

"Just sell the rubies and I'll think about it," Ima said. Her image faded away but her cackling laughter continued for several moments.

"What can you do?" Dorothy asked her grandmother.

The old woman shook her head, then stopped. The headline of the newspaper had changed again:

TORNADO WEATHER OVER KANSAS
HOPE FOR DOROTHY YET

Grandma D grabbed Dorothy's hand. "Let's get out to the barn. Maybe Alex's got the darn thing working."

"Wait," Dorothy said, kicking off the shoes and slipping on her red sneakers. "What about the rubies?" Dorothy asked.

"Put them in the bag and bring them along," Grandma D said. "I'll meet you in the barn."

Grandma D went down the stairs as fast as she could. Ozzie didn't follow her.

"Go on, boy," Dorothy said, picking up the rubies with her hands. "Follow Grandma."

Ozzie just growled at the shape of the witch's hat that had poked through the lid of the trunk behind Dorothy.

"Go on, Ozzie. Go with Grandma to the barn."

Ozzie stood his ground, growling at the trunk. "What are you growling at?" she wondered, turning around.

"Knock, knock," Ima whispered, making the trunk lid thump up and down. The witch's hat went down as the trunk lid went up.

Inside the crystal ball, Ima pressed her face to the glass. Dorothy was so startled that she dropped the rubies.

Ozzie jumped into the trunk and barked at the witch. Ima shook her head. "Take the rubies and throw them out the window."

"No," Dorothy said. "They're going to save my grandma's farm."

Ima moved her fingers back and forth putting Dorothy into a trance. Ozzie pulled at her pants leg but she was falling under the witch's spell.

"You need to take a little nap," Ima said. Dorothy's eyes began to close. "That's good. You're going to just to lie down and never wake up."

"I'm so sleepy," Dorothy whispered, slumping to the floor of the attic. "So sleepy." Her eyes closed.

Ozzie pulled at her sleeve but Dorothy was fast asleep. The headline of the newspaper began to change behind Dorothy's head:

TORNADO TO HIT KANSAS AGAIN!

Dorothy was fast asleep and didn't see it. She also didn't hear the witch cackling inside the crystal ball. The howling of the winds drowned everything out.

Ima snapped her fingers and a troop of mice appeared. "Take the rubies and bury them!" she shouted. Ozzie jumped in front of the rubies and growled.

"If the dog won't move...then eat him!" Ima screamed.

Ozzie barked bravely, moving his head back and forth at the approaching mice.

"Think of that stupid dog as a big piece of cheese," she commanded, snapping her fingers.

In the eyes of the mice, Ozzie looked like a slab of cheddar cheese. Ima grinned as the mice closed in on the brave little dog.

CHAPTER 17

TORNADO

Ima turned her focus on the barn. "Now let's see what those hillbilly bumblers are doing," she whispered, moving her hands back and forth until the image was of the barn.

"Now move inside," she nodded, rolling her hands forward. "That's good," she smiled as the image of Doc and Alexander came into view.

Ima looked closely at Alexander's image. "Four-eyes, eh? Maybe those glasses feel slippery, huh, boy?" she laughed, snapping her fingers.

The boy's glasses slipped down. Alexander pushed them up and they slipped right back down again.

"Leave your specs alone. We got to turn off this machine," Doc said, struggling to turn off Grandma D's big contraption. The windmill blade was spinning in one direction and the propeller was going full blast in the other.

"I can't turn it off," Alexander shouted over the roar of the engine, pushing his glasses back up with his shoulder.

"How did you turn it on?" Doc said into the boy's ear.

"I didn't," Alexander shrugged. "It just came on by itself."

Grandma D came running through the barn doors and was met by a swirl of hay from the loft. "Something's happenin'," she said to Doc, wanting to tell him about the witch in the attic.

"You're tellin' me!" Doc grinned. "This is the darnedest thing I've seen."

Grandma D looked at Alexander. "Did you do anything different?"

The boy shrugged, pushing up his glasses. "Just changed the oil, put on a new filter and..."

Doc looked perplexed. "How 'bout the tires? Did you kick them?"

"Oh hush," Grandma D said. "And what else did you do?" she asked, looking into the boy's eyes.

Alexander hesitated, scrunching his eyes together to keep his glasses from slipping. "Well, I added some weights to the blades and repositioned the levers and...and a few things I read in my physics book and..."

Grandma D cut him off. "Don't matter now whatever you did." She looked at the two of them. "I think we're in for a bad storm."

Doc looked towards the door. "Gettin' pretty bad out there?"

"Nope. The storm's brewing in here," she said, looking at the machine that was pumping and turning behind them.

Outside the barn, the forces of nature were beginning to get out of control. Winds unleashed by Grandma D's tornado machine were bouncing across the prairie, bumping into other winds and building into a larger and larger force.

Lightning cracked and thunder boomed. Doc stood back from the machine. "Think we better get to the storm cellar. Where's Dorothy?"

"She'll be here in a moment," Grandma D said. "She's up in the attic and..."

They were all pulled to the ground as a wind vacuum created by the whirling funnels spinning around Ozcot pulled at the barn.

"Let's go!" Doc shouted.

Inside the crystal ball, Ima was having a witch fit. "Stop, stop!" she screamed, waving her arms around. "I don't want a tornado."

With all the powers of darkness, Ima lifted her arms, trying to command the wind:

"Wind, rain, fire and hail,
Break no wind, not even a gale.
Be so calm that birds can't fly,
And kites and planes fall from the sky."

But the wind was not going to be tamed easily and though one half of the farm fell into a dead calm, the other was racked by savage winds.

Up in the attic, Ozzie bravely nipped and barked at the mice. A blast of wind with the power of a freight train rocked the house on its foundation. An old hat stand swayed back and forth and landed on Dorothy's head.

"Ouch," she said, pushing it off.

Ozzie wagged his tail, then went back to barking at the rodents. "Mice!" Dorothy shrieked at the dozens around her.

She grabbed up an old tennis racket and began swatting at the mice, who retreated back to their corners.

Dorothy looked at the dog. "I must have fallen asleep," she shrugged.

Then she remembered about the rubies and looked around. They were still scattered over the attic floor.

From somewhere outside the house, she heard a roaring sound like a freight train approaching the house.

"What's that?" she said, going over to the window.

She saw her grandmother, Doc, and Alexander come running from the barn. The roof of the old structure was lifting up and down by itself.

Grandma D looked up and saw Dorothy at the window. "Come on, Dorothy. A tornado's comin'! We've got to get to the storm cellar!"

The roof lifted off the barn and spun away. The blades on Grandma D's tornado machine were spinning so fast that the whole machine lifted off by itself and vanished into a black funnel cloud that headed away from the house.

Grandma D watched it go. "Look, it stopped," she shouted, looking over at the calm half of her farm.

Alexander shook his head. "I think it's coming back," he said, pointing towards the other side which was engulfed in wind-whipped fury. His glasses fell off in the wind and he grabbed them before they flew away.

"Oh, goodness," Grandma D muttered, thinking about the tornado that hit the farm sixty years before.

Then the dark winds broke loose, sweeping over the calm side. Within moments, Ozcot was surrounded by a storm.

"Come on, Dorothy!" Doc shouted. "Save yourself."

Dorothy ran back to the trunk. "Quick, Ozzie, we've got to run! There's a tornado coming."

Grabbing up her backpack, she stopped to put in the crystal ball. "Grandma D will want this," she thought.

Ozzie yipped. "I'm coming," Dorothy replied.

She turned to go, then remembered the newspaper. "Can't forget this," she said. She looked at *The Emerald City Times* and the headline changed again:

TORNADO HITS KANSAS AGAIN!

"You're tellin' me!" she laughed. Then it changed again:

DOROTHY'S COMING BACK!

"Not without these," Dorothy said, looking down at the glittering stones. She put the newspaper in her backpack and closed the trunk lid.

Ozzie stood at the stairs and barked. "Quiet. You're making me nervous," Dorothy said, as she stooped to pick up the rubies. She didn't see the shape of the witch coming up through the trunk behind her.

"Come on, Dorothy!" Doc shouted from the first floor. "The tornado's almost here."

He looked back out at the funnel cloud heading towards the house. "Get in the cellar!" Doc shouted.

Dorothy ran to the window. "Oh, my," she whispered. She too saw the black funnel cloud racing towards the house.

She watched the long prairie grass bow before it. Fence posts disappeared and farm machinery flew around like matchsticks. The whistle of the wind was so loud that she wanted to cover her ears.

The shape of Ima went back into the trunk. The witch watched Dorothy's image and muttered, "Just get down to the cellar so that the tornado can blow those rubies to kingdom come."

Dorothy thought about the Wizard. "Someone's got to save him," she whispered.

She looked at the rubies. "I've got to take them to Grandma D."

Ozzie ran to the rubies and barked at the stones. They were moving back and forth, rolling in circles.

Suddenly, the rubies flew across the room and twirled around the swaying light bulb. Before Dorothy could even gasp, the rubies headed straight for her and attached themselves to her ruby sneakers.

"What in the world," she said, looking down at her glittering sneakers. Ozzie barked, wagging his tail. "Ruby sneakers," Dorothy whispered. "I wonder if..."

She looked out the window. The tornado was almost to the house. This was no time to click her heels, but she had to know.

"I feel so foolish," she whispered, standing up straight. She clicked them once. "Oz...whoever heard of such a silly thing."

She clicked them the second time and the room began to sparkle. "Oh, my," she whispered.

At the third click, she was enveloped by a glowing light. "Take me over the rainbow," she gulped, closing her eyes.

"I want to go over the rainbow to Oz," she said, feeling faint. "I don't care how I get there. Just get me there...quick!"

Ozzie jumped into her arms as the tornado neared the house. A strong wind blew her against the wall, dazing her.

The house lifted up and began spinning around in the shrieking wind. "Hold on, Ozzie!" Dorothy shouted.

Then it seemed as if they were floating. The house just seemed to hang motionless in the air. Dorothy could hear the tornado circling around them but the house just seemed to be bobbing on a pond.

The dog barked and strained to get to the window. Dorothy went over and looked out. "We're in the eye of the tornado," Dorothy said. "We're at the top of the tornado."

Everything in the world seemed to be circling around them. Dorothy watched chickens and signs and pieces of fence pass by. "Bet we'll even see the kitchen sink out there," she joked.

What passed by the window seemed beyond belief. *Am I dreaming?* Dorothy wondered.

She saw her father and mother waving, followed by Grandma D, Doc, and the three boys in the neighborhood. She even saw Willa Watkins speed by in her sleek sports car.

"Go back to Orlando!" Willa shouted out.

Dorothy looked at Ozzie. "She makes it sound so easy. Like I could steer this tornado across Missouri and Georgia like a 747 and fly home."

Ozzie yipped. "What else is out there?" Dorothy wondered.

Ozzie began barking madly. "What is it, boy?" Dorothy asked. Then she saw it.

Two large, evil eyes were staring at her through the raging storm. Eyes as big as the houses that passed by.

Then she heard a voice so wicked, so ominous, that it made her cringe. "Dorothy Gale. Don't think I can't see your every move."

"Go away!" Dorothy cried out.

"Never!" Ima snapped. She looked at the girl and shook her head. "So Dorothy's returning to Oz. I never figured on you."

"I just want to go back home to Orlando."

"That's your problem and now you're my problem," Ima said.

"But I don't even know you," Dorothy pleaded.

"Oh, but you do, deary," Ima whispered, her voice booming off the walls of the tornado. "I've always been here in some form and you've always been around to fight me."

"What are you talking about?" Dorothy asked.

"Light and dark...good and evil," Ima sneered. "We're like two Siamese twins locked together."

"I must be dreaming," Dorothy said, pinching herself.

Ima's whole face now appeared through the walls of the storm. "You're not dreaming, but you're about to live out your worst nightmare."

"But I didn't want to leave Kansas."

"Some things are inevitable," Ima whispered. "Soon you'll be in Oz. If you're thinking about trying to save the Wizard, remember this," she said, snapping her fingers.

Lightning cracked and it began raining real cats and dogs.

"And this," Ima growled, raising her hands. Snakes came pouring through the window.

"And this!" Ima shrieked, and a dragon's tongue came licking up the stairs.

"Stay away from me!" Dorothy screamed to the creatures around her. Without thinking, she clicked her sneakers and the creatures backed away.

The large witch's eyes looked to the left and then went wide. Ima saw that the tornado was almost to the rainbow.

Ima clapped her hands and made the creatures disappear. "Go back to Kansas!" Ima shouted, her image fading away.

"Go back to Kansas. Don't cross the rainbow. You can't save the Wizard. You can't..."

Dorothy watched the witch's eyes fade into the storm but her presence seemed to linger on and hold Dorothy in place.

In the darkest room of her castle, lined with stolen gravestones, Ima stirred her cauldron of trouble. Dropping in bits of horrible, nameless, faceless things, the Wicked Witch peered into her seething brew, trying to ruin the future.

"I have the Wizard...and soon Oz will be all mine," she whispered. "I'll bring the world to Oz...and all it's virtues," she chuckled, dropping in a wiggling snake and a cracked skull.

A black cat purred at her feet and Ima snatched it up and dropped it in. With her spoon she pushed back in a claw that reached up from the evil stew. A bat tried to fly out but Ima swatted it down into the bubbling pot.

Waving aside the clouds of steam, Ima whispered her vision of the future that echoed over Oz:

> "Trouble, trouble everywhere,
> Crime in the streets, nobody cares.
> A land with no values
> Is what I seek.
> Where greed is good
> And the rich own the meek.
> Homeless in the Emerald City,
> Kids without hope,
> Few have pity,
> Cities full of dope.
> Bloated budgets,
> Sacred Cows,
> Spend the future.
> Spend it now.
> A theme park of life
> Is what Oz will be.
> Hate your neighbor.
> Close your eyes to misery.
> So batwings and rats
> And bell, book and candle.
> What's over the rainbow
> I'll make into a scandal!"

Dorothy blinked but the witch's face was nowhere to be seen. "What am I going to do, Ozzie? What am I ever going to do?"

"I wish my father was here," she sighed. "He'd know what to do."

Then she saw it and smiled. "Look, Ozzie," she said, pointing to a part of the tornado that had opened up. "There's a rainbow. Daddy's rainbow."

CHAPTER 18

RAINBOW

Shimmering just ahead was a beautiful band of colors, standing oblivious to the storm that was raging before it. As the house bounced up to the top of the tornado, it was propelled forward into the quiet of the jet stream.

Dorothy looked down. "Oh, no," she mumbled. "We're really up in the air." Ozzie jumped back into her arms.

As they neared the rainbow, Dorothy felt she could reach out and touch it. The whole house seemed bathed in beautiful, vibrant colors.

For a moment Dorothy saw her father's image floating in front of the glittering rainbow. "Just remember to treat others like you want to be treated," he said, waving to her.

"I will, Daddy, I will."

"I love you, Pumpkin. I'll always be there if you need me."

"I need you now, Daddy. What should I do?"

"Just follow the golden ruler," Ed Gale said, his image fading away, "and treat all people with kindness."

Dorothy waved for him to come back. "Don't go, please, Daddy."

"Just listen to the rainbow. Trust what the rainbow lady says," her father called out as he disappeared.

"Hold on, Ozzie," Dorothy said as the house entered the brilliant arc of the rainbow.

Time seemed to stand still as Dorothy and Ozzie entered the wonder of nature. Everything was sparkling around them.

"It's so beautiful," she whispered, looking at the colors bouncing off the walls.

"Dorothy Gale," said a sweet, melodic voice from outside the window.

"Yes?" Dorothy said, hesitantly. She looked out the window and saw the most beautiful woman in the world in a flowing gown that seemed woven from the rainbow.

"Who are you?" Dorothy asked.

"I am you and you are me," the lady said.

"I don't understand," Dorothy said, perplexed.

"Oh, you will," the woman nodded. "Think of me as Mother Rainbow."

Dorothy stepped back as the woman's face began changing from tan to black to white to brown. Her features blended from African to Oriental to Spanish.

"How can you do that?" Dorothy asked.

Mother Rainbow smiled. "You can do it too," she said. "We're all like each other. Inside, we're just people. We're all God's people."

Dorothy felt her face changing and looked at her reflection in the rainbow. One after the other she took on the skin and features of the people in the world as the spirit of the rainbow passed through her.

She turned black, then brown. Her hair turned red then hung black and straight. Then it curled tight. Ozzie looked at her, cocking his head back and forth.

"I'm African," she said, admiring her ebony skin. Then her eyes changed to almond-shaped.

"I'm changing again," she whispered, watching her skin color change from tan to brown. For a moment she looked like an Indian, then like a Mexican, and finally she changed from Chinese to Japanese and back through the colors of life.

"See," Mother Rainbow smiled as Dorothy's features returned. "We're really all the same. We just come in different packages," she grinned. "That's the beauty of life."

"But this doesn't seem real," Dorothy said, pulling at a piece of the rainbow which stretched like taffy. "I was black, then I was brown and then I looked Oriental and..."

Mother Rainbow smiled. "It is real. As real as a desire. As real as a dream or a dreamer."

"But where am I?" Dorothy asked. "I've got to get home. I want to go home to Orlando."

"This is a moment frozen in time. It may seem like a small piece of forever, but it will all take place in less than a wink and a blink."

"What? What will take place?" Dorothy asked.

"Your journey to Oz," Mother Rainbow smiled. "But you must hurry, for rainbows don't last forever and there's only one day a year that you can cross through the rainbow into Oz."

"But what should I do?" Dorothy asked, suddenly feeling twelve years old and very alone.

"You've got to save the Wizard of Oz. It's up to you, Dorothy Gale of Orlando, Florida. It's all up to you."

"But I'm just a kid and I want to go back to my family."

Mother Rainbow nodded. "I know, dear. Home is where the heart is."

Dorothy wanted to cry. "I just want to go home to Orlando. Can't I just click my ruby sneakers and go home?"

Mother Rainbow smiled and put her hand on Dorothy's shoulder. "To get there you have to go to Oz. There's no other way."
She took Dorothy by the hand. "Your conscience is your guide. You know that."

"But my conscience says to go home," Dorothy pleaded.

"No, that's your heart speaking." Mother Rainbow nodded. "You have to help the Wizard. It's your responsibility now. You clicked the shoes."

"But I don't want to be responsible. I'm just twelve years old."

Mother Rainbow shook her head. "Twelve or twenty, thirty or ninety, it doesn't matter. Sometimes responsibility seeks us and everyone, no matter what their age, has to face that."

"Do I have to go now?" Dorothy said, feeling more alone than she ever had in her life.

"You have to go now," Mother Rainbow urged.

"Let me get my backpack," Dorothy said, picking it up.

"Take my hand," Mother Rainbow directed, and floated Dorothy and Ozzie out of the room.

Dorothy looked around in awe. "But won't I fall through?" she asked, as Mother Rainbow released her hand.

"You'll be fine. Now go to Oz," Mother Rainbow said, pushing them forward towards the top of the rainbow's arc.

Dorothy held onto Ozzie and looked down the rainbow. It looked like the longest slide in the world, disappearing down into the clouds.

"But where is Oz?" Dorothy called out, trying not to fall forward.

Mother Rainbow sighed. "It's this side of that and that side of your imagination. Hurry now," she said, pushing them. "You don't have much time."

"Take this," Mother Rainbow said, tossing Dorothy the golden ruler that the Wizard had sent to the rainbow for safekeeping.

Dorothy grabbed it as it floated towards her hand. "What is it?" Dorothy asked.

"It's the golden ruler of Oz. It's the measure of all people, big and small. Those who know how to treat others right will measure up. Those that don't will never measure up to much at all."

"This is all so confusing," Dorothy said, looking at the golden ruler.

"Take it to the Wizard. He'll explain. It belongs to him and the people of Oz. It's the golden ruler...you know what it is," Mother Rainbow smiled. "Remember what your father told you."

The gold stick tingled in Dorothy's hand. "Where will I find the Wizard? All Grandma D told me was to follow the yellow brick road."

Mother Rainbow pushed her over the edge. "Things have changed in Oz since your sweet grandmother was here. Ima Witch has stolen the yellow brick road."

"Stolen the road?"

"That's right," Mother Rainbow nodded, "brick by brick."

"But how will I find the Emerald City?" Dorothy asked, looking down at the clouds.

"Follow your heart and don't be fooled. Trust in the golden ruler and trust your own values. That will always bring you red carpet treatment if you're true to yourself. Now go," she said, nudging them forward.

Dorothy held on tight to Ozzie. "Oh, my," she gasped as they slipped a few inches over the edge. Dorothy looked down the steep curve. "I can't see the bottom," she whispered.

"Good-bye, Dorothy," Mother Rainbow called out, floating off into the rainbow. "The fate of Oz is in your hands. Don't lose the golden ruler."

"I won't," Dorothy said, clutching it tightly.

"Some things are worth keeping—like values," Mother Rainbow said. "Never give the golden ruler to anyone but the Wizard."

"Good-bye," Dorothy said, and with a gentle push from the wind they began their descent.

"Oh, Ozzie!" Dorothy shouted as they slid faster and faster, leaving a blaze of sparkles behind them.

"Oh-oh," Dorothy gasped. They were almost to the rainbow's arc. Then they shot over the curve and into the clouds, dropping straight down.

Dorothy held onto Ozzie and braced herself. "Oz, here we come!" she shouted.

Ozzie's barks echoed up over the clouds as they disappeared into a pillowy whiteness, protected from harm by the power of the rainbow and the strength of the golden ruler.

Dorothy was off on a fantastic journey. It was sixty years to the day that her grandmother had made the same journey. A journey in a wink and a blink that would change her life forever.

Dorothy had to return to Oz to save the Wizard. The time she had couldn't be measured by a watch.

She had no idea where she was going and no maps to guide her. All she had to do was hold onto the golden ruler and save the Wizard. The only thing she had to worry about was a witch named Ima.

RETURN TO OZ

CHAPTER 19

A LAND CALLED OZ

When Dorothy opened her eyes, she was sitting in a field of flowers. Ozzie sat by her side, wagging his tail.

"Where is everyone?" Dorothy whispered, looking around. But there was no one to be seen.

She turned to find the rainbow but saw it fading away. "Come back," she shouted, jumping in the air, trying to grab it. "I need you."

When the rainbow was gone, Dorothy looked at Ozzie. "What are we going to do?" Ozzie just cocked his head. "Which way do we go?" she asked.

Dorothy leaned down to tie her sneaker and put the golden ruler down. Ozzie pushed it back towards her hand. "That's right. I'm supposed to hold this until I give it to the Wizard."

"Now then," Dorothy said, straightening up, "I wonder if anyone knows I'm here?" She looked around at the strange, flower-filled field that was surrounded by bushes.

"Come on, Ozzie," she said, walking towards the bushes. Dorothy mumbled to herself, "I kind of thought there'd be a welcoming committee or something. We better go save the Wizard before our time is up."

Ozzie pulled at the cord on her backpack. "What is it?" Dorothy asked.

Undoing the clasp, Dorothy took out *The Emerald City Times*. "I wonder if there's a map in here?" she asked, then stopped. The headline began to change.

DOROTHY'S BACK!

"I guess news travels fast around here," Dorothy said. "But how did they know so quickly?"

There was a rustling in the bushes and Ozzie began barking. "What is it, Ozzie?" Dorothy asked, walking over.

The dog ran into the bushes and began growling. "Leave me alone or I'll spread the word that you're a bad dog!" said a strange, gruff voice.

"Who's that?" Dorothy called out, ready to run.

"The who is not for you to know. I'll ask the questions," grumbled the voice.

Dorothy made a face. "Who are you?"

Ozzie barked again and the bushes began to shake. "I am I and I've got my eye on you for the *Eyewitness News*...that's who."

"Come out where I can see you," Dorothy demanded. "I don't like to play games."

"No," snapped the voice. "And take your dog before I call the dogcatcher."

The branches of the bushes beat up and down. Ozzie came running out with his tail between his legs yipping. "Go find a fireplug to play with!" the gruff voice barked.

Ozzie yelped and ran behind Dorothy's legs. "That wasn't very nice," Dorothy said. She put the newspaper down and patted the dog's head.

"Sometimes the news isn't nice but news is only news if it's new news."

"Well," Dorothy said, putting her hands on her hips. "You don't have to be so snappy."

"Snappy? You must be confusing me with a snapdragon."

"What on earth are you talking about?" Dorothy asked, shaking her head.

"I'm talking about the 'I' like in who I am."

"If you don't tell me your name then I'm just going to walk away," Dorothy said, stepping over the newspaper she'd left on the ground.

The bushes leaned forward than swayed back. "My name's G.V. News is my game and deadlines are my bane. Now leave me alone before I tell the world what a mean dog you have."

"Ozzie's not mean," Dorothy said indignantly, pushing her way into the bushes. But there was no one there and she didn't notice that someone had snuck up and taken her copy of *The Emerald City Times*.

Dorothy looked through the vines, trying not to squish the thick clumps of grapes that were hanging all around. "I guess whoever it was ran off," Dorothy said. "Come on, Ozzie, let's go."

"Ran off, hah!" said the voice. "Not likely! I've covered a hurricane with only a bean pole to cling to. I've faced down thieves wanting to cut my grapes off. Run off? Not on your life!"

Dorothy spun around. "Who said that?" But there was no answer. Eyeing the plants carefully, she turned slowly in a circle. "Where are you?"

From behind her, the voice said loudly, "I'm wherever a story is breaking. I'm wherever the who, what, where and when is happening. Filling in the why with the wherefore and a little bit of what for...if you know what I mean."

"I'd just like to know where you are," Dorothy said, getting irritated.

"Through rain, sleet or snow that's..." then the voice stopped. "Oh, that's the post office. Well, I'm right here with my ear to the ground and my nose sniffing out the news."

Dorothy looked carefully at the leaves, then blinked. "Are you a plant?"

"No," the vine huffed. "Reporters are never stool pigeons."

"I meant, are you a plant plant?"

"Yes," the voice said, acting silly, "I'm a *plant plant*." The leaves shook up and down with laughter.

"Who are you?" Dorothy asked, having never seen a plant that talked. "A Venus flytrap?"

"Venus is a loser. Flytraps can't keep their yaps shut."

"But I thought that only the raisins danced. You know, like in the commercials on television."

The vine shook back and forth. "Can't have raisins hanging from a vine. Only grapes hanging here."

"Then who are you?" Dorothy asked again.

"My name's G.V.," the vine said.

"G.V.?" said Dorothy.

The leaves around the vine nodded. "Yes, indeed," the vine said. A smaller vine unwound and handed her a grape leaf. "My card. G.V. Stands for Grape Vine. People may say they heard it by word of mouth but in Oz, they all heard it on the grapevine."

Dorothy peered into the leaves which appeared to form a face. "I didn't know grapevines could talk."

"Then how else could you hear things on it? Boy, are you dumb," G.V. said, waving her off with a flap of a leaf.

"I am not!" Dorothy said, putting her hands on her hips.

"Then how come you're lost," said G.V. in a smirking voice.

"I'm not lost. I just got here."

"Then where are you and where are you going?"

"I'm in Oz and I'm going..."

"Yes....?" said the plant, drawing out the word.

"Why, I'm here to..."

G.V. started laughing. "I'm not used to plants laughing at me," Dorothy said, making a face.

G.V. giggled. "Well golly. Jeepers-creepers, where'd you get those ruby sneakers," the vine laughed. "You ought to be a plant because you're sure in a jam, and without me you'll be in a grape jam, get it? Grape jam?"

"I get it," Dorothy said crossly.

The plant's leaves shook up and down the vine in laughter. Dorothy heard the chuckle repeated along the vine until it died out in the distance.

"What on earth are you laughing about?"

G.V. snickered. "First, you're not on earth—you're in Oz. And second, there's not much you can tell me that I don't already know."

"Then I suppose you know where I'm going?"

"Sure, that's easy. I heard it on our broadcast, silly," G.V. said.

"Broadcast? What broadcast?" Dorothy exclaimed.

"You mean you don't listen to my talkvine show? It's called, You're On The Line With Rush Vine."

"But I thought your name was Grape Vine," Dorothy asked.

"Rush Vine's my stage name. I know you've heard of me," G.V. said, shining his leaves.

Dorothy shrugged. "I've heard of Rush Limbaugh but I've never heard of Rush Vine."

The leaves turned towards the west. "Shhhhhhh," G.V. whispered, putting a small creeper vine to his face. "A news broadcast is coming through."

"It is?" Dorothy said, leaning forward.

"Here, listen," G.V. said, cupping a leaf. "Put your ear to the grapevine."

Dorothy leaned forward. "I never knew plants could talk," she mumbled to herself.

"That's 'cause you never listened," G.V. snapped.

Dorothy's eyes lit up as she heard the grapevine news. The fast-talking message sounded like an old radio broadcast:

> **"...and this is just in. *The Emerald City News* has learned that Dorothy Gale of Orlando, Florida, has told our correspondent, G.V., that she's on her way to save the Wizard. We'll keep you updated as we get more details."**

Dorothy leaned her head back. "Who told them that?"

G.V. shrugged his vines. "I never reveal a source." Then the leaves leaned forward and he whispered, "You better hurry. I hear that the Wizard really needs you to untie him from the mess he's in."

"How do you know?" then she stopped as the leaves shrugged. "I know, you heard it on the grapevine. Well," Dorothy said, "can you send the Wizard a message."

"Maybe," said G.V., "and maybe not. My job is to tell the news but I can't make people listen."

"Well, would you send a message for me?"

"Sure," G.V. said, unwinding a small vine. The vine pushed into a grape and came back out with grape ink on its tip.

"Tell the Wizard that I'll be there as quick as I can, and..." she hesitated.

"Yes?" G.V. said.

"And tell him I've got the golden ruler and I'll give it to him after I save him."

"That's it?" G.V. asked.

"What else is there?" Dorothy asked.

"Well, you might want to tell him who your next-of-kin is."

"Why should I?" Dorothy said, stepping back.

"Ima."

"What are you?" Dorothy asked, not wanting to play games.

"I'm G.V., correspondent for the grapevine news."

"Okay then," Dorothy said, "why should I tell the Wizard who my next-of-kin is?"

"You know...Ima."

"You're a what?"

"No," G.V. said, shaking his leaves. "Ura's the Wizard and Ima's the Witch. I'm just G.V., the grapevine."

Dorothy sighed. "This is confusing. It's a tough thing to understand."

"No," said G.V.

"No what?" said Dorothy.

G.V. shook his leaves and sang out in an operatic baritone. "Itsa's the dragon that sleeps around Ima's neck. You're-a going to save Ura Wizard and I'ma not kidding, you better be-a careful."

"Will you just send the message?" Dorothy sighed.

"No problem," G.V. said, "but our broadcast is very popular. You never know who's listening."

The grapevine began humming and shaking rapidly. G.V. snapped the message on down the vine.

The message moved through Oz with lightning speed. The vine moved along like a firehose taking water. Leaves twisted and turned and fence posts rattled.

Within a minute, everyone along the vine had heard Dorothy's message and was spreading it around with their roots, leaves, voices and branches.

"You just made the grapevine," G.V. said proudly.

"Good," Dorothy said, "now I'd better be going. I've got to find a map and find where the witch lives."

"Look in the newspaper," G.V. says. "There's always a map there."

Dorothy reached into her backpack but *The Emerald City Times* was gone. "Where's my magic paper?" Dorothy gasped. She looked around. "I set it down over there and, and now it's gone."

G.V. shrugged. "Just get another one from Paper Boy. I saw him pick it up."

"From who?"

"Paper Boy," G.V. said.

"Why didn't you tell me he took it?"

"You didn't ask," G.V. chuckled. "I'm the one in the news business. I ask the questions."

"Where can I find this paperboy?"

"Over there," G.V. said, pointing a leafy stem. "Just through the field and over the hill."

"Oh," Dorothy sighed, "I wish I could just follow the yellow brick road. That sounded so much easier than going off through the fields."

"You should have heard the grapevine shake when Ima stole the bricks. My vine was doing the tango all night, shake, rattle and rolling along with the news."

Dorothy looked and felt lost. "But can someone take me to find this paperboy?" she asked, feeling very vulnerable.

G.V. fluttered his leaves. "They just can't roll out the red carpet every time you come here."

"But I've never been here."

"Hmmmm, well, maybe they will."

"Will what?" Dorothy sighed, tired of the word games.

"Maybe they'll roll out the red carpet for you. After all, it's been sixty years since we had a Dorothy here."

Dorothy thought about Mother Rainbow's words:

> *"Follow your heart and don't be fooled. Trust in the golden ruler and trust your own values. That will always bring you red carpet treatment if you're true to yourself."*

"I'd sure like to have someone roll out a carpet for me."

G.V. shrugged his leaves. "First you've got to find Paper Boy to get your newspaper back."

"Where is this paperboy?"

G.V. pointed with his stem again. "Just head in that direction, partly south, a little west, over some hill and dale and you can't miss him. Tell him G.V. sent you."

"Bye." Dorothy waved, walking off with Ozzie by her side.

At the dark end of the grapevine, in a forest filled only with things that creeped and crawled, Ima Witch squeezed the grapevine, forcing it to reveal the news.

"So you've got my golden ruler and you're coming to save the Wizard," she growled. Itsa Dragon slithered up off the necklace and wrapped around her neck.

"Send this message back," Ima snapped. The vine shrank back but Ima grabbed it.

"Listen here, you worthless vine," she whispered. "If you don't send this message exactly like I want, I'll stuff you and all the grapes I can pull off into an old vat and turn you into rotgut." Ima eyed the vine. "Do you understand?" The vine nodded.

"Now then, you send this message back. Tell Dorothy that the Wizard sends his regards. That everything is fine and wants her to leave the ruler right where she is." Ima paused. "And, oh yes, tell her that she should follow the yellow brick road, and that will take her back to Orlando."

The vine sent the message. All along the vine, plant ears shot straight up because they knew a lie was being transmitted.

But Dorothy didn't hear it. She was off walking through the field towards the hill, holding the golden ruler in her hand.

"Well, Ozzie," she said, "I have a feeling we're a long way away from Kansas, and even further from Orlando. How are we ever going to get home?"

CHAPTER 20

IMA'S CASTLE MOUNTAIN

Ima knew that Dorothy was coming to Oz. There was nothing she could do about it.

"Where is she?" Ima screamed out, trying to focus her crystal ball on Dorothy. "I can't get a clear picture," the witch cursed, because the rainbow was still protecting Dorothy.

"Is Dorothy coming?" Ura asked.

Ima looked over at the trussed up Wizard. "The closer she gets," Ima said, entwining her fingers together in the air, "the closer you'll drop."

The Wizard gasped as he was lowered a foot towards the dark vat of unearthly creatures swimming hungrily below him. An enormous mouth broke the surface.

Ura looked at the creature with one eye who was snapping away at him. "Let me go!" he struggled.

Ima shook her head. "I think I'll just let my little pet keep an eye on you," she winked.

In a puff of smoke, Ima disappeared. The door to the petting zoo slamed shut behind her.

She looked at her grotesque assortment of crossbred animals. Sheep with fangs. Kangaroos with antlers. Bears that climbed trees like monkeys and chimps that growled like lions, scaring the horned camels.

"Ah my little pets," she cooed, stroking the horns of a half-giraffe, half-hippo, "what a little science project you have turned out to be. My own little gene pool of life. I'll make a fortune selling you as designer pets."

Ima felt a terrible pain in her forehead. "Dorothy's here and she's wearing ruby..." she paused, not believing her eyes. "She's wearing ruby sneakers!" Ima screamed, whirling around, swirling her pet's hay and feed until the room was a blizzard.

"How could she put rubies on sneakers? That's not the way it's supposed to be!"

Smoke started to seep from her forehead. The animals shrieked but nothing would stop the pain that Ima felt. "I've got to have those shoes...I want them now!" she cried out.

Ima looked again at the image of Dorothy. "The ruler! Where's my ruler? Ahhhhh, my head is splitting open!"

Her temples began to crack like parched, desert land. "I'm having an Imagrain headache," she bellowed, trying to keep her face from falling apart.

Then she leapt into the air and hovered above her creature creations. "I need my medicine," she whispered, snapping her fingers and disappearing in a puff of smoke.

In her kitchen, Ima frantically opened the cold caskets that lined the walls. One after another she tore open the lids, moving aside whoever or whatever was there.

As she moved down the line, hands, feet and faces looked out from their undead rest, but Ima didn't care. The cracks were spreading across her face and there was little time left.

"Where's my medicine?" she screamed, the intense pain from Dorothy's goodness driving Ima insane.

Then she found it. Pulling out a sack from the last casket on the wall, Ima carefully removed enough slimy creatures to fill a bowl.

Taking out her masher, Ima prepared a batch of one-legged toads and no-legged spiders, blended together with cat's eyes and the stubbly hair from between an elephant's toes.

When it was perfectly mixed into witch's goo, Ima dished out a wiggling spoonful into her mouth. Then another and then another, until the bowl was empty. She licked it clean for good measure. The cracks around her face began to go back together.

"Now I feel better," she whispered, looking around the room. Freak faces from the caskets looked back at her.

"What are you looking at?" Ima screamed, and the caskets snapped shut like a shuffled deck of cards.

Moving her fingers, feeling the focus tingle, Ima brought the image of Dorothy clearly into view. Watching the girl and her dog walk through the fields, Ima wrung her hands.

"So you think this is just some walk through the park, eh?" Ima whispered, as she watched Dorothy pick a flower.

"Come on, Ozzie," Dorothy said in the image. "We've got to find the Wizard."

Ima rubbed her thumb and index fingers together so fast that smoke came out. "This place is no Sunday school picnic," Ima nodded. "I'm in control. Welcome to my world, Ima's world," she said, squeezing her nose.

With a blink of an eye and a burst from her brain, Ima conjured up images that appeared on the wall. Each was like a horror show of what she intended for Dorothy.

> "Cynical, cynical, cynical stew,
> Dorothy, here's what I've got waiting for you!"

Fires, creatures, sinking boats and flaming forests. None of the images were pleasant and none had Dorothy ending up back in Orlando. And they all had the same terrible ending.

> "Life is short and life is sweet,
> Soon Dorothy Gale, you'll be dead on your feet."

With a clap of her hands, the image showed Ima stuffing Dorothy's arm into a casket in her kitchen. "Rest in peace," the image of Ima cackled. "And till death do us unite."

The image faded away. Ima walked back along the line of caskets. "I hope she'll be happy here," Ima said, standing before the last one.

Dorothy's name was already on it.

CHAPTER 21

BILLIKINS

Dorothy stopped at the top of the hill and looked around. "I don't see that paperboy, do you, Ozzie?" Ozzie wagged his tail and spun around.

"What's over there?" Dorothy asked, spying a row of statues leading into the woods. "Let's go see."

On an old granite monument in front of the stone statues was written:

The Billikins Want to Welcome You to Oz
The Land of Things As They Ought To Be

"Must be an ancient city or something," Dorothy said, putting the golden ruler into her backpack.

She walked over to the first statue. It was a bald-headed, stumpy-shaped person, with a pointy, shaved head and a top-knot, sitting on a small, flat throne.

Dorothy walked around the pot-bellied, chubby statue, trying to figure out if it was a man or a woman. She turned to the other statue, which was almost identical except that the long ponytail top-knot hung to the other side.

Then she did a double take. "Ozzie, these statues don't have any...any..."

Dorothy pointed to the statues but Ozzie didn't understand. He just cocked his head and yipped.

"How can you tell if they're boys or girls?"

"Quit it!" said a voice.

Dorothy looked around. Ozzie had his leg lifted against a statue.

"Who said that?" Dorothy gasped.

"Tell the dog to go water the plants. Don't you have any manners?"

"Where are you?" Dorothy asked.

"I'm right here," said the statue.

Dorothy looked again and the statue winked. "I must be dreaming," Dorothy said, rubbing her eyes.

Then the statue on the other side spoke up. "What took you so long?" the Billikin asked. "Don't you know how to work those neat looking ruby sneakers?"

Dorothy was startled. A smile widened across the statue's face. Dorothy did a double take. "How can statues talk?"

Then, from up and down the line of statues that stretched in front of her, came a roar of an answer. "Because we're Billikins."

Ozzie hid between her feet. "What are Billikins?" she asked.

The first statue stood up and stretched. "We weren't sure if you were a witch or not, so we statued up."

"You what?" Dorothy asked, looking in awe at the Billikin who was a moment ago stone and now was coming towards her on two stubby legs.

The other statue hopped down from its throne. "We just freeze up when danger's around. Sort of like turtles do except we don't need a shell."

"Why not?" Dorothy asked, not knowing what else to say.

"Because we turn to stone," a third Billikin said.

"Yeah," said a fourth, "and that's a heavy load to carry around so that's why we statue up."

"But we're rock solid friends," another one joked.

"And if we could when we statue up, we'd like to roll around, but we can't."

"Roll around?" Dorothy asked, shaking her head.

"You know, rock and roll. Get it, rock and roll?" another laughed.

"I get it," Dorothy sighed.

A Billikin spoke up. "And when we saw the ruby shoes, why we thought they belonged to the witch and..."

Another interrupted and said, "But then we saw that they were ruby sneakers and..."

Then another joined in. "And we knew that you weren't a witch coming to hurt the Billikins."

Dorothy was almost dizzy. "What are Billikins?"

The other Billikins got up from their thrones and walked towards her, their long ponytails shaking free. They formed a circle around her and smiled, placing their right palms on top of their heads.

"We're the Billikins," they all chanted in unison.

"And what does that mean?" Dorothy pressed.

"We are the conscience of Oz," said one.

"We help people understand how they ought to be," said another.

"And how do you do that?" Dorothy asked, moving her head like she was watching a tennis match, trying to keep up with which Billikin was speaking.

Then a Billikin who was a bit wider than the rest, stepped forward. "We Billikins try to help the people of Oz accept the things that they cannot change and change the things that they can change, and...." the Billikin solemnly looked at Dorothy, "have the courage, strength and wisdom to know the difference so they don't spend their lives sweating the small stuff."

Dorothy shook her head. "But, but..."

"Go ahead, ask anything," one of the Billikins smiled.

"Okay," Dorothy said, "I don't want to sweat the small stuff, but are Billikins boys or are they girls?" she asked.

They all broke out into giggles. "Dorothy, Dorothy," said the biggest one, "there you go again, worrying about the small stuff."

"But I'm curious." She stopped talking as a thunder of laughter broke out among the Billikins.

"Dorothy's funny, isn't she," the big Billikin nodded to his friends.

"And how did you know my name?" Dorothy asked indignantly.

"Don't blame the messenger," shouted a familiar voice. Dorothy looked over and saw G.V. "They heard it on the grapevine. Miss Ruby Sneakers, have you forgotten what I told you already?"

"No I haven't," Dorothy said, turning towards the vine. "And if you knew you were coming in this direction, I could have come with you," she huffed.

G.V. shrugged its leaves. "Can't ever tell when a hot flash will come in. News travels fast and no faster than on the old grapevine."

"So what's the news?" Dorothy asked.

G.V. straightened his vine out. "The news is that though sometimes no news is good news, in this case, that is the case."

Dorothy blinked. "What did you just say?"

"Er, Miss Ruby Sneakers," G.V. stammered, shaking his grapes to clear his throat.

"Will you quit calling me Miss Ruby Sneakers."

"Okay," G.V. shrugged, "maybe I should put it this way." He paused to shake the dust off his leaves.

"What way?" Dorothy finally asked impatiently.

"Knock knock," G.V. said.

"Knock knock?" Dorothy asked.

"Yeah, don't you know the game?"

"I do," Dorothy sighed, wondering how she was ever going to save the Wizard.

"Okay then. Knock knock."

"Who's there?"

"A-M-I."

"A-M-I who?"

G.V. nodded his leaves. "A-M-I is Ima spelled backwards, and that's who's comin' after you."

"Who told you?" Dorothy gasped, then closed her eyes. "I know, I know, you heard it on the grapevine.

When is she coming?" Dorothy asked, looking around.

G.V. held out a small vine with a sundial on it. "Let's see," he said, trying to position the instrument towards the sun.

"She's either been here before, will be here in a half hour, or...," G.V. said, moving the watch around, "she's already here."

Then the sky darkened and a horizontal tunnel of wind came winding around them like a snake. The Billikins ran as fast as their stumpy legs would carry them, climbing back up onto their thrones and freezing into stone statues.

"What's happening?" Dorothy asked. Ozzie growled and spun around on his little legs.

G.V. pulled his sundial vine back under the leaves. "Let's just say that you've got company. Bad company."

"Who?"

"Ima," G.V. said. "Like in Ima Witch." The wind swirled around the vines, shaking the grapes.

"What should I do?" Dorothy cried out, covering her eyes from the dust.

"Click the shoes and split. Go home. Hide under your bed. That's what I'd do."

"I can't click the shoes," Dorothy said, "not until I find the Wizard."

"Then pull in the welcome mat or put on a flak jacket. Or buy controlling interest in a blood bank. Do something to help yourself," G.V. said, waving his vines around in panic.

The Billikins were all statues again, waiting for the trouble to pass. G.V. rattled his vines, sending the news. "Ima Witch was reported in the Billikins' Land today and..."

Then he saw the black-caped figure, riding her broom in a circle overhead. Flying all around her were dozens of little witches on little brooms.

"Correction," G.V. said, "a confirmed sighting of Ima Witch was reported from the Billikins' Land today."

"What should I do?" whispered Dorothy, watching Ima look down at her. The little witches started flying down, crisscrossing through the line of Billikin statues.

"If I were you," G.V. started, "and of course I'm me and you're you. But if I were you, and I had hands, I'd have that golden ruler in my hand pronto, like quick as a cricket...if you know what I mean."

"The golden ruler," Dorothy gasped. "I wasn't supposed to let it out of my hand." She took her backpack off and pulled out the golden ruler.

"Good luck," G.V. said, covering his vine over with leaves.

"Where are you going?" Dorothy asked, clutching the ruler.

"A good reporter always knows when to run."

"Well, how do you like that?" Dorothy said to Ozzie.

"Drop the ruler and run!" Ima shouted.

"Go away, go away!" Dorothy cried out.

"Okay," Ima grinned. The witch disappeared into a puff of smoke, then reappeared in a blaze of light in front of Dorothy.

"Give me that ruler!" Ima screamed.

Dorothy shook her head. "It belongs to the Wizard."

"And he belongs to me," Ima glared, "so give it to me and go home." From behind her, twenty witches floated up and hung motionless in the air, staring at Dorothy.

"I can't," Dorothy said, wondering where the courage to stand up to the witch had come from. "I can't go home until I've saved the Wizard."

Ima's cackle was so loud that Dorothy had to cover her ears. "Dorothy Gale," she whispered, walking in a tighter and tighter circle around the girl. "That golden ruler belongs to me. It's my right."

"No," Dorothy said, turning in a circle to keep facing the witch.

Ima reached out but wasn't able to snatch it. "She who has the gold rules, and I'm the new ruler so give it to me."

Dorothy waved the golden ruler at the witch to keep her away. "Well, if she who has the gold rules, then I'm the ruler."

"And Ima Witch will never stand for that!" Ima screamed, releasing lightning and thunder into the air. "Now give me that ruler!" she screeched, reaching out for it.

Dorothy ducked and the witch lunged after her. Ozzie jumped up and nipped the witch's arm.

"Ouch!" Ima screamed. The wicked witch drew up to her full height and pointed her finger at the dog.

"Your time is coming," she hissed. Ozzie kept barking. "You're nothing but a hot..." Then she stopped and smiled. "I think I'll turn you into a hot dog," she cackled, raising her arms in the air.

"That's not nice!" Dorothy shouted. "He wouldn't do that to you," she said, pushing the witch back with the golden ruler.

When the golden ruler touched the witch's chest, Dorothy felt it tingle and it appeared to grow smaller.

"Ahhhhhhhhhh!" Ima screamed. "Don't touch me with that!" she cried out, brushing at her chest where the golden ruler had touched her like it was on fire.

"I'm going to get you!" the witch hissed, pointing her finger at Dorothy. "Those stupid-looking shoes and that ruler *will be mine*."

"Go away!" Dorothy shouted. "That's not the way people should treat each other." Ozzie barked his agreement.

Ima wrapped herself in her cape, covering her whole body including her head. The cape stood out and peaked on her head as if it were a witch's hat. Dorothy eyed the peak of the cape, knowing there was more to the witch's power than met the eye.

"Dorothy Gale," Ima whispered, "here is what the future holds for you if you don't give me the golden ruler."

In a billowing ruffle, Ima threw open her cape and held it wide on both sides of her body. Dorothy saw a dozen images of terrible things happening to her.

"Oh, no," Dorothy gasped. The little witches on their brooms howled with laughter.

"Oh, yes," Ima nodded. "What I've got waiting for you is no *Bill Cosby* show." She leaned over to Dorothy's ear. "In case you don't know it, the Huxtables don't live here anymore."

"I'm not listening."

"Give it to me!" Ima said, trying to grab the ruler. "You don't want to mess with the darkness. Go home to Orlando before the moving truck leaves without you."

Dorothy closed her eyes, blocking out the terrible visions. "You can't hide," the witch cackled.

Ima circled around her, whispering evil into her ear. "Listen, Dorothy Gale," Ima hissed, "evil will always fight good. That's what it's all about between you and I. Like it was between my mother and your grandmother."

"I'm not listening!" Dorothy screamed, covering her ears.

"Yes, you are," Ima smiled, flicking lightning bolts up into the air. "Evil has been around since the angels fell. It's what makes good people bad and bad people worse."

Dorothy squinted her eyes as hard as she could and tried to think of something good. *Follow your heart and don't be fooled. Trust in the golden ruler and trust your own values...that's what Mother Rainbow told me.*

Ima picked up her thoughts. "Don't listen to that rainbow woman. I know you changed colors in there, but in the real world, evil is what sometimes divides the world along color lines."

"No!" Dorothy said, determined not to be influenced by the witch. Then she thought of what her father had told her. *I'll always be there if you need me.*

Gritting her teeth, Dorothy thought about her father. Ima caught the thought. "Your father is finished. By now he's given up hope of finding a job in Orlando."

"He has not!" Dorothy said, wanting to cry.

"Sure he has," Ima cackled. "He's already packing up. Your parents are moving to Detroit."

"That's not true!" Dorothy shouted out, drawing strength from her father's words.

She opened her eyes and confronted the witch. "If you don't leave right now, I'm going to have to touch you with this ruler again. So you better leave."

"Read my lips," Ima whispered. "I'll be back," she sneered, wrapping herself back up in the cape. "Adios and break a leg," Ima grinned, winking at Dorothy.

Then she shouted to her witches who were hovering around her, "Back to the castle! Back to Castle Mountain!"

A dark funnel of wind flew in front of Ima before she spun away. The little witches turned into dust devils and followed behind, leaving Dorothy and Ozzie.

"How will I ever get home?" Dorothy whispered as the evil witch disappeared.

CHAPTER 22

RED CARPET

Up and down the line, the Billikin statues blinked their eyes. "Is she gone?" one of the Billikins called out.

"Yes, she's gone," Dorothy said, disgustedly. "And a lot of good all you guys were."

The Billikins began stretching like they'd just gotten up from a nice nap. "We're not guys," one of them said.

"Well," Dorothy said, putting her hands on her hips, "a lot of good you girls were."

"And we're not girls," said another Billikin.

"We're Billikins. We just always were, are, and will be. So who wants to be a boy or a girl when you're a Billikin?"

G.V. unwound his vine and looked out from the leaves. "Think I might win an Oziter Prize for that story."

"And you," Dorothy said, shaking her head, "you sure deserted me when the trouble started."

"You make the news, I just report it," G.V. said, shining one of his leaves.

The big Billikin came up to Dorothy and looked down at the golden ruler. "You've got only eleven good deeds left," he nodded.

"I what?" Dorothy asked, looking at the ruler.

The Billikin nodded. "You started with twelve inches of good deeds and..."

"Twelve inches makes a ruler," another Billikin added.

"Would you let me speak," the big Billikin said, giving the other one a scolding look. "Anyway, you've got eleven inches of good deeds left. So use them wisely. You still have a long way to go before you find the Wizard."

"I hope I have enough to get there," Dorothy said, putting the ruler to her chest.

"You do. But use it wisely," the big Billikin said. "Never let it out of your hand."

Dorothy took a deep breath and let it out slowly. "I wish I could just go back to Orlando. This Wizard-saving stuff might be too much for me."

"Orlando?" said one of the Billikins. "You live at Disney World?"

"There's more to Orlando than just Walt Disney World, you know," Dorothy huffed.

G.V. coughed. "Just click the shoes. That's what a good news hound would do. Click the channel and split."

"I can't," Dorothy said, straightening up and putting on her backpack, "Now, if you could just point me in the direction of where the Wizard is, I'll be going."

"Why don't you stay here with us?" one of the Billikins asked.

Dorothy shook her head. "I miss my mom and dad. I can't go home until I find the Wizard, so I better be going."

"Don't you have a map?" the big Billikin asked.

"I had one in my newspaper," Dorothy said, "but the paperboy took it back. Say, do you know where I can find him?"

The Billikins all shrugged at the same time. "He's probably just down the lane. Just head that way, you can't miss him," the big Billikin said, pointing in the direction Dorothy had originally been heading.

G.V. called out, "I'm sure there's the red carpet treatment waiting for you somewhere."

"You keep saying that," Dorothy said.

The big Billikin sighed. "I guess you do deserve it after all."

"Deserve what?" Dorothy asked, watching two Billikins waddle off.

They brought back a long, wrapped package and set it on the ground in front of Dorothy. "What's that?" Dorothy asked.

The big Billikin smiled and pulled at the paper. Out rolled a red carpet that stopped at Dorothy's feet.

Dorothy stepped back. "What's the rug for?"

"It's not a rug, it's a carpet," G.V. called out. "A red carpet to be exact. You got to have your facts straight in my business, yes-sir-re-Bob."

Ozzie began barking at the carpet. "Hush," Dorothy said, "it's only a rug...er, carpet."

The big Billikin waved her forward. "Now step on it and go."

Dorothy looked at the Billikin as if she was talking to a crazy person. "Just step on the carpet and go? Is that what you said?"

The Billikin nodded. "It's supposed to be rolled out on the yellow brick road, but since there's no road, I guess the ground will do."

"But I've got a long way to go," Dorothy said. "There's not enough carpet to get me there."

"You'd be surprised," G.V. said. "In my business you see a lot of surprises, but this is one of the better ones I've seen."

Dorothy looked at the carpet. "And I just step on it and..."

"Just step on it and go," the big Billikin smiled, pushing her forward.

Dorothy stepped onto the carpet. "What do I do?"

"Just step forward," the Billikin said.

Dorothy took a hesitant small step and the carpet unrolled a few feet. "Oh, jeesh," she smiled. "That's pretty neat," she said, taking another step. The carpet rolled forward each time she stepped and stopped when she stopped.

She turned to the Billikin. "How does it work?"

"Beats me," he shrugged. "How does anything work around here in Oz?"

G.V. couldn't resist showing off. "The red carpet treatment was instituted by a Wizard's decree in 1842, and since that time..."

Dorothy put up her hand. "Stop already. Can you just tell me if there's enough carpet in the roll to take me to the Wizard?"

G.V. nodded his leaves. "According to my Vinencyclopedia, it's never longer than your step in front or the step behind. It never goes forward when you stop. And," he paused, drawing out Dorothy's patience, “there’s enough carpet to get you to where you want to go and then some.”

“This is really, really weird,” Dorothy smiled. “Come on, Ozzie,” she laughed, calling the dog onto the carpet.

The big Billikin gasped. “Is he housebroken?”

Dorothy giggled. “Not that I see any houses around here, but yes, he’s housebroken.”

“Just don’t let him do anything on the carpet,” G.V. sighed. “I’d have to put it on the vine and you know how gossipy some vines are.”

The big Billikin cleared his throat. “Ah, er, we have a little present for you.”

“You do?” Dorothy smiled.

Three Billikins came up shyly and handed Dorothy a small, wrapped package.

“You didn’t have to,” she smiled. The three Billikins blushed.

“Yes, they did,” G.V. interjected. “Part of being a Billikin. Got to be nice to those that are nice to you.”

“Yeah,” said one of them blushing, “we don’t have to statue up when we’re with nice people.”

Dorothy removed the wrapping. Inside was a small Billikin statue. “It looks so real,” she said, examining it closely.

The big Billikin nodded. “Just think of it as a good luck piece to help you on your journey.”

“I’ll always treasure it,” Dorothy said, putting the statue into her backpack.

“Some things are worth saving and some things need to be used at the right occasion,” the big Billikin said.

“Remember,” another Billikin said, bowing slightly, “a little Billikin goes a long way.”

“I’ll remember,” Dorothy said. “Good-bye,” she shouted.

The Billikins all answered at the same time, waving madly as Dorothy and Ozzie headed down the path, the red carpet unrolling before them.

G.V. sighed. “Guess I better vine this story in. Might still have time to make my deadline.” The vines started shaking with the story being sent in.

At the other end of the vine, at the foot of Ima’s Castle Mountain, the Wicked Witch was squeezing the life out of the vine reporter on the other end.

“Deadline,” she whispered, watching the life slip out of the vine. “I think it’s more like a deadvine.”

With the fury of darkness, Ima gave the vine a snap, sending a stinging tingle up the grapevine. She watched the ripple until it was out of sight.

“I just sent in an obituary,” she chuckled, dropping the lifeless vine.

She conjured up the image of Dorothy, flashing it on the rocks in front of her. Dark creatures of the night crawled and slithered forward to watch.

“Look at her,” Ima whispered. “Remember her face.” The creatures growled and grunted.

“She’s only got eleven inches of gold left. Eleven good deeds. Eleven ways she could get home, but she doesn’t even know one of them.” The creatures purred happily, nipping at each other’s flanks, happy that the master of the dark was in a good mood.

Ima patted a beast with one eye that rested its head against her shoulder. “I want you to keep an eye out for her,” she nodded.

“She’ll be coming this way,” she told the creatures. “And if you’re hungry, that tender little Orlando morsel is yours. Finders eaters, losers weepers,” Ima nodded.

“And the rest of you remember Ima’s law,” she said, looking from beast to beast. “It’s a jungle out there, so it’s eat or be eaten. Bite first and ask questions later.”

The beasts growled their approval. Ima waved her hands and sent a shower of electricity into the air. “Now get going and be ready for her!”

CHAPTER 23

PAPER BOY

For the first hundred yards, Dorothy and Ozzie did a lot of stops and starts as they got used to the red carpet. "This is the weirdest place I've ever been to," Dorothy told the dog.

Ozzie barked at the carpet, nipping at the roll, which made it unroll faster. "Oh, Ozzie," Dorothy laughed, "maybe you shouldn't do that."

Dorothy looked around at the beautiful but strange plants and animals that she passed. Sky-blue butterflies with three-foot wings flew alongside blue bumblebees. Strange-looking crimson cats hid in the bushes when Ozzie yipped, and enormous belching frogs let loose with a deafening chorus of grunts, moans and burps.

Dorothy wanted to get off the carpet to look closer at the creatures, but she knew she was pressed for time, so she kept walking on the carpet as it unrolled.

Around the next bend she slowed down. "Look at those iguanas," Dorothy laughed. Sitting on the rocks alongside the road were a group of pink iguanas. "You're very pretty," Dorothy spoke.

From over the hill up ahead she heard a rumbling sound and found a pack of kangaroos juggling apples. "G'day, mates," she giggled, trying to put on an Australian accent.

"Toodles...Toodles," a high-pitched voice called out.

Dorothy stopped. "Is someone calling me?"

Sitting at a table under a tree, as if she was in a fancy café in Paris, Dorothy saw on ostrich with a hat on. "Oh, Toodles, could you find a waiter for me?"

"My name is not 'Toodles' and I don't work here," Dorothy said, then muttered, "wherever here is."

"Well," the outrageous-looking ostrich said, "if you don't work here, then what are you doing here?"

"You mean here in Oz?" Dorothy questioned, coming to a halt.

"No, here in Nature's Café."

Dorothy looked around. "Café? But I see only one table."

"That's why it's so excluuuuuuuuusive," the ostrich said. Then she stuck out her neck which extended like a fire hose. "How do you like my long neckline?" she smiled.

"Oh, my," Dorothy said, watching the head with the hat move around on the end of the long neck.

The ostrich eyed the golden ruler. "Are you some kind of band leader?" she asked.

"No."

"Then what is that *thing* in your hand?"

"It's a...a..." Dorothy stammered.

The ostrich pulled back her head and the hat slipped down onto her beak. Snapping her head back, the hat slipped back into place. "What," she asked, "is an a-a?"

"No," Dorothy blushed, "It's the golden ruler."

The ostrich gasped. "Royalty! I knew it! Oh please forgive me," she said, swooping her neck down to the ground.

"What are you doing?" Dorothy asked.

"I've always wanted to meet a queen and..."

"I'm not a queen."

"Then you're a princess?" the ostrich asked, looking up with one eye.

"No, I'm not a princess."

The ostrich raised her head back up. "Then you're a duke's wife or an earl's daughter or..."

"I'm Dorothy."

The ostrich's hat turned backwards. "Just Dorothy? That's it?"

"That's it," Dorothy shrugged.

"Heavens alive," the ostrich said, pulling her neck back to her body which was still at the table, "what we women have to go through."

"Sorry," Dorothy said, "but that's the way I was born. Good-bye," she called out, walking off.

"Well, you could have changed that, you know," the ostrich snooted. "And where could my waiter be?" she asked, looking around. "I want to know what the specials are today."

Dorothy skipped along on the carpet with Ozzie at her side. "I wish I had my newspaper," she said in frustration. "Then I'd have a map to guide me to the Wizard."

She passed by a babbling brook, which was speaking in a language she didn't understand, as a flock of flamingoes trotted past.

"This Oz is a very strange place," Dorothy told Ozzie. "How does anyone know where they're going if there aren't any signs?"

Over the hill she stopped to ask directions in a village called Georgetown. "Excuse me," she said to the first person she came to.

"Are you speaking to George?" the man asked.

Dorothy was thrown off guard. "I'm speaking to *you*."

The man shook his head. "If you're speaking to *me* then you're speaking to *George*."

"Okay," Dorothy said. "George, can you..."

The man held up his hand. "Hold on, I know you want to speak to George, but which George."

"Which George? Any George," Dorothy blurted out in frustration.

"That could pose a problem," the man said. He cupped his hands to his lips and shouted, "Calling all Georges, calling all Georges."

"Whatever are you doing?" Dorothy asked, then looked around. She was surrounded by men of all shapes, sizes, colors and features.

"Now," the first man asked, "in Georgetown, we're all named George, so which one do you want?"

Dorothy looked from face to face. "Any George will do," she sighed, "I just want to know how I can find the paperboy."

"He's no George," one of the men said.

"And that's a pity," said another, "'cause he'll never know what he's missing not being named George."

Dorothy looked at the first man and said, "Listen, George."

All the Georges around her said, "Yes?"

Dorothy pursed her lips in frustration. "Will someone just tell me how I can find the paperboy? I want my paper back."

"Would you like a copy of the *Georgetown News*?" a man asked.

"Does it have a map to the Wizard?" Dorothy asked.

The man shook his head. "Only has information about George. That's all that really matters."

"Well, I best be on my way," she sighed. "Come on, Ozzie."

After a half hour, Dorothy came to a big bowl on the side of the road. "I hope it's something to eat," Dorothy said, feeling her stomach growl.

She stepped off the carpet to look inside the bowl. "It's alphabet soup!" she laughed, looking down at the six-inch letters that were floating there. Then her eyes opened wide. The soup spelled out, HI DOROTHY.

On the other side of the rainbow, Dorothy would have been startled. But nothing was the same in Oz, so Dorothy giggled.

"Hi," she replied. "Do you know where the Wizard is?"

The letters in the soup bowl began moving around. When they stopped, they'd formed the word: AIM.

"Aim?" Dorothy said, not understanding. "The Wizard's with Aim?"

The letters started bouncing around like the ball in a pinball machine, then came to a stop and formed, SORRY, then bounced around again and spelled: IMA.

"That doesn't help me much," Dorothy said. "Then do you know where I can find the paperboy?"

"Yo," said a voice behind her.

"Yo?" Dorothy said, turning around.

"Yeah, yo with the fashion statement ruby sneakers."

Standing in front of her was an ebony statue that appeared to be made out of papier-mâché. "Yo, I'm here," he said. She looked around to see who was talking to her.

Then she saw the statue smile. "Is that you speaking?" Dorothy wondered.

"Yo, like in yo ho ho," the statue said.

"What are you, a pirate or something?" Dorothy asked.

"Do I look like a pirate?"

"No," Dorothy said, shaking her head. "You look more like an art project gone wild."

"Well, pardon me," the statue said.

"And excuse me," Dorothy said. "Come on, Ozzie, we best be going."

"Hold it there, Ruby," the statue said.

"My name's not Ruby," Dorothy huffed. "My name's Dorothy, Dorothy Gale."

"Okay, red shoes, aren't you lookin' for Paper Boy?"

Dorothy nodded. "Do you know where he is?" she asked hopefully.

"I sure do."

Dorothy waited for an answer, but the statue didn't say anything else. "Well, would you tell me where I can find him?"

"You have two eyes, right?" Dorothy nodded. "And two legs, right?" Dorothy nodded again. "Well, girl, if you just take two steps forward, you'll be lookin' right at him."

"You're the paperboy I'm looking for?" Dorothy asked, walking over to the statue.

"Bad paper, good paper, it's all just paper in my book. Only thing I hate is when they call bad checks rubber checks. They may use those where you came from, but there isn't any rubber paper over here."

"But are you the *news*paperboy?"

"Maybe," the statue said, looking at Ozzie.

"Maybe what?" Dorothy asked.

"Maybe I am and maybe I'm not. Depends."

Dorothy felt like pulling her hair. "It depends on what?"

"It depends on whether you're lookin' to paper train Oscar Mayer there."

Dorothy looked at Ozzie. "His name's Ozzie, not Oscar Mayer."

The statue shrugged. "I don't care if you call that thing Benji. If you're lookin' to paper train that hot dog, then I'm not the paperboy you're lookin' for."

Dorothy crossed her arms. "I just want my paper back."

The statue nodded. "What kind of paper would you like?"

"Paper?"

"You know, cardboard, typing paper, wax paper...that sort of thing."

"Well, I'd like to see my newspaper."

"That's too easy," the statue said. "Think of another kind of paper."

"Why does everyone make me jump through hoops?" Dorothy sighed.

"Hoops? I've never heard 'bout paper hoops."

"Okay," Dorothy sighed, ready to play along, "I like tissue paper."

The statue shook its head. "You don't have a cold, do you?"

"You're silly," she laughed.

"I know," the statue said, "guess I've got a lot of funny papers inside me. Well, here goes," he said, closing his eyes.

Before Dorothy's eyes, the statue turned into a box of tissue paper. "How did you do that?" Dorothy asked.

"Easy," the paper box said. "Now watch."

The box changed into an envelope, then into a notepad then into a greeting card on which was printed, *Anything else?*

"That's pretty neat, but I'd really like to get my newspaper back."

"Okay," and the card turned back into the statue. It was holding Dorothy's copy of *The Emerald City Times.*

Dorothy looked at the headline as it changed:

IMA WITCH VOWS TO TAKE OVER OZ
CAN DOROTHY SAVE THE WIZARD?

"I'm trying," Dorothy said, "but I don't even know where to look."

"Paper Boy knows," the statue grinned. "Just ask and you shall receive."

"Can I see your map?"

Paper Boy nodded and with a whirl, opened up the newspaper to the center pages. There was the map of Oz that Dorothy had been seeking.

"That's just what I need," she said, reaching for it, but the statue snatched it away.

"But you said 'ask and you shall receive.' So I want it," Dorothy said.

"You asked and you received a free look," Paper Boy said, rolling the newspaper back up. He stuck it into a paper sack hanging from his shoulders.

"But I want the paper."

"It'll cost you one dollar," Paper Boy said.

Dorothy looked at the price on the corner of the paper. "But it says it costs twenty-five cents," she said, pointing to the price.

"That was yesterday's price for yesterday's news," Paper Boy said. "And there's been a slight inflation since yesterday."

Holding the paper above his head, he shrugged, "One dollar, take it or leave it."

"I'll take it," Dorothy said, taking off her backpack.

Paper Boy looked at the golden ruler. "'Course you could just give me that gold stick. That'd be a fair trade."

"Hardly," Dorothy snapped. She found one of the five-dollar bills her father had given her and handed it to Paper Boy. "You got change?"

Paper Boy looked at the bill. "Certainly, certainly I got change," he nodded, taking the bill from her hands.

"Let's see. Five dollars less one dollar is..." he said, creating paper money in his hands. "Three dollars," he exclaimed, handing the bills back to Dorothy.

Dorothy looked at the three dollars in her hand. "That's not right."

"Sure it is," Paper Boy said, putting the five dollar bill into his pocket.

"But you said the paper costs one dollar."

"Did I?" Paper Boy said.

"You're trying to cheat me!" Dorothy exclaimed. "I want my money back."

Paper Boy sheepishly pulled it out. "It's only paper money," he said.

"That's not the point!" Dorothy exclaimed. Waving the golden ruler in his face, she tapped him on the shoulder. "Don't you know that it's not right to cheat people? Not even for a penny?"

Paper Boy shrugged. "What could a few bucks mean to you? You're rich. You got a roll of bucks."

"I'm not rich and that's not the point. Would you want somebody to cheat you?" Paper Boy thought for a moment. "Come on," Dorothy pressed, "tell the truth."

"No."

"No what?" Dorothy asked.

"No, I wouldn't want someone to cheat me, so there. You satisfied?" he said, crossing his paper arms.

Dorothy felt the ruler tingle and another inch disappeared. "Oh, no," she said, "what have I done?"

"You made me give you the right change," Paper Boy said, pulling it from his pocket. "Oh, heck," he shrugged, "keep your money and I'll give you the paper free."

"Free? I'm willing to pay."

Paper Boy shook his head. "And I'm willing to pay for the lesson you just taught me. Never felt this way before. Feeling bad but feeling good."

Dorothy smiled. "That's 'cause you did the right thing."

"I guess."

"It's called conscience," Dorothy said.

"What's a conscience?" Paper Boy asked.

"Let me think how to explain that," Dorothy began. "Conscience is like your mother telling you not to do something even when she's not around."

"How can she do that?" he asked. "My mother's not a ventriloquist. And how does she tell me something when she's not even there?" Paper Boy asked, scratching his chin.

"It's in your head," Dorothy said. "Conscience is knowing what the right thing is and doing it, even if it's not what you or your friends want to do."

Then Paper Boy sat down in a slump. "I guess that's why I lost some of my customers. Kept shortin' them on the change. Thought it didn't matter."

"But it does," Dorothy said. "You have to live by the golden ruler. Treat others like you want to be treated."

"Even when they treat you bad?"

"It may sound old-fashioned, but two wrongs have never equaled a right. It never has and never will be. That's just a simple truth, I guess."

Paper Boy shook his head. "You're full of simple stuff, aren't you?"

"I just wish I knew a simple way to find the Wizard."

"You've got the map," Paper Boy beamed. "It's inside the paper."

"Oh, that's right!"

"Do you want to come along with me?"

"To find the Wizard?"

"Sure," Dorothy smiled. "And he'll be able to explain about having a conscience and all that a lot better than I can."

"I don't think so," Paper Boy said. "I'll leave you to go on by yourself."

Then Dorothy felt depressed. "There's only ten inches left on the ruler. I hope I have enough left to find the Wizard."

Paper Boy looked at the golden stick. "A ruler's supposed to be twelve inches."

"I know, but it seems like each time I treat somebody right, or protect us from the witch, I lose another inch." She shook her head. "At this rate, it'll be gone before I can find him."

"Listen to me," Paper Boy said. "If this Wizard can't cut you some slack, say like an inch or two, then what kind of Wizard is he after all?"

Dorothy thought about it, then broke into a big grin. "You know, I think you're right."

"I know I'm right," Paper Boy said. "If he's big in the conscience department then he'll cut you slack, you can bet on that, Ruby."

"My name's Dorothy."

"Okay Dorothy Ruby, now we better get going."

"*We?*" Dorothy said.

"Yeah, we."

"Then let's use the map to find the Wizard."

"It's either that or hang around with the goofy bowl of soup," Paper Boy smiled. "Soup's okay for a few days but after awhile you start lookin' for a cheeseburger in paradise."

Then Dorothy's conscience bothered her. "But it might be dangerous. I haven't even told you about the witch and..."

"I know all about the witch," Paper Boy said. "I read the newspaper and listen to the..."

"I know, I know," Dorothy sighed. "You listen to the grapevine."

"Havin' a good paper around like me will come in mighty handy." Paper Boy hopped onto the carpet. "It sounds like you need some help that only Paper Boy can give and maybe some of that gold will rub off on me."

"I just want you to know what you are getting yourself into," Dorothy said.

"Just don't play with matches and I'll be fine. Good-bye, soup," Paper Boy shouted out. "I'm goin' to see the Wizard with Ruby."

"My name's *not* Ruby," Dorothy sighed.

"Okay," Paper Boy smiled, "I'm off to see the Wizard with Miss Goodie-Two-Red-Shoes, now let's get going."

The soup bowl spelled out, SEE YOU LATER, and they both laughed and skipped along on the carpet.

Paper Boy talked away. "Yes sir, I don't like fire and rain and I don't like the game, Paper-Rock-Scissors. And I might tell jokes, but don't ever start cuttin' up. Makes me nervous."

As they talked, neither one saw the little witch who'd been watching them.

CHAPTER 24

WATCHING

The little witch flew off towards the dark clouds, avoiding the beams of sunshine. When she passed through the gates of Oz, entering the land of the Wicked Witch, she flew low over the ground, scaring the creatures who were waiting for Dorothy.

In the courtyard of Castle Mountain, Ima was initiating a troop of new witches into her coven. "Okay, you witches, repeat after me."

Every bloodshot eye and cockeye in the courtyard was watching her. "Raise your left hand," she commanded and the witches responded.

"Now then," Ima smiled, walking in front of her motley air force. "I want you to repeat after me. Understand?" Fifty ugly faces nodded.

"Okay, this is the Witch oath. It's stronger than Arnold Schwarzenegger, more bonding than Super Glue and lasts longer than a garlic dinner."

She chuckled at her own joke. "This oath lets you join HAG, which stands for Hatred And Greed, the witches union that rules the world."

Then she raised her left hand into the air. Electricity radiated eerily from the tips of her fingers.

"I swear." The witches repeated. "I will do my witch duty for Ima and only Ima, and will obey the witch law." The witches repeated the lines.

The electricity from her fingers shot up further. "To hurt other people and creatures at all times." She paused, waiting for them to finish. "And to keep myself physically repulsive, mentally overbearing, and morally disgusting."

Ima cackled while the witches repeated the rest of the oath. "You are now witches of the night," she screamed, raising her other hand in the air. Wind whipped her cape around. Dust swirls left pentagrams at their feet.

"Now go out and do something bad!" she cried, wrapping herself up in the cape. When she flung it open, her eyes were like hot coals.

The witches mounted their brooms and flew off to every compass point, for evil has no boundaries. The little witch flew up and floated in front of Ima.

"And what do you want, short stuff?"

"Dorothy and a friend are heading this way."

"A friend?" Ima asked. "You mean that dog?"

The little witch shook her head. "No. She's with a boy. A paperboy."

Ima grinned, stroking her chin, scratching at something that was invisible. "Strength in numbers is her game, eh? Well, two's company but three's a crowd. I think I need to go have a talk with them."

With a spin to the right and a spin to the left, Ima vanished and reappeared where the Wizard was tied up. Itsa Dragon was sitting on the edge of the tank, slithering his tongue out, licking the Wizard's chin.

"Let me go!" Ura demanded.

"Calm down, you windbag," she snapped, "or I'll hook you to the end of my broom and use you as a mop."

Ura chuckled. "She's coming, isn't she?"

"Who?"

"You know who," he grinned. "Dorothy's in Oz and she's on her way here. And you can't stop her."

Ima closed one eye and gave him the worst evil stare imaginable. "After I get the golden ruler, I might just sell off the Emerald City and put up a rhinestone palace. So think about that."

"You'll never win," Ura said defiantly. "Dorothy's too strong for you."

"You think *she's* too strong?" Ima said, throwing Dorothy's image up onto the wall.

The Wizard watched Dorothy, Paper Boy and Ozzie travel along. Paper Boy smiled and said to Dorothy, "My mother taught me when the tough get going, the tough get praying."

"We need all the help we can get," Dorothy smiled.

Ima splashed a ball of fire against the image, burning it away. "Prayers, huh? Religion?"

"You'll never win," Ura nodded. "Wickedness will never triumph."

"Don't bet on it," Ima cackled.

Snapping her fingers, her cauldron appeared. Strange looking things peeked out but she pushed them back down with her broom handle.

"What's that?" Ura shivered, seeing a hand try to crawl out of the boiling pot.

"Just a little stew. Call it the blue plate special," she laughed.

The hand reached up again and Ima sighed. "Do you want me to give you a hand?" The hand's fingers wiggled towards her. Ima lifted up two left feet with her broom from the bubbling pot.

"Here, take defeat like a man," she laughed.

Then a face looked up with sorrowful eyes. "You want to get out?" The eyes brightened and the face nodded. "NOT!" screamed Ima, pushing the face back into the cauldron.

"You're not strong enough to beat Dorothy," Ura said.

Ima shrugged. "If Dorothy and that walking litter bag want some religion, that's fine with me."

"It is?" Ura said suspiciously.

"Why should I be afraid of religion, I'm not afraid of anything!"

"You're crazy," the Wizard hissed.

"You just don't want to look in Ima's mirror of life," she whispered.

With a snap, a mirror appeared in her hands. There was no reflection of Ima, but what was reflected was war, starvation, famine and pestilence.

Stirring her pot, Ima cackled over and over, then threw the mirror against the wall. The image from the mirror flashed up on every wall in the room.

"Stop it," pleaded the Wizard. "I don't want to see that. That's not how things ought to be."

"Tough," Ima said. "I'm just a reflection of the real world and the mess people have made of it."

Whispering over her cauldron, she pushed her hands through the steam. As she spoke, the images on the walls changed to reflect what she was describing:

> Methodists, Baptists, Catholics too,
> Muslims, Jews, toss in a Buddhist or two.
> Add in a Mormon, a Moonie and Confucius
> Now all fight for God,
> Make love and peace seem so useless.
> Belfast, the West Bank and downtown Beirut,
> Kill for religion, oh what a hoot!
> Pray for the dead and capital punishment too,
> You have nothing to worry about,
> For God loves only you.
> All men are your brothers?
> Not him, he's black!
> All women are your sisters?
> Only on Sunday, not after that.
> Honor thy mother?
> Not when she's old.
> Love thy neighbor?
> He's got AIDS and it's too cold.
> Now you're saved
> And now you're not.
> Use ethnic cleansing
> To sweep away the rot.
> There're no contradictions
> With just one key to heaven,
> Thank God it's my key.
> How much do I owe you, Reverend?
> And Yea though I walk through the valley of death
> I will fear no evil, for my religion is the best.

"But it shouldn't be that way," the Wizard whispered.

"That's my point and that's why the world is weak and ready for Ima. Divide and conquer. That's the way."

"But that's not right!"

"But that's the way it is. I'm gonna turn Oz into a do-as-I-do-not-as-I-say kind of place. Everyone over the rainbow should feel quite at home," Ima whispered, disappearing from the room.

She reappeared in the head room and looked around. "Let's see," she chuckled, "who do I want to be today?"

Heads of all ages and colors were lined on the shelves from floor to ceiling.

"I love this room," Ima cackled, looking at the head of an old man. "This is the only way to get ahead," she howled at her own joke.

Ima had created her private collection of disguises which enabled her to sneak in and out of the Emerald City at will. That was how she'd tricked the Wizard into leaving his safe haven.

Most of the heads were modeled after nightmares she'd had or tricks she'd come up with, but some were from people Ima had captured. "Use me," whispered the head of an old man.

"No, use me," said the head of a pretty woman.

"Be quiet!" Ima snapped. She looked over her collection, walking down the narrow aisle. The eyes of the heads followed her as she walked.

"Maybe this one will do," Ima said, picking up the head of an old man.

Taking off her own head, she placed the head on her shoulders. "Help me," she whined in an old man's voice.

"No," the witch said, "this one won't do."

"Try me," said the cyclops.

Taking off the head, Ima picked the one-eyed cyclops. Letting out a loud roar, the cyclops head shook back and forth.

Ima's hands then replaced it with the head of a very handsome teenage boy. "This will do," the boy's voice said.

With a snap of her fingers, Ima's black cape and dress disappeared, replaced by stylish jeans and shirt. "Maybe some cowboy boots will help," the boy said, and in a snap, snakeskin boots appeared.

"Oh, not that again," the boy said. Snake's heads were still alive on the tips of the boots. With a snap and a point of a finger, the heads were gone.

"Now, let's go see Dorothy," the boy said, stepping onto a broom and flying off.

CHAPTER 25

BOOK WORM

Dorothy, Paper Boy and Ozzie walked on the red carpet through the woods and over the hills. At the edge of a canyon, they saw a sign that said MELODY LANE.

"Finally, a street sign," Dorothy said. "Let me see the map."

Paper Boy moved and wiggled and the newspaper appeared in his hands. "I think we're right about here," he said, pointing.

Dorothy looked closely, then shook her head. "I don't see this on the map."

"That's 'cause we haven't made a hit song yet," said a voice from behind the rocks.

"What does that have to do with anything?" Dorothy asked. "And who am I speaking to?"

A musical note stepped out. "My name is Dough, and my pals and me haven't had a hit song so we're not on the map yet."

"Oh, brother," Dorothy sighed.

"Hey, guys, do we know that song," Dough called out. From behind the rocks a group of notes skipped out.

"I hope this ain't Name That Tune," Paper Boy whispered to Dorothy.

"Me too."

Dough stepped forward. "Allow me to introduce our group, Melody Lane. I'm Dough," he said, bowing smartly. "And this is Ray, and this is Me and..."

"And I think I know who the rest are," Dorothy smiled. "Can you tell us where we can find the Wizard? Without the yellow brick road, we're lost."

The carpet rolled and unrolled several times. "I think you hurt the carpet's feelings," Paper Boy said.

"Sorry," Dorothy shrugged. "But I'd still like to know if we're going in the right direction."

"It's straight ahead," Ray said.

"Yeah," Me added. "You can't miss it."

"Are there any landmarks we should look for?" Dorothy asked.

Dough thought for a moment, then nodded. "If you're goin' to Ima's Castle Mountain, which is where the Wizard is, then..."

Dorothy stopped him. "How do you know that?"

From the bushes on the side, Dorothy heard a familiar voice. "Because they heard it on the you-know-where."

Dorothy turned and smiled. "G.V.! Am I glad to see you."

"Me too! Everytime I see me I get a thrill, a chill and wonder if I took a good-lookin' pill, to get this handsome."

"It's Rush Vine," Paper Boy gasped. "I'd know that voice anywhere."

The grapes on the vine turned from purple to white to a subtle blush. "Rush is my name and talk is my game."

Paper Boy shook his head. "That's a neat name."

"Just my stage name," G.V. said with a bow.

"Do you have any news for me?" Dorothy asked. "Is the Wizard all right?"

"News? Why nothin' but a hot flash that not even cold cash could force me to reveal." He put a leaf to his lips. "We newsmen can't be bought."

"Well, if you won't tell me," Dorothy huffed, turning away, "I guess I'll just have to stop talking to you."

G.V. unrolled a long creeper vine towards Dorothy. "Not even a teeny-tiny sound bite?"

"Not even a nibble," she said, crossing her arms.

"I'll tell you what I know," G.V. whispered, looking around. Leaves came out and wrapped around Dorothy and Paper Boy.

"Can you keep a secret?" G.V. asked. Dorothy nodded. "Okay, okay," the news vine said, "if you promise to tell the truth, the whole truth and nothing but what the listeners want to hear, no matter what that is, then I'll tell you what I know."

Dorothy crossed her arms. "I'm waiting."

"Yeah, me too, grape juice," Paper Boy said.

"Hold your paper horses," G.V. said. Holding a leaf to the vine, G.V. picked up the vine vibes. "The hot flash of the day is this," he said, then began in a fast, wire-service voice:

> **"...this just in over the grapevine. Dorothy Gale has reached Melody Lane but is singing the blues because she can't find the Wizard. All Oz is holding its breath, turning dark green, wondering when Dorothy is going to get her Kansas act together and get on with the business of saving the Wizard. More on the hour.**

"Oh, man," Paper Boy said, "your hot news is about as hot as yesterday's toast."

"Can I quote you on that?" G.V. asked.

"Come on, Paper Boy," Dorothy said, taking his hand. "Let's hit the road. My act is from Florida," she said snidely.

"Kansas or Florida, what's the difference?" G.V. shrugged. "They're both too hot and too flat to have hills for all the over-the-hill gangs that have put down their entitlement stakes."

"Come on," Dorothy said to Paper Boy, "we've got a Wizard to find."

"But don't you want to hear the latest?" G.V. called out.

"No, thank you," Dorothy replied, skipping along upon the red carpet.

G.V. shot a creeper vine along the ground beside her. "Come on, I'll be discreet. You can trust me. I don't work for a tabloid or nothin' and..."

"And Ruby doesn't want to talk to you," Paper Boy said, "so why don't you go back to Twelfth Street and look for some crazy little women."

The vine slinked back. Dorothy looked at Paper Boy. "Twelfth Street?"

"Yeah, you know, like in the song *Kansas City*," Paper Boy said and began singing. "I'll be standin' on the corner of Twelfth Street and Vine."

Dorothy began laughing and singing along. "They got some crazy little women there and I'm gonna get me one."

"You know somethin' Ruby, you're all right." Ozzie woofed his agreement.

They hadn't gone more than a half-mile when they saw a big dictionary sitting beside the path. "Someone dropped a book," Dorothy said, stopping to pick it up.

Ozzie sniffed at it than jumped back with a yelp. "What's wrong, hot dog?" Paper Boy laughed.

"Help, help! Let me out!" came a high-pitched boy's voice from somewhere near the book.

"Did you hear that?" Dorothy asked her friend.

Paper Boy nodded. "I think we ought to just continue down the road before somebody throws the book at us."

"Aren't you *ever* serious?" Dorothy asked, leaning down towards the book.

Paper Boy shrugged. "It's hard to get serious when I'm hangin' 'round with a girl wearin' ruby sneakers, carryin' a gold ruler, who says she's lookin' for a witch who wiznapped a wizard."

Dorothy ignored him and picked up the book. "Help! Let me out!" came the high-pitched voice again.

"Should I open it?" Dorothy asked Paper Boy.

"Don't ask me. You don't seem to be listenin' to much of anything I've been sayin'."

"Help! I'm stuck!" came the voice from the book.

"Someone needs help," Dorothy said. She slowly opened the book.

"What in the world?" she gasped. Inside the book was a six-inch boy with glasses, who looked like a worm. He was wearing a T-Shirt that clung to his thin, hose-shaped body, that said, *IF YOU CAN FIND WALDO YOU CAN FIND THE LIBRARY.*

"Who are you?" Dorothy asked.

"If I was an ant, I'd have been a dead ant, that's for sure," he said, stretching his thin arms.

Paper Boy looked closely. "What are you, some kind of four-eyed caterpillar?"

"No," the unusual small boy said.

Paper Boy cocked his head, trying to get a better look. "Then are you a maggot, a slug or a grub?"

"No, no, no!" the boy in the book said. He pranced across the page and climbed up on the spine of the book. "Just turn to this page here," he said, pushing his hands between the pages, "and you'll find the answer."

Dorothy was getting used to the confusion of Oz, so she turned to the page. "Now what?"

Paper Boy wanted to go. "Now we should leave."

"Wait," Dorothy said.

The strange-shaped boy said, "Look between *boo-hoo* and *boom*," he said, pushing up his glasses.

"Stop that," Dorothy said, putting the small worm-boy back on the page. "Here's *boo-hoo*, now what?"

"Now find out who I am." the small boy laughed.

"Let's see," Dorothy said, using her finger as a guide. "Are you a book?" The worm-boy shook his head. "A bookbinder? A book-case? A book club? A bookend? A bookie?"

Paper Boy held his ears. "You can make book on the fact that if he don't tell us who he is quick, that I'm going feed him to the birds."

"You're almost there," the worm-boy said, ignoring Paper Boy.

Dorothy nodded. "Ah-ha. Bookman. That's what you are, right?"

The boy shook his head. "Keep going."

Paper Boy put his finger on the next word. "Bookmark. That's it, isn't it?" The worm-boy shook his head.

Dorothy ran her finger down the list of words. "Just nod your head when I get to it. *Bookplate? Book rack? Bookstore?* Or is it..." She stopped and read the definition of the last word before *boom*.

"*The larvae of any of various insects that infest books and feed on the parts of bindings.*"

Dorothy looked up. "You're an insect?"

"Keep reading," the worm-boy smiled.

"*One who spends much time reading or studying.*"

"And what's that the definition of?" Paper Boy asked.

Dorothy looked at the small boy. "He's a...a...bookworm," she smiled.

"And I'm not your average bookworm either," the small boy said, jumping around on the page. "I'm the smartest boy in the world. I'm a genius!"

"And you're very modest too," Dorothy said.

"I know everything there is to know," Book Worm said. "Test me."

"Okay, fish bait," Paper Boy said, pushing the small boy off the book.

"Hey, hey!" Book Worm screamed, "that's my home!"

"Don't hurt him," Dorothy pleaded.

"I won't. Just stand here for a moment," Paper Boy said, lifting the worm-boy down. "I just want to quiz you."

Book Worm stood with his hands on his hips. "I'll have you know that I don't like game shows."

"That's okay," Paper Boy smiled, "'cause I'm just gonna ask you some questions...sort of test you."

"You're wasting your time," Book Worm sighed, "'cause I'm a certified, one hundred and one percent genius."

Paper Boy opened the dictionary and flipped through the pages. "This is a good one," he said, running his finger down the page. "Tell me the names of everyone who died on the Titanic."

"That's not in there!" Book Worm exclaimed.

"Do you know the answer to the question or not?" Paper Boy asked. Book Worm curled himself up into a ball. "Do you know the answer?" Paper Boy asked again. The Book Worm ball rolled back and forth.

"What Paper Boy's trying to say," Dorothy began, "is that it's impossible for someone to know everything."

"But I'm the smartest boy in the world. I'm the Book Worm!" the small boy exclaimed, unrolling and jumping to his feet. His glasses fell off so he picked them up and polished them.

"And it's not polite to brag about yourself," she said kindly.

"But that's the only person I like to hear about," Book Worm said, putting his glasses back on.

"And that's just my point," Dorothy sighed, "if you don't want to hear others talk about themselves, then you've got to understand that others don't want to hear you brag about yourself."

Book Worm thought about it for a moment. "But I know everything."

"No you don't," Paper Boy said.

"It's a fib to say something like that," Dorothy said.

"But it's true!" Book Worm shouted. Dorothy pulled at his nose. "What are you doing?"

"Seeing if your nose will grow, Pinocchio."

"But I've never told a lie and I've..." then he stopped. Dorothy pulled his nose out and out and out until it was longer than his body.

"That's pretty cool," Paper Boy laughed.

Book Worm fell forward but his nose propped him up. "Okay, okay, I did fib and I have fibbed. Make my nose smaller, will you?"

"Bragging and fibbing," Dorothy said, shaking her head. "What a terrible combination."

"I said I won't do it anymore," Book Worm shouted, trying to lift his nose off the ground.

"That's better," Dorothy smiled. "You always want to treat others like you want to be treated." Then she touched him with the golden ruler and his nose started shrinking.

"How'd you do that?" Paper Boy asked.

"It wasn't me, it's the golden ruler."

"Well," Paper Boy said, shaking his head, "I hope you're like a cat."

"Why?"

"'Cause you just used up another one of your good inches."

Dorothy looked. There were only nine inches of golden goodness left. "Oh, no."

"Oh, yes," Paper Boy nodded.

"Oh, what on earth are you talking about?" Book Worm said, rubbing his nose.

"It would take too long to explain," Dorothy said. She stood up and put Book Worm back on his book.

"Now you remember what the golden ruler is and we'll be seeing you."

"Where are you going?" he shouted, jumping up and down.

"We've got to find the Wizard," Paper Boy said, "and we don't have time to waste carrying a yappin' bookworm along."

"But I can help and..." then he looked down sadly.

"What's wrong?" Dorothy asked.

"I guess you don't want me to come along because I'm just a bookworm. That's it, isn't it?"

"Yeah," Paper Boy said. "We might get into some heavy-duty action."

"And you might end up wrapping dead fish," Book Worm taunted back.

"Boys, boys," Dorothy sighed. Then she looked up. "And speaking of boys," she whispered, catching her breath.

Standing next to the road was the most handsome boy she'd ever seen. She had no idea it was Ima Witch in disguise. Paper Boy saw Dorothy's reaction and was immediately jealous.

"You need some help there, pretty girl?" the handsome boy asked.

"I, uh, I..." Dorothy stammered.

Paper Boy looked upset. "What the lady's tryin' to say is, no. No, thank you. No, we don't need any help. So if you don't mind, we're gonna be on the road again. Come on, Dorothy," Paper Boy said, taking her by the arm.

"Not so fast, Paper Boy," Dorothy blushed. She looked at the handsome boy. "Do you know where I can find the Wizard?"

"Funny you should ask," the stranger said, "but I was just on my way to see him. Would you like to come along?"

"We sure would!" Dorothy exclaimed.

"If you know the way," Paper Boy mumbled, not wanting to play follow-the-leader with someone all teeth and muscles.

"I'm terribly sorry," the handsome boy said, "but I've only got room for one."

Book Worm jumped from the book and pulled himself up to Dorothy's shoulder. "Don't trust him. He looks like a rogue," he whispered.

"Don't be silly," Dorothy said, feeling her knees get weak under the gaze of the cute boy.

Book Worm was close enough to hear the pounding of her heart. "You want me to read you the definition of a lady-killer?" Dorothy didn't respond. "How about wolf? Or...or..." He saw that Dorothy was falling in love fast. "Or how about the story of Eve and the apple or the birds and the bees?" he mumbled.

"That's okay, Book Worm," Dorothy said, not taking her eyes from the boy. "Can't you take my friends?" she asked halfheartedly.

The boy sighed. "You're the one who's come over the rainbow to find the Wizard. I'll take just you."

Book Worm almost dropped his glasses jumping up to Dorothy's ear. "How did he know that? What's he got, a crystal ball or something?"

Dorothy snapped back. "How did you know I came over the rainbow?"

The handsome boy gave Dorothy a dazzling smile full of sparkling white teeth. "I guess everyone knows. You're quite famous."

"I can't take any more of James Dean here," Paper Boy said.

"Then I guess you should leave," the stranger said, laying his most heart-melting smile on Dorothy.

"You're on your own, Ruby," Paper Boy said, walking ahead. He hadn't gone more than twenty feet when he looked up in the air. "What's that doin' up there?" he wondered aloud, looking at the witch's broom floating above him.

"The witch must be around here," he said, looking around. Then it dawned on him. "He's the witch!"

Sneaking back around, Paper Boy saw that the handsome stranger had moved in closer to Dorothy. "Now, Dorothy, let me carry your backpack. A pretty girl like you should never have to lift a load like that."

He started lifting it off her shoulders. "And how about that heavy ruler. Let me carry it for you and..."

Paper Boy jumped out, pointing to the stranger's shadow. "Look! He's the witch!"

Dorothy looked at the boy's shadow and gasped. It was the shadow of an ugly witch with a pointed hat. His snakeskin boots seemed to be alive!

Paper Boy strutted up, flexing his paper muscles. "Let me handle this," he said, stepping in front of Dorothy.

"Okay, witch man," he said, raising up his arms like Aladdin, "Shazaaaaaaam!" he shouted, throwing his hands forward. Nothing happened. "Kazaaaaaaam!" Paper Boy shouted, but still nothing happened.

"Anything else?" the stranger said, the tone of his voice changing. The snakes slithered off his boots, hissing at Dorothy.

Book Worm slid down Dorothy's shirt. "Hold on," he said. He opened up his book and fanned the pages. "Look at this," he said to Paper Boy.

Paper Boy read the words, nodded, then took a deep breath and shouted out, "Bing, bang, boom!"

"Try again," the stranger said, his voice becoming more and more like Ima's.

"Okay, abracadabra!"

The stranger yawned. “Look, it won’t work. Why don’t you turn yourself into a tissue so I can blow you away.”

“Try this!” Book Worm exclaimed, pointing to another page.

Paper Boy looked over, then turned to the handsome boy. “Hocus Pocus!”

“I don’t think it’s working,” Dorothy said, shivering under the boy’s glare.

“Wiggle your nose like a bunny,” Book Worm shouted.

“What good will that do?” Paper Boy asked.

“That’s what they did on the old TV show, *Bewitched*,” Book Worm explained.

“Don’t waste your time,” the stranger said. “Now Dorothy, if you’re ready to go.”

“Hold on there, hot stuff,” Paper Boy said, taking Dorothy’s arm.

“Try your nose!” Book Worm said, jumping around.

Paper Boy agreed. “Okay,” he said, feeling foolish. He stood there, stuck his nose out and wiggled it with all his might like he thought a bunny would.

“Oh…” the stranger screamed, falling to the ground, “you got me! You *Bewitched* me,” he said, sounding in total agony. Then he disappeared.

Paper Boy was as surprised as Dorothy, but he kept his cool. “Told you I could handle that witch man.”

Then from out of the ground, a pointed hat pushed up from the earth. Ima broke through the surface and smiled. “Fooled you,” she smiled.

“Wiggle your nose again!” Book Worm screamed frantically to Paper Boy.

Ima shot him a frozen glance. “If you don’t shut up, I’ll turn that book into a flyswatter and you into a fly.” Book Worm gulped.

“Remember,” Ima grinned. “You can pick your friends, but you can’t pick what Ima will do next.”

“She’s lyin’,” Paper Boy said, trying to be brave in Dorothy’s eyes.

"You're right," Ima laughed, sending a fire stream towards Paper Boy.

"Help, help!" he shouted, dancing around, trying to put out the fire on his legs.

"Liar, liar, pants on fire," Ima laughed, then she whirled around to Dorothy.

"Time to read!" Book Worm exclaimed, diving into his dictionary.

"Don't play with fire around them, they'll burn!" Dorothy said.

"If you don't give me the golden ruler, I'm going to have a little book-burning party," she whispered, sending a ball of fire towards Book Worm.

Then Ima spun around again. "And if I don't get the ruler now, I'm going to turn big mouth here into cinders and leave you the ashes to bury," Ima laughed, tossing another fireball at Paper Boy.

"I'm burning!" Paper Boy screamed.

From Ima's Castle Mountain, Ura Wizard watched in horror at what was happening. Ima had left the image on the wall so he could twist in agony.

Concentrating on good thoughts, he sent out a command to the clouds:

Rain, rain, come today,
Come and put the flames away.
Sprinkle, sprinkle little clouds,
Drop your rain, drop it now!

Dorothy looked up at the first rain drops. "Oh thank goodness."

"Don't say that!" Ima snapped, looking up. "Who did that?"

The fire on Paper Boy fizzled out. "I'll never use an umbrella again," he sighed, holding his face up to the cloudburst. Then he began to crumple.

"His papier-mâché is coming apart!" Dorothy shouted.

The Wizard gasped. *Too much rain!*

Concentrating again, he sent out another command:

Stow, stow, stow your raincoat,
Gently put your rain away,
All clouds stop raining now,
That's enough for today.

The rain stopped and the sun came out. "Curses!" Ima said. "There's only one person who could be interfering like this."

"And that must be the Wizard," Dorothy exclaimed. "Let him go!"

"Give me the golden ruler and he's yours," Ima said.

"Don't trust her," Paper Boy whispered.

"Then just click your sneakers and go home," Ima said.

"I want to go home, but I have to save the Wizard," Dorothy said firmly.

Ima chuckled, wrapping the cape around her. "You're too young for responsibility. You should be watching TV or hanging out in a shopping mall. Doing something unproductive like most teenagers do."

"They do not!" Dorothy declared.

"That's 'cause you're not a teenager yet," Ima said. "By this time next year you'll be walkin' on the wild side."

"I will not!" Dorothy said, stamping her feet.

"That's right," Ima smiled. "It won't be next year. You're already walking on the wild side of Oz, but you don't even know it."

Ima turned, then stopped in front of Paper Boy. "See you later, papergator," she grinned, turning him into a green paper beast. "And you," she sneered, looking at Book Worm, "I think you and I ought to go do a little fishing."

"Good-bye!" she laughed, disappearing in a cloud of flames and smoke.

"And good riddance," Paper Boy said, changing back.

"We showed her a thing or two," Book Worm said, jumping around and shadowboxing like a prizefighter.

"Yeah, how weak we are," Dorothy said. "Come on, we better keep going," she said, walking on the carpet.

"Where you going?" Book Worm shouted. "Can I come?"

"Yeah, yeah," Paper Boy said, picking him up. "Maybe the Wizard will teach him not to brag and to tell the truth."

"I forgot," Dorothy said, reaching into her backpack, taking out the snow-shaker crystal ball.

When the snowflakes cleared, she wanted to cry. Ima's face was staring back at her. "I see you!" the witch cackled.

Dorothy stuffed the snow-shaker ball back into the pack and then looked at the ruby sneakers. *Just three clicks and I could go home.*

She looked at her two traveling companions. Ozzie yipped at her feet. *Just three clicks and I could leave these troubles behind.*

She clicked them once and they tingled. *I could be in Kansas in a second.* She clicked them twice and they sparkled. *I could be home on a plane to Orlando tonight.*

"What are you doing?" Paper Boy asked.

"I'm...I'm..." Dorothy stammered. Then she stopped and thought of Mother Rainbow's words: *"The fate of Oz is in your hands. Don't lose the golden ruler."*

Paper Boy looked at the tingling shoes. "Come on, Ruby, don't leave us now."

"I'm not," Dorothy sighed, taking a deep breath. "I'm going to find the Wizard," she said and skipped ahead.

"Come on, guys," she laughed, taking Paper Boy by the hand when he caught up. "We're off to save the Wizard!"

None of them heard the witch curse and scream inside the crystal ball in Dorothy's backpack.

CHAPTER 26

BULLY BEAR

The red carpet took them through many lands with many strange characters.

It wasn't long before they spotted something strange up ahead. "Hold it!" Paper Boy said, putting his hand in front of Dorothy to stop her.

"What's the matter?" she asked.

Book Worm stuck his head out from the dictionary. "Time to read."

"Quiet, Book Plate."

"My name's Book Worm."

"Okay Book Bin," Paper Boy said, irritating his little friend.

"Did you stop us just to horse around?" Dorothy asked.

"No," Paper Boy whispered. "Look at that."

Up ahead was a kid-sized bear standing by the side of the road. "It's a bear!" Dorothy exclaimed.

"A big bear," Book Worm whispered. Ozzie crept up to sniff it.

"It don't look like a Care Bear to me," Paper Boy said.

"What should we do?" Dorothy asked.

"Can't you get this carpet to change course?" Book Worm asked, looking down at the carpet roll.

"I don't think so," Dorothy said. "It just seems to have a mind of its own."

"I hope not," Paper Boy mumbled. "Next thing you know it'll be sayin' 'don't tread on me' and we'll really be up a creek."

"Then what do we do about the bear?" Dorothy asked. "We just can't stand here for the rest of our lives."

"Let's just proceed with caution," Paper Boy said, "and be ready to run like the blazes if that thing's alive."

The carpet stopped at the bear's toes. "It's stuffed," Dorothy said.

"What the heck's a toy doin' out here?" Paper Boy wondered.

"Maybe he was part of a birthday party or something," Book Worm suggested.

Paper Boy shook his head. "He doesn't look like the life of the party to me."

Dorothy touched the bear's stomach. "He feels real."

"Maybe he once was," Book Worm said.

Suddenly, the bear came to life, pointing his paw like a six-gun. Ozzie barked and circled around.

"I don't want to shoot anyone," the bear said, waving his paw around, "but this is loaded."

Paper Boy looked at the paw. "Loaded? That paw's a blank."

The bear ignored him. "All right, all right, throw down that strongbox," the bear demanded.

Dorothy blinked and looked at Paper Boy. "Strongbox?"

"That's right," the bear said. "Either give me the box or I'll blow your heads off. Maybe even wing you in the arm or shoot you in the foot."

"He thinks we're a stagecoach."

"You're no Davy Crockett so don't mess with the bear," the animal said.

"Oh, my!" Dorothy said, backing up.

"Oh, yes!" the bear said. "My name is Bully Bear and if you don't give me what's in the backpack I'll have to rub you out."

He looked at Book Worm and waved his paw. "I'll shoot the grub here first if you don't do as I say." Book Worm hid between the pages of his book.

"Let me handle this," Paper Boy said.

"Stand back before I use you for target practice," Bully Bear warned, pointing his paw. "I'll shoot your headlights out before you even turn them on."

Ozzie started barking and nipped at the bear's feet.

"I eat buffalo for breakfast and use weener dogs for toothpicks," he said, kicking at the dog.

"You're just a bully," Dorothy said, pushing against him with the golden ruler.

Suddenly it tingled and the bear began to whimper, "Don't hurt me. Please, don't hurt me."

"Look at him crying," Book Worm said. "I just looked in the *C* section under crybaby. That's what you are."

"You should be ashamed of yourself," Dorothy said. "Threatening us with that gun in your hand."

"That's no gun," Bully Bear whimpered, showing his paw. "It was just my hand."

"And you threatened to rub us out," Paper Boy exclaimed.

"Maybe a good massage, but I'd never want to hurt you," the bear blubbered.

Paper Boy looked at the ruler. "You've got eight inches left," he said, nodding to Dorothy. "You just lost yourself another inch of gold."

"I did?" she said, looking at the ruler. "Oh, *I did*," she frowned.

"You keep givin' away the gold and we'll have to panhandle our way to the Wiz's place," Paper Boy said.

"I can't help it," Dorothy said. "I just don't like to be pushed around."

Paper Boy looked at the bear and then back to Dorothy. "But do you have to use it on every ragamuffin and fleabag you run into?"

Dorothy frowned. "I hope I have enough to save the Wizard."

"Save the Wizard!" Bully Bear exclaimed. "Are you Dorothy?"

Dorothy nodded. "How did you know?"

"Because I told him, that's how," G.V. said from the bushes.

"G.V., am I ever glad to see you," Dorothy said. Then she remembered she was still upset with the grapevine. "Are you following us?"

"A good news hound always follows leads. That's the way a story is rooted out," he said. "Gosh I hate that expression, *rooted out*. Sounds so cold to me."

"What time is it?" Dorothy asked G.V.

G.V. pulled out his sundial. Holding it up to the sun, he moved his vine back and forth. "Let's see, either you're early or you're late, which would you prefer?"

"That's not much of a choice," Dorothy frowned.

"Not all choices are pleasant," G.V. said. "That's something you learn quick in my business. Like choosing which side to take on a story—who your friends are and which side you want to win."

"I thought newscasters were impartial," Paper Boy said.

"That's 'cause you're in Oz Land, baby," G.V. laughed.

"Am I going to be on the news?" Bully Bear asked the vine, picking lint from his fur.

"Maybe on radio, but not on TV. It's not cool to show someone wearing fur. You understand, don't you?" G.V. said.

Bully Bear shook his head. "I'd get mighty cool if I took this coat off."

"Keep your coat on, I don't want to see a bare bear, my friend," G.V. said.

"Come on, Dorothy," Paper Boy smiled. "It's time we get going."

"You behave yourself," Dorothy said to the bear. "We've got to follow the red carpet and find the Wizard."

"Can I quote you on that?" G.V. asked.

"That was off the record," Dorothy laughed.

"What about me?" Bully Bear asked, kicking his paws in the dirt.

"What *about* you?" Paper Boy said. "Here you just tried to scare us half to death and you expect us to worry 'bout you?"

"Just go home," Dorothy said.

"But I don't want to," Bully Bear sighed, looking like he was about to cry.

"Why not?" Dorothy asked, suddenly feeling concerned.

"I mean, my home's not the kind of place that Goldilocks would want to visit."

The bear looked down. A tear started down his cheeks. "My parents are moving to different caves and it makes me so unhappy. He broke down in sobs.

"There, there," Dorothy said, trying to comfort him. "I can't take you from your parents. They need you now. They both do."

Bully Bear pulled out a key that was hidden in the fur around his neck. "I'm a latchkey bear. My parents both work and I'd really like to have someone to play with. Please?"

"Oh jeesh," Paper Boy said. "Bad 'nough we brought along this worm, and with hot dog and now this bear, we're goin' to start lookin' like a red carpet zoo."

"Please, can I come for just a little while?" Bully Bear begged Dorothy.

"It's going to be dangerous," Paper Boy said.

"And that's dangerous with a *D*," Book Worm said, flipping open the dictionary. "You want to read the definition?"

"Danger doesn't scare me," the bear said, "as long as I'm standing behind you guys."

"Oh, all right," Dorothy said. "Come on. Maybe the Wizard can teach you how to behave towards others."

"Are you housebroken?" Paper Boy asked.

"I'm not a grizzly if that's what you're asking," Bully Bear said indignantly.

"Just checkin'," Paper Boy said. He turned to Dorothy, "Okay, Ruby, let's hit the road."

They started forward and Bully Bear followed behind. "Ruby? I thought your name was Dorothy."

"It is," Dorothy said.

"Good-bye, Dorothy," G.V. shouted. Dorothy waved and they were off.

"But you called her Ruby," Bully Bear said.

"That's just my pet name for her," Paper Boy whispered to the bear as they walked along. "Yeah, Ruby and I are close, real close."

"Like brother and sister?" Bully Bear asked.

"No!" Paper Boy exclaimed.

"You mean like boyfriend and girlfriend close?"

"We're workin' up to that," Paper Boy said.

Book Worm climbed up on the spine of the book. "You saw the way she looked at that handsome boy, didn't you?"

"So?" Paper Boy said defensively. "That was just a witch trick."

"The heart's a tricky thing," Book Worm said. "Don't let your own heart get broken. Dorothy's not going to be here long."

"Maybe," Paper Boy said, "and maybe not."

"Just a warning, my friend," Book Worm said. "Enjoy things while they last."

"This is so much fun," Bully Bear giggled.

Paper Boy looked at the bear. "Just don't try and give me a bear hug, or I'll turn you into a bear rug."

"Do you like to bunny hop?" the bear asked, trying to be friendly.

"Don't go gettin' silly on me," Paper Boy said.

"Why are you guys here?" Bully Bear asked.

Book Worm spoke first. "The Wizard's going to help me tell the truth."

Paper Boy nodded. "And the Wiz is going to keep me from cheating."

"Gosh," Bully Bear exclaimed, "I feel like I'm with some real desperadoes."

"Oh, brother," Paper Boy mumbled, "we got ourselves a real teddy bear comin' along. Should be a real help fightin' the witch."

"I hope the Wizard can make me feel better about myself," Bully Bear said.

"That's a pretty tall order," Paper Boy sighed. "That Wizard doesn't like to bite off more than he can chew."

"Speaking of chewing, I'm hungry," Bully Bear said. "When do we stop for lunch? I just *love* picnics."

"Just don't let your tummy start growlin'," Paper Boy said. "The witch might hear it."

Around the bend they came to a string of signs with a message on them. "What's this?" Book Worm asked.

"Looks like billboards to me," Paper Boy said.

They all read the signs out loud as they passed them:

I KNOW YOU'RE CRAVING BUBBLE GUM.

ALL CHILDREN DO.

SO JUST AHEAD AND AROUND THE BEND

GUESS WHAT'S WAITING FOR YOU!

"Oh, man!" Paper Boy said, "Let's go. I'm ready for some serious chewin'."

"It might be a trick," Dorothy called out.

"And it might be trick or treat," Paper Boy said.

Over the hill they found a bubble-gum baby just sitting by itself.

"How did she get here?" Dorothy asked, looking at the pink bubble-gum baby.

"It's not a she," Paper Boy said, "and it's a big piece of bubble gum that looks like a baby."

"Do you think someone lost it?" Dorothy asked, looking around.

Paper Boy sniffed it. "Who cares? My jaws are tired from talking and need a gum break."

"But it might belong to someone," Dorothy said.

"It doesn't look like it so I say we chew it up," Bully Bear replied.

Paper Boy slapped him on the back. "You're okay, Teddy, you know that?"

Up in Castle Mountain, Ima watched them fall into her trap. "That's right. Come to the bubble-gum baby. Just take a piece of my double-bubble-trouble. Try it, you'll like it," she cooed.

Paper Boy pulled on a gum finger. "I hope this isn't sugar-free," he said, sticking it into his mouth.

"Maybe you shouldn't do that," Book Worm said.

"You do what you want," Paper Boy said, chewing away. "The less you chew, the more for me."

"Do you know how to blow bubbles?" Bully Bear asked.

"Do I know how to blow bubbles?" Paper Boy bragged.

He flattened the gum with his tongue and positioned it behind his teeth. "I'm the bubble king of Oz. Just watch."

Ima smiled at the image on the wall. "I'm watching," she cackled.

Paper Boy took a deep breath and blew. The bubble that came out kept growing and growing until it was bigger than he was.

"That's great!" Dorothy clapped.

"Bigger, bigger!" Bully Bear clapped.

Then the bubble slipped over Paper Boy's body and trapped him inside. "Help! Help!" he said, pounding against the gum walls.

"How did you do that?" Book Worm asked.

"How do I know?" Paper Boy said. "Just get me out."

They poked at the bubble, but no one could pop it. Not even Ozzie's teeth could tear it open.

"Try your ruler," Paper Boy said in panic.

"I'll try it," Dorothy said. She poked the ruler into the bubble but it just bounced off. *Why won't it work?* she wondered, not realizing she had to touch a person with it to make the ruler work.

"Don't you have a hat pin or somethin'?" Paper Boy said, trying to punch his way out.

"I don't even own a hat," Dorothy said, pulling at the gum.

Ima's trick had worked. She watched the children struggle, enjoying every second of their misery.

"Time to be a party popper," she sighed.

Ima took a big needle out of her cape and pointed it at the image in front of her. "I hate to burst your bubble," she whispered.

"Hurry, Dorothy!" Paper Boy said. "I think this was a trap."

"I'm trying," Dorothy said.

Ima poked the pin closer to the image. "Sorry, blotter head, but it's time to blow this place."

Ima stuck the pin straight into the bubble image and it exploded with a bubble-gum kaboom. Dorothy and Bully Bear were knocked over by the blast.

"What happened?" Dorothy asked, sitting up.

"Where's Paper Boy?" Book Worm asked.

He was nowhere to be seen. "Someone blew him away," Book Worm said.

"Don't blame me," Bully Bear said. "I didn't do anything. My paw's aren't even loaded."

Dorothy took off her backpack. "We've got to find him. He's got to be around here somewhere."

Then she heard a faint voice. "Is that you, Paper Boy?" she called.

"Did you hear something?" Book Worm asked.

"Listen," Dorothy said.

Bully Bear cupped his ear. "It sounds like it's coming from your backpack."

"Oh my gosh," Dorothy said, opening the flap. She pushed aside the little Billikin statue and lifted out the snow-shaker crystal ball. She shook it until there was a blizzard inside.

"Help, help, Dorothy!" came a tiny voice from inside it.

"That's Paper Boy's voice," Book Worm whispered.

When the snowflakes settled down, they all gasped. Inside they saw Paper Boy, hanging from the bottom of Ima's broom, wrapped up in gum.

"Trick or treat," Ima shouted, "Give me the golden ruler or I'll turn him into paper dolls."

"No...you wouldn't!" Dorothy said. Ozzie barked.

"Just try me, sunshine girl."

"Help, Dorothy!" Paper Boy shouted.

"Help yourself," Ima cackled, snapping her fingers. Paper Boy unraveled into a string of five paper dolls. "He's such a cutup," she grinned.

"Oh, please don't do that," Dorothy said. "Paper Boy, are you all right?"

Five paper dolls shouted back. "Save me!"

Ima laughed, pointing her finger at Dorothy. "Drop the ruler and click those shoes. Leave while the leaving's good."

"I can't," Dorothy said.

"You can if you want to. The choice is yours," Ima laughed. She looked at the paper dolls. "Maybe he'd look better as a spitball," she said. Paper Boy turned into a tight roll of wet paper at the snap of Ima's fingers.

"We'll find you, you mean witch!" Bully Bear shouted.

"And you're next," Ima said, pointing her finger at the bear. "I've been needing a good bearskin rug."

Bully Bear cringed behind Dorothy. "I won't let her hurt you," Dorothy said.

Ima laughed. "And if you want to join me for a little paper bonfire later, courtesy of scrap paper here, why, I can even turn it into a weener roast for that mutt of yours." Ozzie reared back and barked furiously at the crystal ball.

"The party starts at midnight, the bewitching hour, so don't be late!" she taunted.

"What should we do?" Book Worm whispered.

"I'll trade junk mail here for the golden ruler. You've got until midnight to decide," Ima grinned. "Like the rabbit said, it's a very important date. Call it a fire sale," she cackled.

"Save me, Dorothy," Paper Boy cried out, as Ima changed him back into the papier-mâché boy.

Ima threw back her head in laughter, then flew off towards Castle Mountain which loomed darkly in the distance.

"Help me, Dorothy," Paper Boy shouted until his words faded out.

"He's gone!" Bully Bear exclaimed. "That mean witch took him."

"Dorothy will think of something," Book Worm said. Then when she didn't answer, he climbed up on her shoulder. "Won't you, Dorothy?"

Dorothy looked at the crystal ball and then at the golden ruler.

"I've only eight inches left," she whispered.

"Is that enough to save the Wizard and Paper Boy?" Book Worm asked.

"I don't know," Dorothy said.

"If you don't know, then I don't know what we're *ever* going to do," Book Worm said. "Answers like that can't be found in a book."

"I think I should feel scared," Bully Bear gasped.

"What are we going to do now?" Dorothy asked, holding the snow-shaker crystal ball in her hands.

Then she thought of what Mother Rainbow had told her:

> *"You've got to save the Wizard of Oz. It's up to you, Dorothy Gale of Orlando, Florida. It's all up to you."*

She looked in the backpack and saw the little Billikin. *What good are you?* she wondered, then thought of what the Billikins had told her:

> *"A little Billikin goes a long way."*

"You're just along for the long ride," she said, putting the crystal ball beside it and closing the backpack.

G.V.'s vine crept up from the ground and wrapped itself around her in sympathy. "It's okay, kiddo."

"Oh, G.V. What am I going to do? I wish my father were here."

"But he's not, so it's all on your shoulders," G.V. said. "So just take your time. Rome wasn't built in a day."

"But we don't have much time, G.V.," Dorothy said. "I've got to save the Wizard and Paper Boy. Rainbows don't last forever," she said.

"Not longer than a wink and blink of an eye," G.V. mumbled. "You want the good news or the bad news?"

"I don't care," Dorothy said. "You choose."

"Okay, the good news is that you know that Ima has the Wizard."

"What's the bad news?"

"You've got to go save him," G.V. smiled.

"And that's what I better go do," Dorothy asked, stepping onto the carpet.

"Any news you want to broadcast?" G.V. shrugged.

Dorothy took two steps, then stopped. "Tell them that Dorothy Gale of Orlando, Florida, is coming to save the Wizard!"

G.V. watched Dorothy and Bully Bear with the dictionary under his arm march off down the carpet path. "Good luck," he said to himself. "You'll need it."

Then the vines began to rumble with the news. Dorothy was coming.

CHAPTER 27

DEADLY GAME

"Hey, you old witch, let me go!" Paper Boy screamed.

Ima turned. She'd hooked him to the wall with a paper clip, which really amused her. "Another word out of you and I'll stick you on the paper holder on my desk," she warned, pointing to the sharp spike.

"What have I ever done to you?" he asked.

"You were with Dorothy," she said. She snapped her fingers and disappeared.

"Pssst," Ura said, trying to get the boy's attention.

"Are you callin' me?" Paper Boy asked.

"Are you all right?"

"I've been clipped before, but never like this," Paper Boy said, wiggling around, trying to get out.

"Is Dorothy coming?" Ura asked.

Paper Boy nodded. "She's on her way here to find the Wizard. Once he knows we're in trouble, we'll all be saved." He looked at Ura. "Who are you, anyway?"

"I'm the Wizard."

"Oh, great," Paper Boy sighed. "I'm clipped and you're whipped. If you ask me, Ruby ought to click those sneakers and say 'I'm outta here.'"

"Who's Ruby?" Ura asked.

"She's a pretty special girl," Paper Boy said.

Then the wind began to blow through the room. "The witch is coming back," Ura said.

Ima appeared in a flash of light. "Miss me yet?" she grinned.

"Like a toothache," Paper Boy frowned.

"You're askin' for it," she said. "Maybe I should just line my kitty box with you."

"You got a kitty?" Paper Boy asked.

From inside the petting zoo a lion roared loudly. "Want to meet him?" Ima asked, batting her eyes.

"No thanks, I'm allergic to cats," Paper Boy gulped.

"Let's play a game," Ima smiled. She flicked her fingers at the floor and a bottle appeared.

"What game's that?" Paper Boy asked, suspiciously.

"Spin the bottle! Haven't you ever played it before?"

"No, can't say I have!" Paper Boy said.

"I've invited a few party animals to play with you." Ima grinned.

The hall door burst open and a line of creatures straight out of a nightmare lumbered in. "Lift that obnoxious paper kid down and put him on the floor." The creatures did as ordered, lifted the paper clipped boy down, and set him next to the bottle.

"Now," Ima chuckled, raising her eyebrows, "who's got hot lips?"

A dozen creatures with drooling, horrible lips puckered them up to show her. One of the creatures' lips were smoldering like he'd been on fire. "You're first," she said, tapping the smoking beast.

Paper Boy cringed at the faces that stared at him. "Ah, I never kiss on the first date. Sorry, fellas." The creatures began to howl with delight.

"I'll just spin the bottle for you," Ima said, leaning over. She gave it a flip with her wrist and it whirled around and around, stopping on a one-eyed creature.

"Come on!" Paper Boy cried out. "This ain't fair."

"You don't like kissing?" Ima smiled, then turned as she noticed one of the little witches pulling at her cape. "And what do you want?"

The little witch screeched out in a high-pitched voice, "Have you heard the news?"

"What news?" Ima said, irritated.

"It's all over the grapevine. Dorothy's coming to save the Wizard," the little witch said.

"Tell her to hurry," Paper Boy said, looking at the creature getting ready to kiss him.

"We'll see about that," Ima said.

With a flash of electricity, Ima threw the image of Dorothy and her friends up onto the wall. "That girl doesn't know when to quit," Ima mumbled to herself.

Ima zeroed in closer on the image of Bully Bear, then clapped her hands three times, shouting, "Witches, witches, witches! All HAGs report to me."

From every door and window, dozens of witches of all shapes and sizes flew into the room. "Okay, girls, listen up," Ima said, pacing the room.

Then she stopped as another door flew open. "Sorry I'm late," said a ten-foot-tall witch with the ugliest face in the world. The wart on the end of her chin was twelve inches long with pig-bristle hairs sticking out.

"I wasn't sure you'd make it, Pig Foot," Ima said.

The big witch carried a crooked broom and dragged a third, deformed leg behind her. "I'm in a bad mood," she growled.

"Good," Ima cackled. "That's just the mood I like you in."

Ima looked at the other witches. "You see Yogi Bear there," she said darkly, pointing to the image of Bully Bear. The witches nodded.

"I'd like to have a nice bearskin rug and Teddy there would make a nice one." She pointed her finger at the crowd. "I want you all to go bring that fleabag to me right now!"

"Can I eat the dog?" Pig Foot asked.

"Later, if you're really, really bad," Ima smiled. "Now off with you. Go get me that Bully Bear."

With shrieks and howls, the witches turned their brooms and flew off.

"Does that mean we can stop the game?" Paper Boy asked. The creatures grumbled their disapproval.

"Let's play another game," Ima said.

"How 'bout let's play Where's Paper Boy?"

"How do you play that?" Ima asked.

"Well," Paper Boy said, "you just take this paper clip off me."

"Then what?"

"Then you close your eyes like Sleeping Beauty for 'bout a month and then you come lookin' for me."

The witch stood up and sent Paper Boy a look so chilling it made him shiver. "Ima doesn't play that game."

With a clap and a snap, Ima pointed to her desk. A pair of scissors lifted into the air, followed by her paperweight rock.

"Paper Boy doesn't play that game either," he moaned.

"Shut up before I shred you," Ima said. She twirled her arms and filled the room with smoke. When it cleared, the pair of scissors and the rock had taken form and were standing there, blinking their eyes.

Ima cackled and moved both her fists up and down. "One, two, three," she said, over and over. The scissors and rock began to get into the rhythm. "One, two, three," they said in unison with the witch.

"Now *you* say it," Ima commanded Paper Boy.

"No, thank you. I'd rather play spin the bottle with the Addams Family you invited over."

Ima took the paper clip off and sat the boy in front of the rock and scissors. "Now play!"

The rock and scissors counted, "One, two, three," and stood there with their fingers pointing to themselves.

"This is rigged!" Paper Boy said.

"And why's that," Ima chuckled.

"I lose no matter what I do." Paper Boy pointed to the rock. "I don't mind him always bein' the rock, 'cause paper wraps the rock."

"So what's wrong with that?" Ima asked.

"Nothin', it's him that ain't playin' fair," Paper Boy said, pointing to the scissors.

Ima looked at the scissors and shrugged. "You want him to be something he's not?"

Paper Boy sighed. "Scissors always cuts paper. That doesn't give me a chance and that's not fair."

"Life's not fair," Ima grinned, "but that's how the game's played anyway." Behind her, the image on the wall showed what Dorothy was doing.

Dorothy and Bully Bear kept an eye out for trouble as they walked along. "I hope that witch doesn't hurt Paper Boy," she said.

"Me too," Book Worm spoke up. Ozzie barked in agreement.

"Maybe she just wanted some paper to write you a note," Bully Bear said, trying to be helpful.

"Those are nice shoes," said someone behind them.

Dorothy stopped. There was a girl in a wheelchair coming up the path and she looked familiar.

"Well, thank you," Dorothy said. "I didn't hear you coming."

"These wheels are as silent as an Indian in moccasins," the girl grinned.

"Do I know you?" Dorothy asked, trying to place her face. Dorothy didn't notice the colors of the rainbow reflecting in the girl's hair.

"Are you following us?" Bully Bear asked.

"It's not always easy getting around in this thing," the girl smiled. "But that carpet you're walkin' on sure knows the best path."

Dorothy stopped and looked around. "Where are you going anyway?"

The girl shrugged. "Wherever life will take me. It's not easy being me when the me inside me wants to run and play. But I've learned to live with it."

"What happened to you?" Book Worm asked.

"I wasn't wearing a seat belt and..." the girl looked down. "I don't like talking about it."

Dorothy tried to change the subject. "I'm glad you like my shoes."

The girl's eyes brightened. "Those are the kind of shoes I'd love to wear if I..." she took a deep breath..."if I could walk again."

"Don't give up hope," Dorothy said, not knowing anything else to say.

"I don't," the girl said, "but it's hard, you know."

"You can follow behind us," Dorothy said, clutching the golden ruler.

"I won't be a pest," the girl smiled. Then the sky darkened above them. "Witches are coming," the girl whispered, looking around.

"Where?" Bully Bear asked. The girl pointed to the horizon. Hundreds of witches were approaching.

"What are we going to do?" Book Worm shouted, pulling at his hair and dropping his glasses.

"I'd run," the girl said. "That's what I would do if I could."

"Come on," Bully Bear said, "let's get outta here!"

Dorothy started to turn. "Good luck," the girl said.

Dorothy stopped and turned. "What are *you* going to do?" she asked.

The girl in the wheelchair shrugged. "I'll get by. If I can find a clear path to go down, I'll have a chance." Then she shook her head and smiled. "You run off as fast as those red flashy sneakers will carry you."

Dorothy looked down. "You want to wear them for a little while?"

"But they're yours."

Book Worm jumped up and down. "But those are your magic shoes and..."

Dorothy shrugged. "We look like we wear about the same size."

"And you want to walk in *my* shoes?" the girl asked.

"I'll never know what that's really like," Dorothy said, slipping off her ruby sneakers, "but these may help you get around." Dorothy placed the sneakers on the girl's lap.

Ozzie barked at the approaching witches. "Hurry, Dorothy," Bully Bear said.

The girl leaned over and slipped off her sneakers and handed them to Dorothy. "This is not a fair trade."

"It *feels* like the right thing to do," Dorothy said, slipping on the plain sneakers. "Listen, click the ruby sneakers together three times and you can get over any obstacle in your path."

"The witches are almost here!" Bully Bear cried out, running in circles.

"Click them now," Dorothy whispered.

"Are you sure?" the girl asked.

"I'm sure," Dorothy said.

The girl slipped them on and clicked them once.

"We've got to hide," Book Worm shouted.

The girl clicked them twice.

"Come on, Dorothy, or the witch will get us!" Bully Bear cried.

"I want to go to a land without barriers," the girl said, clicking her shoes for the third time.

"Good luck," Dorothy smiled, touching her with the golden ruler.

As it tingled in her hand, the girl in the wheelchair waved and disappeared in a blaze of color. For a moment Dorothy thought she saw a rainbow, but it was gone before she knew it.

Dorothy looked at the ruler. "Another inch is gone," she said to herself. She had only seven inches of good deeds left.

"Watch out!" Book Worm screamed.

Ozzie barked, jumping at the air. Suddenly, dozens of witches were upon them, pulling, hitting, biting and squealing.

"Help me, Dorothy!" Bully Bear screamed.

"I'm trying!" Dorothy shouted, but she was pinned down by two ugly hags who drooled in her face.

"Take the bear!" the ten-foot witch cried out.

Ten little witches grabbed at Bully Bear, pulling him by the fur.

"Ouch, ouch!" Bully Bear shrieked, trying to fight them off.

"I'm coming," Dorothy shouted, but the ten-foot witch stepped in her path.

"I'll deal with you later, girlie," the big witch hissed. Ozzie nipped at her black dress. "And I'll eat you later, mutt!" she shouted.

In another minute they were gone, carrying Bully Bear away with them. Dorothy watched them fly off.

Bully Bear cried out, "Save yourself, Dorothy."

"Maybe you should," Book Worm said, sitting down on his book. He looked very depressed.

"I can't do that," Dorothy said.

"Sure you can," Book Worm sighed with his face in his hands. "Just click the shoes and go home. I might do that if I were you."

Then he looked at the plain sneakers on Dorothy's feet. "Looks like you're stuck in Oz."

"But what should I do?" Dorothy asked, suddenly feeling very alone. Then the rainbow lady came to mind and Dorothy remembered their conversation:

> *"You've got to save the Wizard of Oz. It's up to you, Dorothy Gale of Orlando, Florida. It's all up to you."*
>
> *"But I'm just a kid and I want to go back to my family."*
>
> *"To get there you have to go to Oz. There's no other way. You have to help the Wizard. It's your responsibility now. You clicked the shoes."*

"And I just gave them away," Dorothy muttered to herself.

She looked off in the distance at the witches carrying Bully Bear. "It's all up to me," she whispered. "I've got to save them all."

CHAPTER 28

GATES OF OZ

Inside Ima's Castle Mountain, Bully Bear found himself stretched and pulled until he was flat as a rug. "You'll make a nice rug," Pig Foot the giant witch growled.

Bully Bear couldn't move his arms or legs but his mouth still worked. "But I don't want to be a rug."

"Tough luck, Yogi," Ima laughed.

"Where do you want him?" Pig Foot asked.

"Put him right there," Ima ordered, pointing to the space in front of her desk.

"Take it easy!" Bully Bear shouted as the little witches carried him roughly across the floor.

"Right there will do," Ima smiled. When they had spread Bully Bear out, Ima leaned down and looked at his face. "Are we comfy?"

"No!" Bully Bear said indignantly. "I don't want to be stepped on."

Ima made a sad face. "Maybe I should let Pig Foot use you for a three foot warmer."

Bully Bear looked at the huge witch. "Keep her off me!"

"Just be good and keep my tootsies warm at night, and maybe I won't turn you into a coat," Ima cackled, walking off.

Bully Bear saw Paper Boy, or what was left of him, sitting next to the rock and scissors. "What happened to you?" Bully Bear called out, moving his head around on the floor.

"Nothing a little Scotch tape won't fix," Paper Boy said.

The rock nudged him. "Let's play."

"Can't we rest for awhile, fellas?" Paper Boy asked.

Scissors shook his head. "Ima said we had to play until you were confetti."

"Oh, great," Paper Boy grumbled.

Pig Foot came up and tapped Ima on the shoulder. "You better look at this," she said, lumbering over to the image on the wall.

Ima looked at Dorothy's image. "What's it gonna take to stop this girl?"

Pig Foot snarled, "Why don't you cast a spell and turn her into a toad?"

"Look, you big dummy," Ima snapped. "If I were to turn her into a toad, then I'd be stuck with her in Oz forever."

"But she'd be just a toad," Pig Foot said.

"And she'd probably toadie up to some Prince Charming and turn back into her old, obnoxious self."

Ima walked around shaking her head. "If she'd just click the shoes and go home, everything would be all right."

Then an idea came to Ima's mind. "I've got it!" she shouted, snapping her fingers.

Ima disappeared with a poof. The door to the broom closet slammed closed and a boom of thunder shook the walls of the castle as she flew off.

Dorothy carried Book Worm's dictionary under her arm. She looked from side to side, more nervous than she'd ever been in her life.

"I hope this carpet knows where it's going," Book Worm moaned.

"Without a map, we've got no choice but to follow it."

"What's that?" Book Worm said, pointing to the two large soldier statues that the carpet was rolling towards.

"I don't know," Dorothy whispered.

She walked quietly until the carpet stopped between the large soldiers. Hanging at one side was a sign that said, GATES OF OZ.

"Halt!" shouted the statue on the left.

"Double halt!" the other one said.

Dorothy and Book Worm jumped to attention.

"Why are you trying to leave Oz?" the first soldier asked.

Dorothy gulped. "We're trying to find the Wizard."

"Then you're going in the wrong direction," the second soldier statue said flatly. "The Emerald City is in the other direction."

"You mean the Wizard's back in the Emerald City?" Dorothy exclaimed. "Did Ima let him go?"

"What are you talking about?" the first soldier said. "No Wizard ever leaves the Emerald City."

"Do you guys get the news out here?" Book Worm asked. Both of them shook their heads.

"Haven't you heard anything about what's going on?" Dorothy asked.

"What's going on?" the first soldier asked. "Oz is Oz. It always was, is, and will be."

Book Worm jumped up and down, trying to keep his glasses on. "But it's been all over the grapevine and..."

Both soldiers sighed. "We're allergic to grapes," the first one said sadly.

"Can't even get near a raisin or I break out into hives," the second one said.

"Well, the Wizard's been Wiznapped," Dorothy said.

"Wiznapped!" the first soldier exclaimed.

"Who's going to save him?" the second one shouted, dropping his gun.

"I am," Dorothy said flatly. Ozzie barked in agreement.

"You?" the first statue said.

"You're just a girl," the second said, sighing deeply.

"Girls can do anything you can do," Dorothy said indignantly.

"She's pretty tough," Book Worm added.

"But once you cross this line," the first soldier said, pointing to the black line on the ground. "You're entering the Witch Zone."

Dorothy looked at the line. On the Oz side, everything was green and lush. But on the Witch Zone side, everything was dead and brown.

"The Wizard's at Ima's Castle Mountain," Dorothy said.

"That certainly is in the Witch Zone," the first solider said, shaking his head.

"You sure you have the right address?" the second soldier asked.

"I'm sure," Dorothy said.

"Maybe you should call the Emerald City to see if the Wizard is back yet," the first soldier said.

"Do you have a phone?" Dorothy asked. Both soldiers shook their heads no. "Then why did you suggest it?"

"Just felt like it," he blushed, looking down.

Ima flew a wide circle overhead, listening to Dorothy's conversation. "So Dorothy would like to use a phone, would she?" With a twist and a turn, Ima's broom left a stream of smoke behind.

"Look up there!" Book Worm shouted, pointing towards the sky.

Written in big letters were the words:

DOROTHY PHONE HOME!

"I wonder if something's happened?" Dorothy gasped.

"But they don't have a phone here!" Book Worm frowned. "What are you going to do?"

"I guess there's nothing I *can* do," Dorothy said.

"What's that?" Book Worm shouted, pointing to the sky. Floating down on a parachute was a cellular phone.

"That's strange," Dorothy said, as the phone floated right into her hands.

Dorothy dialed her number and waited for someone to answer. Riding on her broom high up in the air, Ima held her fingers to her ears, using it as a phone.

"Dorothy, Dorothy, are you there?" Ima said, imitating Dorothy's mother.

"It's me, Mom! Can you hear me?" Dorothy said, feeling her heart thump.

"Oh, Dorothy, can't you come home right now? The moving truck is here and we don't want to leave without you."

"Mom, please don't move. Wait until I get home and..."

Ima put her hand over her mouth to hold back a laugh. Then she switched voices. "Dorothy, this is Dad. Come home now."

Tears rimmed Dorothy's eyes. "Daddy, Daddy, don't leave without me."

"I'm sorry, Pumpkin," Ima said in Dorothy's father's voice. "But if you don't drop the golden ruler and come home, we may never see you again."

Dorothy gasped. *That can't be my father talking. But his voice sounds so real.*

"Just click the shoes, Dorothy. Just click the shoes and come home. We don't want to lose you."

Tears came down her cheeks. Dorothy felt her whole world was breaking apart. "I miss you."

"I miss you, Pumpkin. And if you don't come back now, I'm afraid your mother and I will have to get divorced."

"No!" Dorothy cried.

"Yes," Ima said, throwing her head back in silent laughter. "So drop the ruler, click the shoes, and come home."

"But I can't, Daddy," Dorothy whispered. "I gave away the shoes."

"You what!" Ima shouted in her own voice, then changed back. "You what, Pumpkin?"

"I gave my shoes to a girl in a wheelchair. Now I don't know how I'm ever going to get home."

Ima flew into a blind rage, then zoomed straight towards the ground. "You'll never get home!" she shouted, diving straight into the ground.

Dorothy jumped back. "It was a witch trick!" Book Worm said, climbing up onto her shoulder.

"Do something!" Dorothy said to the soldiers, but they just ran off into the woods.

Ima tunneled just under the surface, turning up the ground like a mole wearing a witch's hat. Then she was gone.

"Where did she go?" Book Worm asked.

Ozzie sniffed at the ground and then began barking. "What's wrong, Ozzie?" Dorothy asked.

But before the dog could bark again, the ground underneath him exploded. Ima came flying up and grabbed the dog!

"Ozzie!" Dorothy cried.

Ima zoomed straight towards Dorothy, worms and fresh earth flying off her. "Duck, Dorothy!" Book Worm shouted.

Dorothy ducked just in time. Ima reached out to grab the ruler but snatched Book Worm instead.

"Don't let her take me," Book Worm screamed, trying to wiggle out of the witch's grasp.

"You can't take them!" Dorothy screamed, trying to grab the witch.

Ima moved around her like a sheep dog and then snatched Dorothy's backpack. The little Billikin statue fell out and landed near the black line.

Ima hovered just in front of Dorothy's face. "Now you listen to me, girl. I've got your friends, litter boy and bear rug, and now I've got this worm and hot dog."

"Let them go!" Dorothy demanded.

"I will," Ima said. "All you have to do is toss the golden ruler over the black line, over into the Witch Zone, and I'll let your friends go."

"What about the Wizard? Will you let him go?"

"The Wizard's mine," Ima cackled. "Now you either do what I say or all your friends will be dead before the bewitching hour."

"Never!" Dorothy shouted defiantly.

With a flash of light and a flurry of dust and wind, Ima flew in a tight circle, then sped off towards her castle.

Book Worm's voice echoed in the distance. "Save yourself, Dorothy." Ozzie kept barking until they faded away.

Dorothy sat down and began to cry. "That Wicked Witch took all my friends. And she even took the crystal ball," she sobbed.

"What am I going to do?" she said, wishing someone was there to help her.

Pulling herself together, Dorothy looked at the witch's castle in the distance. "I want my friends back," she said determinedly, holding the golden ruler into the air.

She walked over to the black line, the line that separated good from evil in the land called Oz. "All I have to do is leave the golden ruler and all my friends will be back," she whispered.

The ruler tingled in her hand as she neared the black line. "If I don't have my shoes to get back home, at least I can have my friends with me in Oz."

Stopping at the line, Dorothy held the golden ruler in the air. "Someone's got to save them," Dorothy said, trying to justify her actions.

"Don't do it," came a voice at her feet.

"Who said that?" Dorothy asked, looking around. Then she saw the little Billikin statue.

"Did you say something?" she asked, picking it up. But the statue didn't move.

"Guess it was just the wind," she mumbled to herself.

Dorothy looked at the golden ruler and gripped it tightly. "I can't let Oz down," she said. "Everyone is depending on me. I've got to go save them." The ruler vibrated in her hand, giving her strength.

Dorothy stepped onto the black line with the little Billikin in her hand. The winds in the Witch Zone began to moan ominously.

She nudged the red carpet forward but it wouldn't cross the line. "Now what am I going to do?" she worried. "I've been following your lead. Won't you go with me to the witch's castle?" But the carpet wouldn't budge.

"Well, thanks for everything," she said, reaching down to pat the carpet.

Straightening up, Dorothy looked at the Billikin statue. "It's just you and me, kid," she smiled, stepping into the Witch Zone.

The winds howled so loudly that she didn't hear the statue answer back. "A little Billikin goes a long way."

Dorothy had entered the most dangerous place in Oz. A place she had no choice but to enter.

Dorothy had been heading there since she entered Oz. She was on a collision course with fate that couldn't be avoided.

To save the Wizard, to save her friends, Dorothy had to enter the Witch Zone. There was no other choice and no other way home. If she was ever to go home again.

CHAPTER 29

HORRIBLE HOGS

Ima entered her castle window in a terrible mood. She could feel it in her soul. Dorothy had crossed the black line and had entered the Witch Zone.

"Put me down," Book Worm shouted.

Ima opened her hand up. "Quiet or I'll stick a fishhook through you, fish bait," she said, closing her fingers.

Ozzie jumped from her arms and hid behind a stack of old brooms. "You can run but you can't hide forever," she said, peering at the dog through the broom handles.

Putting away her broom, Ima burst through the door. "Did you bring me the dog?" Pig Foot asked, walking towards Ima. Her third, misshapen leg hung behind her.

"He's in there," Ima said, nodding towards the broom closet. "Find him and he's yours."

Pig Foot loped off, smacking her lips. Ima opened her hand and dropped Book Worm onto her desk. "Now, let's play a game, shall we?"

Paper Boy looked over. "Don't trust her," the little piece of him that was left said.

"What happened to you?" Book Worm asked.

"She rigged the game against him," Bully Bear answered.

Book Worm turned. His eyes went blank when he saw the bear rug laying on the floor.

Ima chuckled. "Ready to play, my little maggot?"

"Play what?" Book Worm said, looking around for a book to hide in.

"Let's sing first, okay?" she smiled.

"What song?" Book Worm said.

Ima Witch smiled and imitated Mr. Rogers. “Boys and girls. You know the song:

> ‘This old witch,
> She played one,
> She squished the maggot
> With her thumb...’ ”

Ima brought her thumb down towards Book Worm who rolled around on the desk. Ima laughed and continued:

> “With a smack it, whack it
> Give a witch a broom,
> You will never leave this room.”

“Keep running, Book Worm,” Bully Bear said, wishing he could help.

“Will someone go spill something hot on fleabag over there?” Ima said.

Pig Foot stuck her head out of the broom closet. “You call me?”

“You just catch the weener dog,” Ima snapped.

She looked at Book Worm. “Ready to sing some more?” she asked.

“You’re no Mr. Rogers!” Book Worm screamed from behind her pencil box.

“And you’re not a lucky duck today,” she laughed, then began to sing again:

> “This old witch
> She played two,
> She stomped the maggot
> With her shoe...”

In a flash she slipped off her black shoe and began banging the desk, trying to squash Book Worm. She sang as she pounded:

> “This old witch
> She played three
> She put me in her mouth
> And swallowed me...”

With a quick grab, Ima scooped Book Worm up and dangled him above her mouth.

"No!" he screamed.

"Yes!" she cackled, and popped him in her mouth. With a gulp he was gone.

"You ate him!" Bully Bear cried.

"You're a cannibal!" Paper Boy screamed.

Ima cleared her throat then belched loudly. "Ura is over there," she said, pointing to the Wizard. "Itsa is here," she smiled, holding up her necklace. "Ima is here," she nodded, touching her chest. "And you both know about Inna."

"Inna?" Bully Bear and Paper Boy said in unison.

"Yeah," Ima grinned. "Book Worm. He's inna here," she cackled, pointing to her stomach.

Ura moaned. "You shouldn't have done that."

"But I did and it's over."

"You'll never rule Oz. Not in a million years!" Ura shouted, struggling to get the snakes to let him go.

A noise like falling brooms sounded from the broom closet. "Did you catch that stupid dog?" Ima shouted.

Pig Foot knocked over a stand of flying brooms. "Not yet! But when I do, I'm gonna eat him," she growled.

Ozzie crawled under the tables, behind the chairs and around the broom stands.

"You can't hide forever," Pig Foot said, getting down on her hands and knees.

Ima burped. "I should have washed him first," she said, shaking her head. Inside her stomach, Book Worm slipped deeper and deeper into the darkness.

Ima belched again. "Pig Foot, forget the dog and tell the Horrible Hogs to saddle up."

"You want to let the *hogs* loose?" Pig Foot said, her eyes wide with fear.

"Tell them to go get that little girl and bring her back here. Dead or alive."

Pig Foot stumbled off down the hall, her useless third leg dragging behind her. Down through the dark and dank castle hallways she went, past locked rooms of monsters and terrible things.

In the stable, Pig Foot stopped at the door. "Ima wants you to go now," she said, shivering at the sight of the Horrible Hogs.

Standing before her, ten big Horrible Hogs, crusted with warts and covered with battle scars, grunted towards her.

"Ima says to go get the girl named Dorothy and bring her back."

"Alive?" grunted a grungy Horrible Hog, moving its tusks up and down.

"Dead or alive," Pig Foot answered. "But I think she'd rather have her alive."

"Let's go," grumbled the biggest Horrible Hog. Pig Foot slipped away, not wanting to watch the mean warriors of darkness put on their battle gear.

Within minutes, the Horrible Hogs rode out on their half-horses-half-rhinos to get Dorothy.

In the dark, leafless forest that surrounded Castle Mountain, Dorothy walked along feeling shivers and goose bumps run up and down her arms.

"This is worse than going to the principal's office," she said, trembling as a half-horse-half-coyote galloped by howling.

A vulture looked down and flapped its wings. "Leave me alone," she said, ducking as a pack of two-headed bats and flying rats shot past.

She passed a sign which said, SCENIC ROUTE, but closed her eyes at the burned-out houses, gallows and graveyards she passed.

Signs for ELM STREET, FEAR STREET and other bad places lined the way. A calendar on a tree said Friday the 13th. Dorothy ripped the page down but the one under it was the same.

Images of all the horror movies she'd ever seen or heard about passed through her mind. "I'll never watch another bad movie again," she whispered.

"I wish I were home," she said, her lip quivering. "I wish I were back in Orlando with my mom and dad."

She felt the ruler tingle in her hand. "I won't let you down," she said. "But without the ruby sneakers, I don't know how I'll ever get home."

Then she looked at the little Billikin statue. "I wish I had someone to talk to," she whispered.

"Will you give me an exclusive story?" G.V. asked from behind, startling her.

Dorothy spun around. "G.V.! Am I ever glad to see you."

"Don't think I'm bringing you good news, 'cause I'm not," the vine said, as he crept along the ground.

"Why on earth are you here?"

"I keep telling you, you're in Oz."

"But this is the Witch Zone. You shouldn't have come," Dorothy said.

"Look, I have a chance to host *Eyewitness News*. With the story I've already filed, I know I'll get the job."

"Already filed?" she said.

"Sure," G.V. shrugged. "This can only end in disaster. So I wrote a general piece about how hard you tried and how you died fighting the witch."

"That's *not* very encouraging," Dorothy said. "Then why are you here?"

"'Cause I just wanted to get some pictures of myself with you before all the action starts. It'll look good in my bio."

"Pictures?"

"Yeah," G.V. said, taking out his camera. "This thing's got an automatic flash, so if you'll just stand there," he said, putting the camera down, "it'll get a good picture of us both."

G.V. set the timed shutter and crept over to Dorothy. "Smile," he grinned. "Say grapevine."

"I don't know why I'm doing this," Dorothy grumbled.

"Everybody wants to be a star for fifteen minutes in their lives. Your tragic story will make a great movie of the week."

The camera clicked. G.V. crept along the ground and took the photo out. "Let's see how we look," he said, waiting for it to develop.

"Ah, look at this," he said, handing the picture to Dorothy.

She watched the picture come into focus. "You look good," Dorothy said.

G.V. nodded. "And so do you," he said, looking at Dorothy's image. "And so does..." G.V. turned around, "he."

"Oh my gosh!" Dorothy exclaimed, looking at the face of the Horrible Hog in the picture. G.V.'s vine curled up and shot towards the brush.

"Grab her," the hog grunted from behind. Dorothy tried to shake herself loose but the Horrible Hog's grip was too tight and she didn't want to drop the golden ruler or the Billikin.

"What's this?" the hog asked, looking at the statue in Dorothy's hand.

"Get rid of it," said another.

The hog holding Dorothy knocked it from her hands. "Let's go!" he shouted. "Ima's waiting."

The Horrible Hog put Dorothy across its saddle and the band of evil creatures rode off in the darkness towards Castle Mountain and Ima's bewitching hour.

G.V. stuck his head out from the dead brush. "Guess I better go," he said, wishing there was a different ending.

Then he saw the little statue come alive. "Where you going?" G.V. shouted, as the statue began running after the Horrible Hogs.

"Dorothy needs me," was all the statue said.

G.V. fluttered his lips. "I hope they're payin' me by the word," he grumbled, creeping along the ground, trying to keep the little Billikin statue in view.

CHAPTER 30

CAPTURED!

The Horrible Hogs carried Dorothy to Ima's upper dungeon room. "Here's the girl," the biggest hog grunted, putting Dorothy down.

"Well done, handsome," Ima smiled, looking up from her newspaper. The hogs marched off leaving Dorothy standing there.

"Have you read the paper today?" Ima asked.

"What paper?" Dorothy asked.

Ima held up a copy of *The Witch Times*. The headline read:

DOROTHY FAILS TO SAVE OZ!

"It's time to give up, little girl," Ima whispered. "Just give the ruler to me and I'll let you go."

"Where are my friends?" Dorothy asked, looking around.

"I'm over here, Dorothy," Bully Bear called out.

"Oh, no. You poor thing," Dorothy said.

"I'm over here," Paper Boy cried. All that was left of him was a small piece of paper. The rest of him was in shreds.

"What have you done to them?" Dorothy shouted, trying to hit Ima with her hands.

"Stand back!" Ima shouted.

"Where's Book Worm?" Dorothy asked.

Ima shrugged. "He had a dinner date."

"She ate him!" Bully Bear screamed.

"That's not exactly true," Ima said. "I swallowed him. Maybe if I'd chewed him up a little, I wouldn't have such indigestion," she sighed, rubbing her stomach.

The Wizard called out from over the tank of swimming monsters. "Dorothy. Dorothy. Over here."

"You must be the Wizard," she said.

"Sorry we had to meet this way," he said. "But I'm glad you came."

"This is not old home week," Ima snapped. Then she looked at the ruler. "You've only got seven inches left! Give it to me!"

"Not on your life," Dorothy said, backing up.

"Then it will be on *your* life," Ima said, creeping forward.

Pig Foot came into the room. "Let me have her."

"Later," Ima whispered. "First I need to have the ruler."

"Don't let her have it," Ura shouted.

Ima stopped and smiled. "I know how to handle this," she grinned. "Pig Foot, you come with me."

Ima made Pig Foot dissolve, then snapped her fingers and disappeared. The door to the head room slammed shut behind her.

Dorothy turned to the Wizard. "Let's get out of here," she said.

"Can't," the Wizard sighed. "Look over there." Sitting in front of the doorway was Itsa Dragon, who blew a long stream of fiery smoke towards them.

"How did you ever get into this mess in the first place?" Dorothy asked.

"Because I failed to listen to good advice and instead, just ruled Oz with my finger to the wind and bent like a tree trying to please everyone."

Dorothy shook her head. "And now we're all in a jam because you wanted to please everyone."

"I know," the Wizard sighed. "I really blew it."

"There's got to be a way out," Dorothy said, looking around.

In the head room, Ima handed Pig Foot a man's head. "Now put this on," she said. Pig Foot took off her own head and put on one that was identical to Dorothy's father. "Just keep that third leg up under your coat," she warned.

"I will," Pig Foot said in Dorothy's father's voice.

Ima took off her own head and lifted one that looked like Dorothy's mother off the shelf. Slipping it on, she adjusted it, then asked, "How do I look, dear?"

"You look wonderful." The face of Dorothy's father smiled.

Dorothy knelt next to Bully Bear. "Does it hurt?"

"Only when someone steps on me," he sighed.

"What can I do?" she asked.

"Just think of something. That's why we came with you in the first place."

Then the door of the head room banged open. Dorothy turned and gasped. Standing there were her mother and father.

"Dorothy," the head of her mother said. "Let's go home."

"That's right," her father's head said, "aren't you tired of all this?"

Dorothy felt like her heart was bursting. She closed her eyes, trying to remember what Mother Rainbow had told her:

> *"Follow your heart and don't be fooled. Trust in the golden ruler and trust your own values."*

She saw through the trick when she spotted the third leg under Pig Foot. "You're not my parents. You're just another witch's trick."

Ima snapped her fingers and her own head appeared. Then she snapped at Pig Foot and the tall witch's own head appeared, only it was on backwards. "Oh, rats," Ima said. "I'll fix you later," she told her, pushing the huge witch away.

Ima stepped towards Dorothy. "Don't hurt her," Ura pleaded. "Oz needs her."

"Time for you to take a little swim," she hissed, throwing up her hands. The snakes dropped the Wizard down into the tank of monsters.

Ima walked over and parted the waters. Ura fell to the bottom. On both sides, the monsters swam, trying to reach him.

Then she grabbed up Bully Bear and tossed him in with the Wizard. "What are you doing?" Dorothy asked.

"You'll see," Ima cackled, scooping up what was left of Paper Boy with a dustpan and dropping him into the vat. The pieces of paper fluttered down like confetti.

Dorothy grabbed the witch's arm. "Don't do that again," Ima hissed.

Grabbing a bucket, Dorothy filled it with water and tossed it on the witch. Ima spun around screaming, smoke rising from her.

"I didn't want to have to do that," Dorothy said, watching the witch writhe in agony.

But then Ima stopped and burst out laughing. "That worked in the old days, but not any longer!" she shouted.

Ozzie came running up and jumped into Dorothy's arms. "Oh, Ozzie," she said, cuddling the dog.

"Oh, Ozzie," Ima mimicked. "You make me sick." She walked over to the tank. "Are you all ready to play a little Marco Polo?"

"Don't do that, please," Dorothy pleaded.

"Oh it's *please* now, is it?" Ima said.

"Yes. Please let us go."

Ima shook her head. "I want the golden ruler. Then we'll talk."

"I won't give it to you," Dorothy said firmly.

"I want it *now*!" Ima said, grabbing at Dorothy.

"No!" she shouted, pushing against Ima's stomach.

Ima coughed and belched. "I think I'm getting sick," she said, then coughed up Book Worm.

Pulling him from her throat, she tossed him down into the tank. "Now all your friends are together."

"Let us go," Dorothy said.

Ima pointed her finger at Dorothy and lifted her and the dog into the air. She left them dangling above the tank, then set them down with the others.

"I'll be back in five minutes. That's the bewitching hour. If you don't give me the ruler, then I'll let you all play with my fishes."

"Come on, Itsa," she said, calling to the dragon. With a slow flap of its wings, the dragon flew back onto the necklace around the witch's neck. With a puff of smoke, Ima was gone.

Bully Bear sighed. "What a revoltin' development this turned out to be."

"You can say that again," the Wizard said, looking at Dorothy.

"What are we going to do?" Dorothy said, looking at her friends and then at the monsters swimming around them.

"Grab this!" shouted a tiny voice from above.

Dorothy looked up and saw the little Billikin tossing them a rope. "Little Billikin," she said.

"Hurry," he whispered, "you don't have much time. The witch will be back soon."

"Don't leave without me," Paper Boy said. "Just splash some water on me."

"Water?" Dorothy said.

"I'm papier-mâché. I'll come back together."

Dorothy splashed water on the bits and pieces of paper then watched in amazement as they fused back together. "Nothing like gettin' your act together," Paper Boy winked.

"Come on, Dorothy," the Wizard said, "we've got to go."

"What about Bully Bear?" Dorothy asked, looking at the rug.

The bear wiggled his neck around and life came back into his body. "How did you do that?" Dorothy asked.

Bully Bear sat up and stretched. "It was just like hibernating. Don't you guys ever read *National Geographic*?"

Book Worm looked up at the Billikin. "I need a bath so let's hurry."

Each one helped the other up the rope. After they had all climbed out, Dorothy looked around the room. "The hallway is clear," she whispered. "Let's go."

"What about him?" Bully Bear asked, pointing to the statue.

"Good-bye, Dorothy," the little Billikin waved. "That's all I can do," he shouted, and then he disappeared.

"A little Billikin really did go a long way," Dorothy said.

"Better than the cavalry," Paper Boy said. "Now let's split!"

Ima watched their images from her darkest room in the castle. She turned to Pig Foot. "They're all yours," she cackled. The ten-foot witch with the third leg lumbered off.

CHAPTER 31

ESCAPE!

G.V. crept slowly up the staircases of Ima's castle. "I should never have come," he mumbled. "I should have left well enough alone. Now I'll be stuck writing obituaries for the rest of my life."

To keep from getting scared, G.V. thought up headlines for his stories. "Let's see, G.V. GOES INSIDE THE WITCH'S CASTLE. No, that's not strong enough. How about, FEARLESS REPORTER BRAVES DEATH AND DESTRUCTION. No, maybe it should read, DARING REPORTER PUTS GRAPES ON THE LINE TO GET STORY!"

He shook his head. "Still sounds kind of wimpy."

G.V. cocked his leaf. He heard a strange buzzing sound and curled up under a chair. "Doesn't sound like happy chatter to me," he mumbled under his breath.

A group of the witch's Warrior Wasps flew slowly down the hall, moving their stingers up and down. "Buzz off," he whispered.

One of the Warrior Wasps turned towards him. G.V. froze, pretending to be a regular plant. After they'd gone by, his vine was still trembling inside. "I don't like going undercover to get a story. Too dangerous."

"What's that?" he whispered, feeling a breeze. Coming towards him was a pack of little witches.

After they had flown by, G.V. shook his head. "There's a lot of who, what and when happening somewhere in here, and I think I'm about to find out the how and I don't like it," he moaned, wishing he had never come in the first place.

"Maybe the headline should read, G.V. IS THE MOST FEARLESS REPORTER IN THE WORLD! That sounds better." He nodded.

Creeping along, staying as close to the wall as possible, G.V. heard the sound of approaching footsteps. "What next?" he mumbled.

Hiding behind a big urn, G.V. whispered a broadcast into his vine:

> **"This is G.V. and I'm right in the middle of the biggest story of the century. Dorothy is locked somewhere in the witch's castle. I hope to get her final words before they finish her."**

Then he squeezed the vine. "Cancel that copy," he whispered into the vine, "and run with this:

> **This is G.V., the world's most fearless reporter. I've fought off the witch's demons to bring you a firsthand account of the death of Dorothy Gale. She died in my arms, thanking me for my bravery, urging me to go on a high-paid speaking tour to tell her last words to the world."**

"What are you talking about?" Dorothy said, tapping him on the vine.

"Dorothy, I thought you were...you were...well, you know," G.V. blushed.

"No, I'm not dead."

"Do you know the way out?" Paper Boy asked. "The witch party hour is coming at midnight and I want outta here."

"I'm just a news hound," G.V. said. "I just came here to follow the leads."

"That means no," Paper Boy said, disgustedly.

"What happens at the bewitching hour?" Bully Bear asked.

"You don't want to know," G.V. said. "All I can tell you is that you'll wish you were a teddy bear or one of the Three Bears when they get through with you."

"But how do we get out of here?" Book Worm said, pushing his glasses back up.

"I think I know the way," the Wizard said.

"Good, I'll follow along," G.V. said, winking at Dorothy.

"Do I have time for another quick broadcast?" G.V. asked.

Paper Boy shook his head and followed behind the Wizard. "This is like the blind leading the blind," he mumbled to himself.

They crept slowly down the hall. "Lions and tigers and bears," Bully Bear mumbled.

"Will you be quiet," Book Worm said.

"Yeah," G.V. frowned, "that's an earlier story."

"Okay," Bully Bear whispered, pointing into the room they just passed. He began humming.

"What are you trying to tell us?" Paper Boy asked in disgust.

"Follow the yellow brick road," Bully Bear sang out, pointing with both paws.

The room was filled with yellow bricks. "There's my road!" the Wizard exclaimed.

"That's a front page story!" G.V. shouted. "I gotta call this story in."

He put his mouth to the grapevine and started sending out the story:

> **"This is G.V. and I have just found the yellow brick road. All of Oz will have G.V., the world's greatest news hound, to thank for bringing back one of the great historical treasures of Oz."**

Then G.V. stopped and made a face. "Funny, I can't get a message through. Feels like the vine's down or somethin'."

"Good. Now say good-bye and hit the bricks. We gotta get outta here," Paper Boy said.

"But my yellow brick road!" the Wizard exclaimed.

Dorothy shrugged. "We can always come back for it."

Bully Bear looked at her like she was crazy. "That'll be the day. Let's get out of this castle before they turn me into a Care Bear."

"What's wrong with my vine?" G.V. said, shaking it. "It feels kind of loose," he puzzled, pulling on it. *"It is loose!"* he exclaimed.

"Come on," the Wizard said taking two steps. Then he stopped dead in his tracks. The others bumped against him.

"What's wrong now?" Paper Boy said in disgust.

"L...l...look," the Wizard whispered. Standing at the end of the hall was Pig Foot. She was holding a pair of scissors in her hand.

"She cut my vine!" G.V. exclaimed. "That's vine service property. I'll sue!"

"I'm going to get you!" Pig Foot bellowed.

"Come on," G.V. shouted, "next thing she'll be saying is Fe..."

Pig Foot took a step forward. "...Fi, Fo, Fum, I smell the blood of..."

"Run!" Bully Bear screamed, and they all followed behind him.

Pig Foot came howling behind them. Ima watched from her room. "That's good. Chase them up here, you big clodhopper."

Pig Foot picked up her useless leg so she could run faster. "I'm gonna eat the worm, *and* the bear *and* the dog," she screamed.

"Big appetite that woman has," Paper Boy said. "Glad she's leavin' me out."

"And I'll use *you* for a napkin!" Pig Foot shrieked.

"She's gaining on us!" Book Worm screamed, holding onto Dorothy.

G.V. wrapped himself around the Wizard's leg and held on as tightly as he could. "I wish I had a cellular vine," he mumbled. "What a story this would make!"

Bully Bear came to a hallway with three directions to choose from. "Which way?" he wondered out loud in panic.

Dorothy took over. "Follow me!" she shouted. Ozzie followed behind, barking as loudly as he could.

Soon the Warrior Wasps, little witches and Horrible Hogs were following behind. The howling and growling echoed throughout the halls of Castle Mountain.

There was a tall door at the end of the hallway. Dorothy banged against it, trying to get in.

"Open it!" the Wizard shouted.

"It's stuck," Dorothy said.

"Hurry," Bully Bear said, watching the horde of beasts led by Pig Foot come rushing towards them.

Dorothy threw her body against the door and it opened. Standing in front of them was Ima, and behind her the strange, ugly shadow with the witch's hat.

"I've been waiting for you," the witch cackled. "It's one minute 'til midnight. Give me the ruler or you all will die a horrible death!"

Bully Bear and Book Worm cowered behind Dorothy. The Wizard stood beside them. Only Paper Boy had the courage to stand next to Dorothy.

"Don't give it to her," he whispered, squeezing her hand.

Behind them, the creatures of the night crawled into the room.

"Give me the golden ruler," Ima said, stretching out her hand. The winds of the open window behind them howled as a storm began building.

Ima's nailed fingers clawed the air in front of Dorothy's face. Drawing all the strength of her being, Dorothy pretended to hand the ruler to the witch.

"That's a girl," Ima whispered.

"Here!" Dorothy shouted, smacking the witch's hand as hard as she could. The ruler blazed and seemed to stick for a moment to Ima's skin.

"Nooooooooo!" Ima screamed, then she slumped to the floor. Suddenly the room was wracked with thunder and bolts of electricity.

Ima's beautiful face began to crack open. "What's happening?" Book Worm asked.

"Looks like an ugly coming out party," Paper Boy whispered.

As the pieces of her face fell off, her true nature emerged. The face of the ugliest witch in the world blinked and hissed, still dazed from the golden ruler.

On her head was a peaked witch's black hat. Her long, stubbly chin had bristle hair that twitched on the end of a four inch black wart.

"Where's a camera when I need one?" G.V. moaned.

"She'd break the lens," Paper Boy whispered. "Man, is she ugly."

Then Ima collapsed onto the floor. "Is she dead?" Bully Bear asked.

The Wizard shook his head. “I think you stunned her.”

“What happened?” Dorothy asked.

The Wizard put his hand on Dorothy’s shoulder. “She used a spell to hide her ugly face.”

Paper Boy looked at the ruler. “You lost another inch.”

All the little witches in the castle hovered around Ima’s body. The Wizard looked at Dorothy. “Free the Munchkins. Save them from this fate.”

“I’ll try,” Dorothy said.

Taking a deep breath, she waved the ruler in a long sweeping arc and touched each one. They all began to glow and in a burst of color, changed back into the Munchkins.

Paper Boy shook his head. “There goes another inch,” he sighed. “You’re down to just five inches.”

Dorothy waved the ruler at the beasts, who backed away. “Don’t waste it on them,” Paper Boy pleaded.

The beasts in the room ran off in fear with Pig Foot leading the way. The Munchkins blinked and rubbed their eyes.

“Thank you, thank you!” they shouted, hugging Dorothy.

“There’s no time for that!” the Wizard shouted. “Go get the yellow bricks and meet us at the Gates of Oz.” The Munchkins ran off.

Bully Bear looked at the ugly Wicked Witch. “She’s coming to.”

“Now what do we do?” Paper Boy asked.

“Should we take her broom?” Book Worm asked.

The Wizard shook his head. “We can’t all fit on it.”

Paper Boy looked out the window. “I’ve got an idea,” he said.

“What?” Bully Bear asked.

“You’ll see,” Paper Boy said. Standing at the window ledge, the papier-mâché boy began changing shape.

“My gosh,” Dorothy said, watching him stretch and stretch until he was shaped like a paper airplane.

“Get on,” he said.

“Are you sure you can carry us all?” the Wizard asked.

"I'm the only game in town," Paper Boy said. "And she's waking up." Ima's hands were grasping at the air like a creature pawing in the dark.

"Get on, quick!" Book Worm shouted.

Ima got to her knees. "I'll get you!" she hissed, looking at Dorothy. "You'll never escape from me!"

Dorothy saw her backpack in the corner and grabbed it. "You leave us alone. You've done enough damage."

"I'll follow you to the ends of Oz."

"Come on, Dorothy," the Wizard shouted.

"Where should I sit?" she asked, standing beside the paper plane.

"Sit here," Bully Bear said, pulling Dorothy beside him. Ozzie barked and jumped onto her lap.

"What about me?" G.V. said, feeling left out, looking over his leaf at Ima crawling towards him.

"Get on up here," the Wizard said.

"See you later, you uglygator," Paper Boy said, winking at Ima. "Everybody hang on," he shouted, flying out the window with all his friends on board.

"Do you know where you're going?" Book Worm shouted.

"Little late to be asking the pilot that," Paper Boy snickered, heading straight into the clouds.

Itsa Dragon flew into the room and licked Ima back to her senses. The wicked witch looked at the clock. There were thirty seconds left to the bewitching hour.

"I've got to stop them from leaving the Witch Zone," she said, pulling herself up. Itsa crawled back into her necklace.

Using her broom as a cane, she adjusted her witch's hat, climbed up onto the ledge and muttered into the night an evil chant:

> "Star light, star bright,
> Witch's star that lights the night.
> Wish I may,
> Wish I might,
> Catch them at the stroke of midnight."

With a shriek she jumped out and sped through the darkness on her broom after Dorothy and her friends. The dragon's red eyes glowed in the darkness.

"Hold on!" Paper Boy shouted.

The wind was so strong that it took all Dorothy's strength to keep from falling off. "I'm falling!" she screamed.

"Grab her!" Paper Boy shouted, trying to stay on course.

Dorothy's fingers slipped away. The Wizard reached out but couldn't grab her.

"Bye, Dorothy," Bully Bear whispered.

G.V. took a breath and mumbled. "Faster than a speeding computer. More powerful than CNN. Able to make it to the Oprah Winfrey show..."

He uncurled his full vine and shot forward. "It's G.V. to the rescue!" he shouted, winding around Dorothy's waist and pulling her back up.

"Thanks, G.V."

"Just don't tell my editor. We're not supposed to get involved with a story."

"Hold on, Ruby. We're gonna make it."

"She's coming!" Book Worm shouted, pointing behind them. They all heard the witch's shrieking screams and turned. Ima Witch was zooming towards them, her black cape flapping behind her.

"Are those her eyes glowing?" Bully Bear whispered, watching the glowing red eyes come closer.

"Those are her dragon's eyes," Paper Boy shouted.

"Hurry," the Wizard said. "The edge of Oz is just ahead."

In front of them were clear skies. Behind them was the Witch Zone and the end of them all.

"Please let us make it," Dorothy prayed.

"Hold on like a possum in a storm," Paper Boy said and dipped down, flying loop-de-loops and figure eights across the sky, trying to elude the witch.

"Give me the ruler or I'll shoot you down!" Ima shouted, throwing lightning bolts from her fingertips. Itsa shot his tongue out, trying to grasp the ruler, but he missed.

"Don't do it, Dorothy!" Paper Boy shouted, diving away from Ima's grasp.

But Ima's broom was faster than the paper airplane. "We're not gonna make it," Bully Bear said. Ima was now in front of them, blocking their way.

"Yes, we will!" Paper Boy shouted, diving straight towards the ground.

Ima tried to block their way but Paper Boy pulled up within inches of the ground and slipped under her. The dragon's tongue slithered over Dorothy as they loop-de-looped around the witch.

"Hurry, hurry!" Dorothy said. The edge of Oz was only a hundred yards ahead.

"You'll never make it!" Ima shouted, kicking her broom into high gear. Doing a witch's wheelie, Ima came straight at them with her broom pointing up. Itsa hissed fire and breathed smoke.

"Look, it's a rainbow," G.V. said.

"In the Witch Zone?" the Wizard wondered.

"You got luck, Ruby," Paper Boy said.

"Just good friends," Dorothy smiled as the rainbow came between them and the witch.

From inside the rainbow, Dorothy saw a face. "Hurry," Mother Rainbow said, "you don't have much time."

Ima crashed against the shield of goodness that surrounded the rainbow and twirled towards the ground.

"When she hits the ground, she's a goner," Book Worm exclaimed.

Itsa let loose a burst of fire and Ima pulled herself up at the last moment and flew back up.

"I'll get you, Dorothy Gale! You're not through with the Wicked Witch yet!" Itsa stuck his tongue out, but it couldn't get through the rainbow.

Paper Boy glided down to a safe landing just past the black line that divided Oz from the Witch Zone. "We made it!" Dorothy shouted.

"And look who's coming!" the Wizard smiled.

The Munchkins were racing towards the Gates of Oz with all the bricks from the yellow brick road.

The red carpet rolled up and stopped in front of them. "You waited," Dorothy smiled.

Paper Boy changed back into his papier-mâché boy body. "I think we better make tracks," he said, pointing to the rainbow. "That thing's fading fast."

"To the Emerald City!" the Wizard shouted, stepping onto the red carpet.

"But I want to go home," she said, trying to hand the Wizard the golden ruler.

"Give it to me when we get to the Emerald City," he said. "Now lead the way."

G.V. shouted to anyone who would listen. "If Oprah or Phil Donahue call, I'm available any time."

Dorothy stepped onto the carpet, followed by all her friends. The Munchkins brought up the rear, laying the yellow brick road behind them.

CHAPTER 32

THE EMERALD CITY

The citizens of Oz lined the streets of the Emerald City to welcome the return of the Wizard. Dorothy had never seen such a happy crowd of people.

"You're a hero," Paper Boy smiled, stepping up onto a platform erected for their return.

"No, you are," she said. "We all are," she smiled, hugging her friends.

"Speech, speech!" came shouts from the crowd.

The Wizard climbed up to the podium and held up his hands for silence. "I owe it all to Dorothy," he shouted. "She saved me and the land of Oz."

"Long live Dorothy!" shouted the crowd.

"And," the Wizard said, putting his arm around Dorothy, "I hope she will live with us for the rest of her life."

"But I want to go home now," she said.

"What did you do with the ruby sneakers?" the Wizard asked, then stopped. "I can see it in your eyes. That was a thoughtful thing to do."

"I just felt like helping her out," Dorothy said, thinking about the girl in the wheelchair.

"You can give me the golden ruler now," the Wizard said.

Dorothy started to hand it to him, then stopped. "Will you help my friends get what they want in life?" she asked.

Bully Bear kicked the ground. "That's all right, Dorothy. We'll get by."

Dorothy shook her head. "Will you?" she asked the Wizard.

"I'm not sure I can," he said, wanting Dorothy to discover what was inside her.

"Then what kind of Wizard are you anyway?" she challenged. The crowd hushed.

"That a girl, Ruby," Paper Boy whispered, giving her a wink of encouragement.

"What a story," G.V. said from the side. "Definitely an Ozitzer Prize."

Dorothy held the golden ruler up and stood in front of her friends. "Each of you gave of yourself. Each of you wants to be better," Dorothy said.

She looked at the ruler. There were just five inches of gold left. *Maybe one will get me home*, she thought. She counted her three friends. *That leaves two for safety*, she nodded.

Standing in front of Bully Bear, Dorothy said, "Bully Bear, for helping me save the Wizard and learning the true meaning of compassion, I urge you to treat others like you want to be treated."

With a tap on his shoulder, a golden glow came over the bear. "Thanks, Dorothy," he smiled.

Dorothy winked. "You deserve it," she said, kissing him on his fuzzy cheek.

Next she stopped in front of Book Worm, who had managed to find another dictionary to live in. "And you, Book Worm. For your courage and intelligence and for learning the importance of being humble and telling the truth, I urge you to treat others like you want to be treated."

She tapped him on the shoulder and he too was enveloped by a golden glow. "Thank you, Dorothy," he grinned.

"I couldn't have done it without you," she smiled, kissing him also on the cheek.

"What about me?" Paper Boy said.

Dorothy stopped in front of her paper friend. "And you, Paper Boy. You who has learned the value of not cutting corners and being honest, I urge you to treat others like you want to be treated."

With a sweep of her arm, Dorothy brought the golden ruler down onto his shoulder. Paper Boy sparkled in the golden glow of goodness.

G.V. crawled up from the side. "Dorothy, the rainbow's fading. Word on the vine is that you better try to get back into it or you'll never get home."

Paper Boy stood there, waiting for his kiss, but Dorothy forgot what she was doing in her panic. "Where's the rainbow?" she asked, looking around.

Then she remembered about Grandma D losing her farm. "Oh, Mr. Wizard," she said, "I can't go home until I figure out how to save my grandma's farm."

G.V. tugged at her pants leg. "Look, Dorothy, I've been doin' a little snoopin' on my own and..." He stopped and pulled a notebook from under his leaves.

"Under Kansas law, section 44339, under title 1024, which is found in book twenty-two, section eleven, page thirty-three...ah...paragraph two, it says that if a person doesn't receive their tax notice by the U.S. mail for reason of theft, then the tax sale of their property is rescinded."

"But who stole Grandma D's tax notice?" Dorothy asked.

G.V. pulled out an envelope from under his other leaves and handed it to Dorothy. Inside were pictures of Willa Watkins stealing Grandma D's tax notices from her mailbox.

"How on earth did you get these?"

G.V. shook his head. "I keep tellin' you, we're not on earth around here. This is Oz. Anything's possible here. And..." he said, pausing to find the words, "seems like they're converting defense plants into peace plants where you come from."

"You mean my father has a job?"

"You never know," G.V. said, swinging his vine around.

Dorothy hugged G.V. as hard as she could.

"Hey, hey! You're squeezin' the juice outta me! My vine's short enough as it is," he said, wiggling the end which Pig Foot had cut.

Dorothy laughed. "G.V., best news hound in the world, I give you the exclusive who, what, where, when, why and how of my story."

"Really?" G.V. beamed.

"On just one condition," Dorothy said.

"And what's that?"

"Just be fair in what you write."

"You got it, kiddo," he smiled. "I can't wait to go on *60 Minutes* with this one."

Dorothy touched him with the golden ruler and gave him a kiss on the leaf. Paper Boy watched as the golden glow enveloped the vine, connecting it back together.

She didn't kiss me, he pouted, feeling left out.

"But how will I get these pictures back to my Grandma?" Dorothy asked, suddenly remembering she was a long way from Kansas.

"I'll get them there," the Wizard said. "Along with this."

"What's that?" Dorothy asked.

"It's your Grandma D's birth certificate. The one she's always been wondering about."

"Where'd you get it?" Dorothy asked.

"Don't reveal your source," G.V. warned, his leaves blushing.

Dorothy held the ruler out to the Wizard. "There's just one inch left. I'm sorry."

The Wizard suddenly looked sad. "What's wrong?" Dorothy asked.

"My heart hurts," the Wizard said, thinking of Grandma D.

"What's wrong?" she asked.

"Just a long lost love that won't let me find her," he said.

Dorothy straightened up and touched the Wizard with the ruler. "And with the last inch left on the golden ruler, I give you all the happiness that your years have left."

The aging Wizard felt the tingle as the ruler touched down his shoulder. "Thank you, Dorothy," he whispered. "I'll always be eternally grateful."

Then the ruler disappeared. "Oh, no!" she mumbled, looking around for it. "I didn't mean to use it all up."

"You didn't save any for yourself," Book Worm said.

"How are you going to get home?" Bully Bear asked, starting to cry.

"That's okay," Dorothy said, her eyes welling up, "I did something for each of you that came from my heart. That's what really counts."

"You can stay here and live," the Wizard said.

"I appreciate the offer but...but I really want to get home." Dorothy looked at her feet. "But without the ruby sneakers, I guess I can't."

Paper Boy looked towards the horizon. "That rainbow's fadin' fast. But you can still make it."

"How?" Dorothy asked. "I don't have the shoes."

The golden ruler reappeared in the Wizard's hands. It was twelve inches again. "You can make it," he said, waving the ruler over Dorothy.

"But I thought I used it all up," she whispered.

"The golden ruler never disappears...you just have to believe and it's always with you. That's why it's the golden ruler."

"Come on, Dorothy," Paper Boy said. "You gotta try to make it."

The Wizard turned to Dorothy. "You have shown us all what it means to live by the golden ruler. Run as fast as you can and get into the rainbow. Your family is waiting for you."

"It's too far," Dorothy said, crestfallen. "I'll never make it in time," she whispered, looking at the fading rainbow.

Paper Boy grabbed her by the hand. "Come on, Ruby, I'll get you there."

"But how?" she asked.

Paper Boy changed back into a paper airplane. "Climb on," he said, "there's not much time!"

Dorothy grabbed onto him and looked at her friends. "Good-bye," she said, tears falling down her cheeks.

"Good-bye doesn't have to be forever," Bully Bear blubbered.

"We'll see you again, won't we?" Book Worm whimpered, the tears pushing his glasses down his nose.

"I hope so," Dorothy cried.

"Hang on, Ruby," Paper Boy said, stepping up to the edge of the platform.

Ozzie came running up, barking. "Hop on," Dorothy said, taking the dog into her arms.

"Good-bye, Dorothy," G.V. called out, "you made great copy."

"Good-bye," Dorothy called back, and then they were off.

Hanging onto the back of the paper airplane, Dorothy held Ozzie tightly. "Will we make it?" she called out through the wind.

"I think so," Paper Boy said. "But it's gonna be close."

As they approached the rainbow, they could see Ima Witch's ugly face clearly from the other side. "I'm gonna get you!" she screamed.

"She oughta chill out," Paper Boy mumbled.

"Hurry, please hurry," Dorothy whispered.

"You can't hide from me, Dorothy Gale!" Ima screamed. "If you come back I'll be waiting for you."

From inside the rainbow, Mother Rainbow waved her arm. "I told you it would all be over in a wink and a blink. Hurry, Dorothy. The rainbow is fading fast."

"Hang on," Paper Boy shouted, flapping his tail for speed.

Just as the rainbow's edge was fading, Paper Boy glided into its protective glow. "We made it!" Dorothy said, feeling the goodness of the rainbow wrap around her.

"This is weird," Paper Boy said, as they both changed colors and features. He looked at Dorothy. "We changed colors," he laughed. "You look like me and I look like you."

"We're inside the rainbow," Dorothy smiled. Then they changed back.

Mother Rainbow changed colors and shapes and for a moment looked like the girl in the wheelchair. Then she held out her hand. "It's time to go. Say good-bye to your friend."

Dorothy looked at Paper Boy. A tear was running down his cheek.

"I'll miss you, Ruby. I really will," he said, wiping the tear with his fist.

"And I'll miss you," she whispered, kissing him on the cheek.

"You have to go now," Mother Rainbow said.

"Good-bye," Dorothy called out. "I'll be back."

"I'm countin' on that, Ruby," Paper Boy said, waving as she and Ozzie floated off through the rainbow back into Grandma D's house.

In a wink and a blink she was back in Kansas.

BACK TO KANSAS

CHAPTER 33

HOME AGAIN

When Dorothy came to, she was lying in bed in Grandma D's house. She blinked her eyes and looked around.

"Dorothy's awake!" Doc shouted.

Grandma D came into the room. "My dear, what a fall you must have taken."

Dorothy rubbed her head. "But the tornado? What happened?"

Doc shook his head. "The dang thing was over in a wink and a blink." Dorothy caught the words and looked at him. "It just passed by the house."

"Found you in the attic with your backpack on. Ozzie here was standin' beside you like Lassie," Grandma D smiled. Ozzie put his paws up on the bed and yipped.

"'Course, we couldn't figure out what happened to your red sneakers. You must have dropped them somewhere," Doc said. "We just found you up there in your stockin' feet."

"Don't you need to go check the mail?" Grandma D asked, giving him a stern look.

"Okay. Guess you girls need to do some hen talk."

When Doc left the room, Grandma D sat beside her. "You went there, didn't you?"

Dorothy nodded. "I'm sorry."

"Sorry? Sorry for what?"

"For losing your crystal ball and newspaper and...and..." Dorothy hesitated.

"And what?"

"I lost your rubies. I guess you won't be able to pay off the farm now."

Grandma D grinned. "Sheriff came by just after we found you. Said someone sent him pictures in the mail."

"Pictures?" Dorothy asked.

"Of Willa Watkins stealin' my tax notices. Doc says he'll work everything out for me tomorrow."

"He really loves you, you know that, Grandma?"

Grandma D sighed. "I know it. Maybe if I could figure out where I come from, I'd feel better makin' the decision about where I'd go for the rest of my life."

"He wants to marry you."

"I know that," Grandma D said. "It's just that bein' an orphan and all has kept me from gettin' married again. I can't explain the feeling of not knowing who I am."

Doc walked into the room. "You better sit down," he said.

"I am sittin' down," Grandma D said.

Doc handed her the letter. It was a copy of her birth certificate and a family tree, which showed that her parents had died in an accident.

"Now your family tree's got roots," he grinned.

Grandma D hugged him. "Oh, Doc," she whispered.

"Guess all those letters you wrote to the newspapers for information finally paid off. Shows what puttin' the word on the grapevine will do."

Dorothy felt a tingle and thought of G.V.

Doc took Grandma D's hand. "Now that you know who you are, will you marry me? Heck, I'll even believe in Oz and be the Wizard himself if you'll just say 'I do,'" he said, trying to be funny.

Grandma D turned and nodded. "I do. I'll marry you, you old coot."

The phone rang in the hall. Grandma D went to answer it. "It's for you, Dorothy."

Dorothy got up from her bed and went to the phone. "Hey, Pumpkin, guess what?"

"Dad? Is that you, Dad?"

"It's me! Listen I got my old job back. They're converting the plant into a civilian company. We don't have to move from Orlando. I want you to come home right away."

Grandma D smiled. "Good news?" she whispered, crossing her fingers.

Dorothy nodded. "If you want you can come home now!" her father said.

"I just got here," Dorothy said. "Grandma D and I have a lot of catching up to do."

"It happened, didn't it?" her father whispered over the line.

"What?" Dorothy said.

"You know?"

"What?"

"You went to Oz, didn't you?"

"I'll tell you all about it when I get home next week," she grinned. "I'll call you later."

"I love you, Pumpkin," her father said. "When you get home we will burn the FOR SALE sign!" her father laughed as she hung up the phone.

For the next week Dorothy and Grandma D compared their two incredible journeys. They had both been to Oz, the place where things are as they ought to be.

A land just over the rainbow, no further away than a wink and a blink. A place somewhere between childhood and growing up that is within the heart of all of us.

For Dorothy Gale of Orlando, Florida, life would never quite be the same. She had left good friends over the rainbow and wanted to see them again.

But there was only one day a year when everything was right to go over the rainbow to Oz. Dorothy was already making plans with her grandmother to return, so they both could be ready to go back to Oz.

You see, Dorothy had learned the true meaning of the golden ruler. If you give from your heart, not expecting anything in return, good things will come to you.

If you treat others as you want to be treated, you can change your life and the lives of those around you. Two wrongs don't make a right. Greed is not good.

If you really treat others like you want to be treated, you can be at peace with yourself. It is the simple things in life, like giving of yourself, that are worth more than all the riches in the world.

On her last evening in Osawatomie, Dorothy stood on the porch, looking out across the endless prairie. *Kansas is in my blood*, she thought, feeling the pull of the land. *It's where my roots are.*

In the distance she saw the faint glow of a rainbow and thought about Mother Rainbow and all her beauty.

Dorothy smiled. *Paper Boy, Bully Bear, Book Worm, G.V. I miss you all so much.*

"I'll be back next year," she whispered. "You can count on it."

And in the twinkling of the twilight, in no more than a wink and a blink, Dorothy thought she saw the rainbow brighten over Oz.

About the Author

THOMAS L. TEDROW is a best-selling author, screenwriter, and film producer. He prides himself on stories that families can read together and pass on to friends.

He is the author of the best-selling eight-book series, **The Days of Laura Ingalls Wilder**, which is being made into a television series, and the four-book series, **The Life and Times of The Younguns**.

Dorothy—Return to Oz is the first book in the new series, New Classics For The Twenty-First Century.™

With a Journalism/Public Relations degree from the University of Florida, Tedrow lives with his wife, Carla, and their children in Florida. He occasionally can be found in Oz...if you know where to look.